Cabinets of Curiosities

John Thieme

Title: **Cabinets of Curiosities**

ISBN: 979-8-88676-527-4

Author: John Thieme

Cover image: https://pixabay.com/

Publisher: Generis Publishing
Online orders: www.generis-publishing.com
Contact email: info@generis-publishing.com

Contents

'Blood tells many stories.' That's what the pathologist would say to me less than a week after I first went to The Weavers, but she didn't elaborate. Perhaps she felt she'd already gone beyond the bounds of professional discretion. By then most of the story was known, but not all. The other elements had to do with blood too, but not the blood she had examined. 'If you put a razor in your mouth, you will spit blood.' Where did that saying come from?

.   .   .   .

A black-and-white mongrel, some kind of terrier-mix, had been wandering into my garden two or three times a day. I didn't know where he came from and he'd run off hastily when I went outside. I never got close to him, but I identified with him. A stray who didn't commit easily. That's what they say about me. Quick to withdraw, and when cornered too passive, too phlegmatic. Perhaps they're right. I've never been able to wear my heart on my sleeve and I don't like to make waves. But that morning a bolt from the blue sucked me into the quagmire of the White family and their 'curiosities', and after that it was hard to stay uninvolved. 'If you put a razor in your mouth, you will spit blood.'

I'd been marking time for a while. My sporadic work, as an investigative journalist took me to various parts of the world, but for the most part my assignments were unfulfilling, as well as intermittent. It'd been a month since I'd come back from reporting on tax avoidance in the Caymans and my previous job, investigating labour conditions in the Emirates, had left me out of pocket. A lacklustre relationship had ended a couple of weeks before, because she wanted me to be 'more decisive'. And that in many ways was the story of my life. I was now in my early thirties and living alone in a shabby genteel cottage in the Home Counties. Not exactly what Sam Whoo had had in mind for himself a few years earlier.

I turned on the radio. Van the Man. Slipping and sliding. Just where *did* we go, days when the rains came? I put on the PC. Perhaps the world had been in touch. That's to say, perhaps someone other than airlines, supermarkets, booksellers and people telling me I'd just inherited a million or more dollars, pesetas or naira, provided I sent them my bank details, had been in touch. The inbox was better than some days. Just a handful of those messages and three 'real' ones: from an uncle, a former colleague who had never been much more than an acquaintance, but who now, apparently addicted to e-mail, wrote semi-regularly and a mail from Isabel White. My uncle was going for a colonoscopy; my former colleague was going to Greece for a month and Isabel was going … nowhere, it seemed. It'd been so long since I'd had any contact with the White family that it took me all of three seconds to place her.

Remember Me?
Date: 29 June 2009. GMT 08.55.
From: IsabelWhite@cabinet.com
To: SamWhoo39@gmail.com

Dear Sam,

I hope you won't mind receiving this message out of the blue. You probably won't remember me. I'm Stuart White's sister. I knew you a bit when we were at college. My friend Lily and I started when you were in your final year. And you were here a couple of times, when you came to visit Stuart in the vacations. Once we spent a day together, when Stuart drove us all – you, me, my mother and Alice to Woodhall Spa. We didn't do much, but it was a nice day all the same and I'm mentioning it, because that's probably what you'll remember me most from. Anyway, I do, do hope – and then I hope a bit more – that you remember me and that this doesn't seem like an intrusion.

I don't know if you've heard that Stuart's not with us anymore and, if you haven't, I very much hope that it's not a shock to hear this now. Forgive me if I don't go into detail just at the moment.

The reason why I'm writing is because we've got some papers of Stuart's. Some folders that seem to be meant for you. I know it's a bit odd, but it'd be great if you could come up here and look at them. Do say 'no', if it's a bad time or awkward for you in any way. I hope you won't mind me writing to you out of the past like this, Sam. That past is very much our present. I should fill you in on the family news. Dad died at the time I left college (you probably knew that), Mum is well and Uncle Wilf is absolutely great, as incorrigible as ever, not showing his age at all. Alice and Jules are fine – if you remember them, that is. And we're all still in the old house, all except Martin and Steve … and Stuart, of course.

Anyway, I hope you'll write back and that you may come. It would be really great to see you. Apart from the folders, all I can offer is filling you in on a bit more of our news and protecting you from Alice's home-made scones. Seriously, though, they're not so bad now and she doesn't make them much anymore … and well, like I said, it would be great to see you. I'm repeating myself and so I think that means I should stop. Do write if /when you can.

Warm good wishes,

Isabel (White)

P.S. I remember YOU so well! Do you remember our cabinets of curiosities?

Re: Remember Me?
Date: 30 June 2009. GMT 09.24.
From: SamWhoo39@gmail.com
To: IsabelWhite@cabinet.com

Dear Isabel,

Thank you for your message. It's good to hear from you and of course I remember you. How could I forget you all? I didn't know about Stuart and so it's a terrible shock. Just 32, like me. I don't know quite how to ask, but what happened? Was it natural causes?

I remember a cabinet of curiosities, but not very well. It was that collection you had in the long room at the side of the house, wasn't it? What exactly do you want me to do? Do you just want me to read the folders? Do you know what they're about? I suppose they aren't something you could send? I'm not too busy at the moment and so, if you really think I should come up, I could. But could you tell me a bit more?

In any case, it would be great to see you all again. Regards to your Mum and everybody in the family.

Best wishes,

Sam

P.S. Do you ever see Lilith? Is she alright?

Re: Remember Me?
Date 30 June 2009. GMT 10.05.
From: IsabelWhite@cabinet.com
To: SamWhoo39@gmail.com

Dear Sam,

Thanks ever so for writing back so quickly. I wondered if you'd get the message and if you did whether you'd reply. I'm so glad you have. It's hard to talk about this, so can we leave details until I see you?

I'm glad you've remembered the cabinet and yes, that's where it was. Now it's much bigger, of course. And it's a 'them', not an 'it'. It got pluralized. I think 'it' would have mainly been Dad's when you were here. Then Stuart and Uncle Wilf started adding bits and pieces, until it seemed 'it' was theirs too and so they branched off and they both got their own rooms. Now we've 'extended' and there's a room for everyone, but some are bigger and fuller than others, of course. These days Uncle Wilf is our chief curator and he keeps us all up to the mark, in his own wonderful way.

When I wrote last night, I think I got a bit carried away. You should see the folders and I would like to see you, but can we put this on hold for a few days? I hope you won't think me odd, asking one minute and then not being quite so sure about it the next day. I'll definitely be back in touch soon, but give me a day or two, and please don't write back until I get in touch again.

I nearly forgot. One thing is easy to write about. Yes, I still see Lilith. She's fine and quite nearby – in Lincoln. I saw her there last month. She's with Spike. They used to be married and they're still together. I've lots of news to tell you, but this other business is getting in the way just at the moment, so it'll have to wait just a while. Can you bear with me? Please don't reply to this message. I'll be back in touch. I promise to write very soooooooooooon.

Love,

Isabel

The morning was beginning to seem a lot less ordinary. Had Stuart's 'little sister' been strange like this all those years ago? Not that I remembered. All that really came to mind was that she was a quiet teenager, who came alive when she began to speak about faraway places, imagining them with the intensity of a Scheherazade telling tales to defeat death, and that she'd disappeared from college very suddenly. What might she be like now? Hard to imagine her a dozen years older. Most of all, though, I needed to know about Stuart and she'd said nothing more about him in her second message. It was hard to absorb. Over the years I'd learnt to insulate myself from most hurts, but this was touching a nerve.

I went outside and threw down the remnants of my morning toast. No sign of the dog. Back indoors, I watched hopping blackbirds squabble over the toast, devoting more attention to chasing one another than securing food, while sparrows darted around their feet and made off with most of the better scraps. Then pragmatic starlings spotted the opportunity, swooped in and, pointed beaks to the ground, walked their independent way through the toast, demolishing the remains in a matter of seconds. A dove was collecting twigs for what I guessed was its second nest of the year, but was I right? I'd spent most of my life in towns. I wondered if I'd ever again have a home that I could share with someone.

I respected Isabel's request not to write, but in the days that followed, I thought of little else.

It was a week before she wrote again.

Re: Remember Me?
Date: 7 July 2009. GMT 14.23.
From: IsabelWhite@cabinet.com
To: SamWhoo39@gmail.com

Hello again Sam,

I hope you won't think me odd for writing to you like I did and then sort of breaking off. Things aren't easy at the moment. Some of the family think I should be inviting you, but as usual not everyone agrees, and I want to be sure. You know what the White family are like! I think the best thing is for us just to write to one another for a few days – if that's OK with you and you don't think I'm mad. I'll understand if you do. Then perhaps we can arrange for you to come up, like I said. But, of course, only if it's not imposing and you want to.

We were all very shaken up by Michael's death – so sudden, so terrible. I wonder what they'll decide happened, whether or not it was the pills. I watched the memorial service on TV last night. Did you catch any of it? Very moving I thought, especially when Germaine sang 'Smile'. I had no idea that Charlie Chaplin had written it and that it was Michael's favourite song. It's so hard to believe he's gone. It's all seemed a bit unreal to me. Uncle Wilf is going around the house moonwalking. At his age! He's 87 now, you know. Still, I guess you can't keep a good alcoholic down.

I know you'll think I'm crazy, writing to you about this, when it has nothing to do with the folders and what I'm really wanting to talk to you about, but it's necessary, Sam. I need to do it this way. Bear with me, will you? Write back now, OK? I'm completely sane. Don't worry about that. I'll see you soon. It'll be a while, but not too long. I promise. You should be here, or I wouldn't have raised the possibility.

I forgot to ask. I'm guessing you're still living in London, but with e-mail you could be anywhere in the world, couldn't you? It may be very difficult for you to come up here. Do let me know, assuming your address isn't a closely guarded secret. I promise I won't descend on you unannounced!

Your friend,

Isabel

Re: Remember Me?
Date: 7 July 2009. GMT 17.36
From: SamWhoo39@gmail.com
To: IsabelWhite@cabinet.com

Dear Isabel,

Thanks for your message, No, I'm not in London. I was out of the country for years, but now I'm back in the UK. I'm not too far from London. I bought a little cottage in Essex a couple of years ago. Not much to write home about and the mortgage is a pain, but at least it's vaguely rural and there are days when I feel I can think.

It sounds like Uncle Wilf is in good form. No, I didn't see the Michael Jackson memorial event. From what I've heard, it was a mixture of show business and religious service. There's a lot to come out there. Anyway, I'm here for you when you need me, provided it's fairly soon. Work has been taking me abroad quite a bit and it's likely I'll be off on another assignment in a month or two.

Take care,

Sam

Re: Remember Me?
Date 7 July 2009. GMT 18.49
From: IsabelWhite@cabinet.com
To: SamWhoo39@gmail.com

Hi Sam,

I'm sorry it's taken me so long to reply. OK, I know it's only an hour and I left it for ages before, but it seems more urgent now.

I think we should talk about Michael. All the contradictions and cross-overs: a boy-man, who never quite jumped the line that takes you out of youth, or a man-boy, dying at the age of fifty; black trying to turn a whiter shade of pale; the children – his children? – the public image and the private life; the bankrupt multi-millionaire; the cosmetic surgery, making him an androgyne as well as white-black. And did you know he was a friend of the Incredible Hulk? Man turning into monster. 'Thriller' – a nice guy at the beginning, who turns into a Gothic I-don't-know-what. But I do believe the monster was the disguise and the real Michael *was* Peter Pan. Nobody could beat Michael when it came to disguise, not even Stuart, though of course he could be a bit like Michael.

Guess what I've just done? I had to stop Uncle Wilf moonwalking and so I showed him 'Thriller' and he's getting himself up as a ghoul. He doesn't look much like Michael so far and he's not got all the moves yet, but I fear the worst.

Don't you think they sanitized Michael a bit for the memorial service? Even Uncle Wilf, bless him, says so. He understood that none of the participants could do the dancing and anyway it wouldn't have been appropriate, and that's why they went back to little Michael, but he thinks they should have shown a bit of footage of the crotch-grabbing Michael. Well, I guess that's the minority report, but I can see his point a bit. When in doubt, go for the children's story? I wonder what you think, Sam. Can't wait to hear.

Still friends?

Yours,

Isabel

Re: Remember Me?
Date 7 July. GMT 23.11
From: IsabelWhite@cabinet.com
To: SamWhoo39@gmail.com

It's me again. I can see why you haven't replied. You do think I'm crazy, wittering on about Michael, when I should be, could be, talking about other things. Trust me, I'm OK. Write when you can – anytime in the next six minutes will be good.

Much love,

Isabel

Re: Remember Me?
Date 7 July. GMT 23.32
From: IsabelWhite@cabinet.com
To: SamWhoo39@gmail.com

OK, see if I care. Talk to you tomorrow.

Iz

Re: Remember Me?
Date 8 July. GMT 10.02
From: SamWhoo39@gmail.com
To: IsabelWhite@cabinet.com

Hello Isabel,

Sorry. I was out last night and didn't check messages when I got back. I don't know what to say about Michael. I haven't thought about this as much as you or, from what you say, Uncle Wilf has. But one thing intrigues me. You compared him with Stuart. And there's something else: you spoke about Stuart in the present tense, as though he's still with us. I'm starting to get a bit confused, but I do appreciate your messages and would like to see you.

How are your Mum and Alice, Jules, Steve and Martin? It'll be so good to see them all, of course.

Best wishes,

Sam

Re: Remember Me?
Date 8 July. GMT 10.21
From: IsabelWhite@cabinet.com
To: SamWhoo39@gmail.com

Dear 'best wishes, Sam',

Well, la-de-da. Big deal. You don't even bother to check to see if I've written and then you send best wishes, even though you are one of the family. Who needs these BEST WISHES? I can see I'm going to have to abandon my plan to take my time over this and get you up here as soon as possible. Stand by. I'll be back in touch soon with a formal invite for 'best wishes, Sam', so that he can see for himself what's going on and ask mother and Alice and Jules how they are himself, since 'it'll be so very good to see them all, OF COURSE'. And bwS should be reading my messages more carefully. I told him Steve and Martin aren't here.

You know, I was only being polite when I started out asking if you remembered me. OF COURSE, you remember me. Once seen, never forgotten. It's time to come out of hiding now, Sam. Tell me what you remember about Tony's café and then you'll earn your invitation to Bubbleby and you can haul your tail up here, 'best wishes, Sam', and start to grow up. I don't plan to charge you for the education, but I can't speak for the others! You'll have to take your chances. So bring your wallet, 'bwS'.

Lots of love,

Is-a-bell?

P.S. There's something weird in your message. You seem to think Stuart's dead. I didn't say that. All I said was that he's not here anymore. He went travelling and we're out of contact. That's all. I miss him terribly and I worry, but I'm sure he's alive and well. Maybe he's fly fishing in the Highlands, or having root canal work done in Budapest or writing the greatest novel ever in a hut somewhere in the pampas.

P.P.S. Apologies, Sam. I don't mean to be rude. But, leaving aside the not-so-small matter of your not reading my messages carefully enough, you really should have written back last night. I knew you were there and I hung around by the computer for hours. Just cos you're worried about my sanity, that's no reason for not writing. And btw, just in case you're wondering, I'm boringly sober these days, and I never did do drugs. I'm OK, really I am.

It was good to see a flash of the 'old' Isabel in her postscript about Stuart's possible whereabouts, but I was baffled by the volatility of her e-mails. I decided to keep things as simple as possible when I replied.

She was more or less right 'of course' – those two words now began to seem taboo. I *had* been out, but I'd got back home fairly early the night before and left the computer off.

Re: Remember Me?
Date: 8 July 2009. GMT 17.36
From: SamWhoo39@gmail.com
To: IsabelWhite@cabinet.com

Dear Isabel,

It's a big relief to know Stuart is OK, even if you're out of touch with him at the moment. Let me know when you'd like me to come up and I'll do my best to fit in with whatever you think best. I remember you all fondly. Stuart wasn't my only friend in the family and from what you say Uncle Wilf alone will make the visit worthwhile.

I remember Tony's well. I think that he probably gave us life-long resistance to germs, by exposing us to so many.

Warm good wishes,

Sam

Re: Remember Me?
Date 8 July. GMT 20.21
From: IsabelWhite@cabinet.com
To: SamWhoo39@gmail.com

Well, I suppose 'warm good wishes' is progress of a kind. I regard it as a platform for further negotiations. Am getting to work on arrangements now. Initiating top-level discussions with all parties concerned.

Over and out,

Isabel

I wondered if she'd be back in touch in minutes, hours, days or weeks. It was five days.

Re: Remember Me?
Date 13 July. GMT 8.08
From: IsabelWhite@cabinet.com
To: SamWhoo39@gmail.com

Last night Isabel White conferred with certain members of the White family currently residing at Bubbleby and she has been formally mandated to send the following:

> Ms. Isabel White and her family have great pleasure in inviting Mr. Sam Whoo to be their house guest at The Weavers, Bubbleby during the months of July and August 2009. This invitation is valid from 13 July onwards and the period of stay may be extended by the agreement of both parties.

Sam, no need to RSVP. Get your arse into your car and come up here immediately, before somebody changes their mind again. Just get here – OK? I'm not fooling around now. I'm deadly serious. Come now, before something goes seriously wrong. If you don't stop, you could be here in about three hours – three and a half at most. If you're held up, ring me. OK? 01699 777319.

Love,

I

P.S. I just wrote 'if you're held up', but I don't know what I was thinking of. Don't be! I shouldn't even raise the possibility. Divert around jams, go through fields, take short cuts! YOU ARE REALLY NEEDED HERE … NOW ISN'T SOON ENOUGH! So there CAN'T be hold-ups. Don't try to tell me there have been. I'll NOT believe you.

Re: Remember Me?
Date: 13 July 2009. GMT 8.10
From: SamWhoo39@gmail.com
To: IsabelWhite@cabinet.com

OK, but a brief answer. I'll be with you around lunch-time. I don't use the mobile when driving, but I'll check for messages when I stop – just in case. It's 07763 941941.

Re: Remember Me?
Date: 13 July 2009. GMT 8.12
From: IsabelWhite@cabinet.com
To: SamWhoo39@gmail.com

OMG, I think HE expects lunch!

I packed a bag quickly and set out on the drive north. Along the motorway my mind went back to my days as a student: to Stuart, to Isabel, and to Tony's café.

Tony's

We usually went to Tony's backstreet café for lunch. It was a windowless greasy spoon, reached through a narrow basement door at the foot of an equally narrow flight of stairs. Somehow Tony had eluded the prying eyes of Health and Safety and his café was all the more magical as a result. An Aladdin's cave that now seems to belong to prehistory, though the period I am writing about is little more than a decade ago. The dimly-lit interior boasted just six tables, each of which could seat four people. If you didn't get there just after noon, you didn't get a table.

Skipping any of our college lectures scheduled for twelve o'clock, Stuart and I would usually find others to make up a quartet, so we didn't have to share a table. Always Stuart and I. Sometimes with Dave and John (A), or Grace and Jill, or Arthur and John (H), or Harry and Spike – crazy Spike, who couldn't be serious if he tried, though I don't think he ever did. Then in our last year as students, which was their first year, we would sometimes go to Tony's with Isabel and her friend Lilith – solemn Lily, who couldn't be crazy if she tried, though I don't think she ever did. Isabel was studying geography. She was slow to start conversations, but unstoppable once started, a born monologist who painted alchemical word-pictures of Wapisiana settlements in Guyana, irrigation in the Okanagan, urban renewal schemes in Shanghai. I never knew how much she invented and how much was taken from her geography textbooks, but the poetry of her tales was clearly original. She cast spells, as she wandered languidly from the contours of Saharan dunes to the choreography of mating penguins, from elegies on the demise of steelworks to odes on crepuscular oaks. Space was the raw material of her art; she transformed hitherto empty places into the interiors of Dutch masters. And Tony's was the perfect setting for her storytelling, its subterranean world as near as we could ever have expected to get to King Shahryar's palace in the London of the last years of the twentieth century.

I can't remember when Isabel dropped out of college, but it must have been somewhere in her second term. At the time I didn't know why and I don't remember ever asking Stuart. I think I vaguely speculated that she must have departed for one of those far-off places she had conjured into existence for us, but if I thought that I would have been wrong. After that we saw very little of Lilith. A few years later, I would hear that she'd committed suicide in a cathedral close somewhere in the east of England, but by then I'd lost touch with Stuart and his family and so this remained no more than a rumour. Mourning my own lack of self-awareness during our student days, I hoped it wasn't true. Surely it couldn't be. Wouldn't the drama of the setting have generated news coverage? But when I heard this, I realised with some alarm that, though I'd hardly known her and hadn't thought about her in years, I needed Lilith to be alive, somewhere in the world. If you'd asked me why I don't think I could have told you, but maybe it was because she had been a rock of unsmiling reliability amid our student idiocies. At the time, though, I didn't think much about Lilith. I'd fallen under Isabel's spell, as she crowded Tony's tiny basement with the magic of her landscapes.

Back then as students, before and after Isabel and Lilith, Stuart and I were inseparable. Isabel was, as I said, a Scheherazade, with a marvellous gift for evoking otherworldly places, but Stuart was the centre of my lived personal geography. We had met before we went to the college, but we'd hardly known one another and it was during our first week there that we bonded. We went to see a movie with one another, found we had similar tastes in films, food, drink, people, almost everything, and spent more and more time together, without consciously thinking about it. Or at least that was how it seemed to me at that time, in that place. We never shared a flat, but we did almost everything together. So that interlude with Isabel (and Lilith) was the most natural thing in the world, since Isabel was Stuart's sister. We talked about 'the others', placing them in our mutually agreed taxonomy of human types, but we never questioned ourselves or our friendship. At least I know that *I* never did. Now, though, looking back, I wonder: could Stuart really have been as unself-questioning as I was?

We went to Tony's, because it was nearby, because the portions were huge and because it was cheap. Most of all, though, we went there because of Tony himself and the entertainment he provided. He was really Antonio, a portly Neapolitan of about fifty-five, everything we could have wished for in an Italian restaurant owner. He wore a chef's apron, usually soiled with juices or gravy, though seldom, if ever, really dirty; and he spoke English like someone parodying an Italian speaking the language, generously adding vowels to the ends of words: 'So whata you boys wanta eata today'; 'I maka very special mixta grilla, if you lika'.

Every Monday the 'Potato Man', a scruffy besuited individual with a hessian sack over his shoulder, would appear at the foot of the stairs, silhouetted against the dim daylight outside. He would hesitate in the doorway and an elaborate farce, which underwent minor variations in its weekly performance, would ensue, as he negotiated with Tony. Tony would throw up his hands in horror; the Potato Man would smile and mumble ingratiatingly, 'Real cheap today, Tony', or 'A special price for you this week, Tony'. Without advancing, Tony would turn his hands towards the man, pushing his palms forward in a gesture of rejection. A ritual of remonstrations would follow, before Tony inched towards the door and the Potato Man dared to shuffle a couple of steps forwards. They would both drop their voices and, after a minute or two of haggling, the deal would be done; the potatoes that would launch a thousand chips during the course of the next week would pass quickly into the recess that was Tony's kitchen, to the apparent horror of his longsuffering, but frequently combative wife, Milly.

Milly was perhaps ten years younger than Tony. She was really Emilia from Catania, a dark-skinned, African-looking Sicilian, who, we joked, had good connections in both the Mafia and the Vatican. She and Tony jostled for space as they cooked, and sometimes sang, together in the small kitchen that was the innermost sanctum of the cave. Their duets were always Italian, or pseudo-Italian – they were smart enough to know their clientele – and never quite predictable. An inspirational 'Volare' or a raucous 'Buona Sera, Signorina, Buona Sera' would lead onto a sorrowful 'Mama', in which Tony's tenor always took the lead, or a mournful 'O Sole Mio', in which Milly, with her better English, sang solo contralto verses of the words Elvis had popularized decades before. When this delayed the arrival of our lunch, we would join in. A mocking out-of-tune chorus, wailing 'It's now or never'. Tony knew we would wait, but usually obliged by accelerating his cooking, sometimes stopping singing altogether. Milly, less accommodating, was his perfect foil. She would simply sing louder, turn down the gas and generally assert her disregard for 'stoooo-dents'. There were, after all, only six tables and they were always full. Tony may or may not have had ideas of a quicker turnaround time for customers; Milly definitely didn't. She was entirely her own woman and, from our limited glimpses into their world, her only compromises in life were made for Tony's sake. She indulged his weaknesses: forays to the next-door betting shop, an even smaller hole-in-the-wall; and a weakness for their chips, which were an archetypal thing of beauty.

As I said, we went to Tony's for the entertainment, and it never disappointed. The singing was, however, really just a sideshow. The main attraction was Tony's menu, lovingly rewritten every week on a series of elongated cardboard strips that slotted into ridged holes in a wooden board on the wall. Its frame advertised Campari, though, of course, they didn't have a liquor licence and this was never on offer. Many of Tony's menu items remained the same from week to week, but just as great actors never give the same performance twice, variations in the orthography and calligraphy of Tony's menus ensured that they, too, offered endless variety. Spaghetti was always on the menu, but the number of curling, copperplate *g's* with which Tony spelt it was less reliable. Usually there were two – 'spagghetti' – but sometimes his enthusiasm allowed this to expand into three and on one memorable occasion he added an extra aitch as well: 'spaggghhetti'. Tony's spellings suited the size of the sizzling, pan-fried portions that he would deliver from kitchen to table with a theatrical flourish. His love of *g's* was coupled with an aversion to *c's*. On his wall 'custard' became 'gustard', 'cabbage' turned into 'gabbage'. Spike, a dedicated graffiti artist, wanted to alter the first *b* to an *r*, but we persuaded him that it would be sacrilegious to deface Tony's murals: 'gabbage' *must* remain 'gabbage'. As time went by, Tony's creative spellings became ever more exciting: captivated by the appearance of 'apple grumble' on his menu, we ordered double portions that rendered us comatose for the rest of the afternoon.

Then, one rainy Monday lunchtime, Tony offered transubstantiation. We'd been sitting in his café for a minute or more before Stuart spotted a new addition to the menu and nudged me. I looked up and there it was: 'God and chips'. I began to giggle. Stuart kicked me under the table, but my giggles gave way to uncontrollable laughter. Stuart was wiser. He simply smiled, glancing towards the kitchen, as if to advocate caution. But I was not to be contained and John (H) and Arthur, who were making up our foursome for the day, caught my mood and began to laugh too. Tony appeared from the kitchen and, keen to share our joke, began to grin, though he had no idea what we were laughing at. Stuart remained discreetly silent, but the other three of us were cackling hysterically. Tony looked puzzled. At that moment Milly appeared and following my line of vision quickly understood the source of our laughter. *She* was not amused. Milly had a talent for dry irony, but today her approach was altogether more direct.

'So you think it's funny, do you? You come here. You share Tony's wonderful cooking and … and you laugh at him? What kind of leee-tle boys are you? Let me tell you something. He is a hundred times the man any of you will ever be. He is a good man. A very good, good man. And what are you? Stoo-pid. Stoo-pid stoooooo-dents. That's all. Filling your bellies with his fine food and learning nothing about life except what you can find in your sill-eee school-books. Ohmicod! Please get out of our gafé right away or great harm may come to you. (She was holding a carving knife.) You know what you are? You are … cod-awful.' She seemed to turn her gaze, and the knife, towards me as she said this.

Was I being singled out, because I had laughed even louder than the others? And something else struck me. Stuart's restraint seemed to complement her mood, as if he was somehow in collusion with her, sharing her innermost feelings. But I must have been imagining this. Milly and Stuart belonged in different worlds.

Our stomachs still empty and our laughter dispelled in an instant, we went back to the college and a one-o'clock lecture on Leibniz and his monads. I didn't concentrate. To this day I couldn't tell you what a monad is, but I've come to think of it as a kind of nomad. I never went back to Tony's. I think Stuart did, but I'm not sure about this. We remained friends, but never spoke about that day in Tony's again. We finished our course. I graduated with a poor degree, Stuart was more successful, and we went our separate ways. In the years that followed I became something of a nomad myself and I had no more contact with the Whites until that day when Isabel sent me the first of her e-mails. I had no idea how Tony's world had cast a shadow over mine.

Turning Off

I turned off the motorway, but left the radio on for a while. I'd turn *it* off and plug in the sat nav for the last bit of the drive, once I'd left the A-roads. It'd been raining, but now a rural sun broke through, illuminating hitherto gloomy fields. I turned the windscreen wipers off. I'd only been to Stuart's house two or three times, years back now, but in the past I'd have simply glanced at a road atlas for a few seconds and found my way straight there. I wondered how much Bubbleby might have changed and how different Isabel and the various members of the White family would be. I'd know soon enough. The Isabel of Tony's café would probably have had a repertory of images to illustrate, and perhaps explain, how places are transformed. But the Isabel who had been writing to me had only offered a fleeting glimpse of the student who imagined worlds into being. Still this new erratic Isabel was as yet only a virtual being and I wondered if she wore an Internet mask. It had been hard for me, with my real-world mask of caution and politeness, to cope with her flamboyance. The traffic programme cut into the music on the radio and a local channel told me there were delays at the roadworks in Grantham and a minor accident south of Lincoln. I turned *that* off.

After the flattened inclines of the motorway, I felt released, almost light-headed, as the car swept up and down welcoming hills, round bends, under trees. The radio seemed to catch my lyrical mood. Van the man was following me. Now I *was* on the bright side of the road. We'll be lovers once again. Was it possible my life was being controlled by a deejay in the sky who was finding music to match my mood? But no, I told myself. That was a pathetic fallacy in both senses of the adjective.

I was still running on cruise control, but the bends started to become a bit sharper and so I turned *that* off. Lincolnshire is mysterious – two mysterious worlds really: the flat agricultural south with the fens to the east and the more northerly wolds that I was entering now. In this part of England most of the villages have names ending in '-by'. Was that an Anglo-Saxon or a Viking suffix? Either way it gave these villages a shared character, making them both communities and worlds apart. The Whites had lived near Bubbleby for generations, but I remembered that they'd spoken of themselves as outsiders, referring to the local villagers as 'they' and 'them'. I'd asked Stuart about this the first time I'd visited, and he'd side-stepped the question, muttering something about their forebears having been Huguenot refugees; and I'd made a stupid joke, which unintentionally changed the subject: 'Four bears! We were poorer than you. We only had three and no Goldilocks to eat their porridge.' So I remained unsure why the Whites saw themselves as separate. They were obviously better off than many of the locals, but I felt sure class wasn't an issue. Maybe it was just a matter of temperament. In a world of reliable but often reticent people, perhaps they were viewed as artistic, incongruously fanciful. Stuart had an encyclopaedic interest in everything under the sun, and the breadth of Isabel's imaginative travels had sometimes made her seem his female equivalent. Now, as I drove towards Bubbleby, I began to think that the family's curiosities might make them all oddities in dependable, salt-of-the-earth middle-England.

I've never had Isabel's gift for populating space, but like most people I suppose I imagine places through their cultural associations and namings, shared fictions recycled over the decades – Hardy's Wessex, the Brontës' moors. Sometimes signposted for us – Shakespeare's county, Nelson's county, not so very far away from here. Constable country, Wordsworth's Lake District. So many clichés, shaping responses and I've absorbed more than my fair share of them, having been a literature 'stoo-dent'. Then there are the resonances of more contemporary names – Soham and Flixborough, south and north of here; Old Trafford and Anfield; Glastonbury – well at least that was complicated by Arthur and the matter of Britain, as well as Springsteen, Blur and whoever else had performed there in recent years. Hadn't they paid a tribute to Michael this year? I wasn't sure. But what mythologies did Lincolnshire conjure up? Fruit and flowers. Wasn't it the home of Interflora? Perhaps, but that didn't have quite the same resonance. Some famous World War II airbases, but could I name even one of them? The cathedral in Lincoln, but I didn't know much about that and anyway the town probably didn't have much in common with the rest of the county. Margaret Thatcher had come from Grantham. Forget that! Her legacy, the England she'd spawned, was part of what had sent me into exile, scurrying around the globe, trying to find a more congenial 'home'. So what was left? What literary associations? Wasn't Chesney Wold, the bleakest house in that dreary novel, somewhere in Lincolnshire? (Lady Dedlock, Lady Dedlock, / Had a child out of wedlock.) And Tennyson. I wanted to resist his influence too. Victorian doubt and insecurity. His miserable poem, born out of the loss of his friend, that turned a single death into an excuse for an elegy for himself, his age, for … everything. No, I preferred to see this landscape without associations, under-peopled, or at least inhabited only by the farmers, fruit-growers and tradespeople that the Whites seemed to have so little in common with. Most of all I wanted it to be a blank landscape where the Whites were drawing their own map of England, creating a place that defied clichés. And I wanted to be coming as a traveller without cultural baggage.

I turned off onto a B-road, with a few miles to go before I'd be leaving this for the lane – little more than a dirt track really – that led down to the village and up to the Whites' house, The Weavers. Now there were dead pheasants on the road, while others scurried in and out of the hedgerows, males accompanied by two or three young. Birds with no road sense, unlike the worldly-wise crows that fed on the abundant roadkill, taking flight instants before cars reached them. It all seemed so familiar and, as I gradually adjusted my driving pattern – brake when you see a pheasant; don't worry about the crows, they'll look after themselves – time seemed to collapse. I could have been driving along this uncrowded road a dozen years before. The success of pan-European 'logistical solutions' had changed England's arterial routes out of all recognition, but here it appeared that time had stood still and I fantasized that I was driving along roads that were insulated from 'progress'.

The drive became even slower. This was the time of year when tractors, hauling trailers that now did seem larger than those I remembered, took to the road, creating small convoys behind them. Other cars, familiar with the bends, waited for the moment when they knew it was safe to pass, overtook and accelerated away at speed. Twice I found myself ready to follow, but lacking local knowledge left it too late to do so before the next bend or dip. I sensed that the remaining section of the convoy behind me was identifying me as an outsider. The fields in the south of the county were said to be reliant on Eastern European labour, but these roads didn't seem to welcome migrants. The forward movement of time was manifesting itself after all. Nothing, it seemed, stays static; and again I wondered to what extent Bubbleby and the Whites could have remained the same. Eventually I came to the old wooden signpost – definitely the same one that had 'always' been there – that pointed to the lane to Bubbleby and I turned off, feeling no impulse to look at my sat nav now. I was wanting to journey back in time, so why did I need it? 'Bubbleby 5 miles'. Another ten minutes, because now the road was very narrow, a single track with passing places every few hundred yards. It was quiet, but I had to reverse into one of the passing spots before I'd covered the first mile. I switched on the mobile to see if Isabel had sent a text. She had. 'Where R U.' I turned *that* off. I was near enough not to need to reply. A dove flew out of a hedgerow, a diversionary manoeuvre to protect its young? I was unused to this kind of driving, the sudden braking and gear changes for blind bends and the acceleration into fifth gear for a few hundred yards where the lane was straight. This section was taking more than ten minutes, but I slowed right down, partly so that I wouldn't arrive frazzled. She would be waiting for me. I turned the radio on for moral support and he was there again: Van the Man. 'Slim Slow Slider'.

The Weavers lies just beyond Bubbleby. As I drove into the village, I wondered if it would have changed. The pub was still there: The Hope Inn. 'Abandon hope, all ye who enter here!', Stuart had once quipped. I couldn't remember anything Isabel had ever said about the place, but then I'd spent much less time with her and perhaps this was too close to home for her topographical flights. Now, though, I couldn't wait to hear her talk about this little world, so embroiled in the intricacies of Englands past and present, but, for all my travels, so remote from anything in my own experience. Just beyond the pub, there was the general store that had doubled as a post office, but now seemed to have lost that role. The grass on the little bit of village green in front of it looked untended and abandoned. But then it would have grown quickly in the warm, wet weather and so this wasn't necessarily a sign of total neglect. Twenty or thirty houses had been, and yes, still were, clustered around the green. No more than cottages really and more nondescript than picturesque, but just quaint enough to masquerade as the centre of a picture postcard village. Above them, casting its shadow on more than half the houses, a massive church, with Norman origins and, it was rumoured, a few Saxon stones. What fear it must have struck into people's hearts at one time. And now? In most parts of England it would simply have been an anachronism, but here, I was guessing, it still had a residual power, vying for primacy with satellite dishes that ensured instant global information amid this isolation. And, I assumed, Isabel must have a good broadband connection. Solitude clearly wasn't what it used to be and yet The Weavers *was* a cul de sac. Just one way in and one way out and every time one either went in or out, a drive past the inquiring eyes of the three widowed women who lived in neighbouring cottages by the green. Stuart had called them 'the witches', chanting 'Hubble, bubble, Bubbleby / They're watching over you and me', when we passed their houses. Now as I drove in, I wanted to believe they were still looking on, as it were confirming my presence, in a very different manner from the broadcasters who seemed to be pursuing me with Van. The cottages had patches of grass in front of them, two beautifully manicured lawns framing a delinquent uncut mop of grass in the middle. What human stories might these tell? Neighbourly disputes or a mutual understanding arrived at over decades?

The village is in a dip and after that the lane continues on up to Bubbleby, climbing precipitously for a hundred yards or so, before settling into a steadier ascent. This part of the lane leads nowhere except to the Weavers and a couple of neighbouring farms. Not far now I thought, but I wasn't remembering precisely. I'd always been with Stuart, rapt in conversation, and it might be further than I imagined. With the village behind me, I found I was going even slower, though the lane was deserted. There were overgrown hedgerows on both sides now and occasionally the car was brushing against them. The ten minutes I'd estimated it would take me from the sign to Bubbleby were turning into twenty-five. Finally I reached the top and there it was, The Weavers – a late Georgian two-hundred-year-old, three-storeyed house of less than manorial proportions, but of a size that set it apart from those in the village. At the front there was a huge dirt drive. Two cars were parked there: an ageing Mercedes and a 2007 Ford Focus. This was 4x4 territory, but the Whites had never been predictable, never succumbed either to fashion or practicality. Tire tracks suggested other cars were regularly parked there. On the right-hand side there was a double garage. Its door was open, but there were no vehicles inside. Just a collection of lawn mowers and garden tools, some of which one could tell, even from a distance, were rusty and disused. I remembered that The Weavers had never had much of a garden at the front, but there were a couple of acres at the back. I tried to recall the rear garden and several of its features came back. A well-kept lawn, a paved area with a barbecue pit, an apple orchard, a carefully maintained rockery, and behind all this a wilder, less tended expanse of grass, and at the rear of this several conifers, a willow (or were there two?) and some unkempt fruit trees. Looking at the façade now, I reflected that places have usually shrunk when we go back after years away, but The Weavers appeared bigger.

What would Isabel be like? The student I'd known was wispy and delicate, not given to complaining and silently disapproving of anyone who whinged. She'd been quiet and reserved until she launched herself into her imagined worlds. But the Isabel of the e-mails had been very different and I could envisage being greeted by a bellicose termagant, shouting 'Where on earth have you been? You're later than late. Three hours, fifty minutes. Couldn't you have rung?' What I didn't expect was to drive up to a house that could well have been unoccupied, to have to ring an old-fashioned bell, wonder if it was still working and wait thirty seconds before her mother, Laura, came to the door, older than I remembered her, but still looking anything but old, offering me first her left and then her right cheek to kiss, while saying nothing at first. An immaculately poised, tallish, slim woman with swept back strawberry blonde hair. A woman whose deportment was all of a piece with her impeccable, albeit slightly strained, manners.

'It's good to see you after such a long time, Samuel. Isabel is expecting you.'

'And it's really good to see you, Mrs. White. You're looking well.'

An awkward silence. Then she told me the house 'must have grown', since I'd last visited. An extension had been added to the left-hand side. Six or eight new rooms. I guessed that the individual cabinets, which Isabel had spoken about, explained the expansion. As Laura and I spoke, our voices echoed in the spacious hallway. The Weavers seemed haunted with history. Not a Gothic pile, but nevertheless permeated by a past. It had had about fifteen rooms, and now there were more than twenty.

'Come into the lounge, Samuel. I'm so glad you could come.' And as we walked into that room, which seemed unchanged – the same Hogarth prints on the walls, the same suite with the wooden armrests, the same faded gold curtains – she added, 'You must be tired after the drive. Will you have something to drink?'

'That'd be nice. Thank you.'

'Tea or coffee, or perhaps something cold?'

I was about to answer when Isabel materialised in the room, appearing as if from nowhere. She was wearing unremarkable faded jeans and a longish T-shirt. The T-shirt's pristine whiteness suggested it had been put on in the last hour or two. She seemed entirely 'normal', neither the student I remembered, nor the bipolar Isabel of the e-mails. Average height, slightly frail in build, nothing that would stand out in a crowd. The hennaed hair of her student days had turned into a mid-brown. Her natural colour or another dye? All that was remarkable about her was the nervous animation of her speech. Was that typical or was it prompted by my arrival?

'Sam, thank you, thank you, thank you for coming. It's so good to see you.' She planted a kiss on my cheek and looked for me to return it, something the student Isabel would never have dreamt of doing, but it was nervier and more self-conscious than her mother's two-cheek conventionality.

'He doesn't need a drink, Mum. I'm taking him to the Hope Inn for lunch.' And then to me, 'We'd better get going before the food runs out down there. They don't have too many customers at lunch-time and so it's very much a case of the early bird …. You can bring your stuff in afterwards. Mum can talk to you when we get back and I expect Uncle Wilf will claim you for a while and show you his prize exhibits in the cabinets, and Alice and Jules will be back from work. I'll explain things … later.'

The words came in quick succession, but the tone was measured, making me think that she'd been assuming a persona in her e-mails. If not, why had the urgency of her messages evaporated? Mrs White looked on, composed, allowing her daughter's chatter to speak for both of them. A mother, skilled in diplomacy, who had brought up six children and been widowed just over a decade before.

Isabel in contrast was rushing to say more. 'Do you mind if we walk to the pub? It's all downhill.'

I grinned. 'That means it'll be uphill coming back.'

'That's true, but walking will give us a chance to talk.'

We set out, walking quickly, but now she was speaking more slowly. She was carrying a rolled tartan umbrella. 'Look at that cloud. Let's hope it doesn't rain.'

'We should have driven, you know.'

'No, I didn't feel like driving and I think you've done enough for one day. And the umbrella is big enough for the two of us.'

We went down the hill, walking on a narrow verge between the road and hedgerows at this point. Further on we'd be in the road itself. For at least two minutes we lapsed into total silence, and that was a relief from the small talk.

Eventually I plucked up courage. 'Why am I here, Isabel?'

'Because you agreed to come?', she ventured.

'I agreed to come because you asked me to. It's been years.' I inclined my head to ask the question again.

'Because Stuart left folders for you. Because I love you. Because we all love you. We always did, you know. Well, most of us anyway.'

'Even Uncle Wilf?'

'Yep, definitely Uncle Wilf. As much as any of us. He loves you heaps and heaps, like his own son. You'll have to face it, Sam. You are greatly loved in the White family.' As she said this, she flashed me a smile that I'd forgotten, but instantly recognised as the one that lit up her face as she imagined places into being in Tony's café. It exuded warmth. It promised homecoming. At that moment, the sun re-emerged from behind the threatening cloud and the various possible Isabels converged into one.

'Not that you deserve us. All those years abroad. Why did you desert us?'

'I guess I gave up on England,' I shrugged. 'It wasn't personal. It had nothing to do with you or the family.'

'Nothing to do with us. How can you say that? Stuart missed you desperately. You must have known. It had everything to do with us.'

'No, don't be silly. Stuart and I had drifted apart and I hadn't seen him for a year or two before I went abroad.'

'And *where* did you go? *Why* did you go? I need to know all the details. I stayed home and I bet you've been to spectacular cities, ginormous jungles and dazzling deserts. I hope you've been absolutely everywhere, so you can tell me all about the whole world. I haven't travelled like you, but if you tell me about all the stunning places you've been, I can imagine I'm there. I still pore over my atlases you know, and I google places that have a webcam. Yesterday I was in Krakow, watching a little dog run across the Main Square, people drinking coffee, and a pigeon shitting on the statue of Eros Bound. I wandered up to the craft stalls too. But you, Sam, you have *been* to these places.'

'I've never been to Krakow.'

'OK, but you've been places. You can help me imagine them. You can bring them to me, by telling me whether the air is fresh, whether the people are hospitable, whether the police are fierce, whether they're wet and windy or hot and dry, whether there are beggars, drug dealers, mime artists, rare animals, dwarfs, unicorns, stray dogs, magic carpets.'

'Well, I've never seen a unicorn or a magic carpet. That's for sure. I've been here and there. I can tell you if you like, but I've nothing very interesting to say. I came, because you called and I'm here. That's what's most important, and now it'd be good to know why you want me here.'

She turned away, like a sulky schoolgirl. And we were silent again.

Then after another minute or two, 'It's good to see you again, Sam.'

'That's what your mother said. You're sounding like her.'

She pulled a face. 'I know, I know. You are old, Father William and I'm old, old, old, like my mother. Only I'm a spinster lady and she has a fine family.'

'Your mother doesn't look old, Isabel, and you certainly don't.' I wasn't flattering her. If anything, she looked girlish.

'Sam, can you keep a secret?'

'Yes?'

'I don't want to be like my mother. Don't say that again, please.'

'OK.'

'Did you marry, Sam?'

'Yes.'

'Once, twice, thirty-three times?'

'Just once.'

'Are you still …'

'No, can't you tell?'

'No, I wouldn't have asked if I'd known. No, that's not true. You're right. I could tell. But did you love her?'

'Well, I thought so for a while.'

'A while! How long is a while?'

'Not long. Just a short while. Then it seemed like there had never been anything there in the first place and I think she thought so too. And then she ran off with this Mexican …'

'*This* Mexican, not that one?'

'Well, no, though you're right to ask. There were quite a few around at the time.'

'So you got divorced? Just like that?'

'It wasn't difficult. We were married in Vegas, divorced in Reno – the day after we knew there was nothing there anymore.'

'So you were living in Nevada?'

'No, not exactly. We were living in Arizona. But let's stop this conversation. I didn't come here to talk about myself.'

'OK, that's fine. You never did much, did you? But I'm so glad you got rid of her, Sam. I hate to think of you married among all those clothes-stand cacti and lunar hills and maybe dying in Death Valley …'

'That's in California.'

'I know, I know. Don't forget you're talking to the world's greatest geography student …'

'Who didn't finish her course.'

'And who is having salt rubbed in that wound, all these years later. You certainly know how to make a girl feel good, Sam. But I *do* know about places. Always did, always will. If you were living in Arizona and getting married and divorced in Nevada, it wouldn't take much imagination to pop over the state line into California to die desperately, but in an aesthetically pleasing way, though as I hope you're realising, I … am … mightily … glad … that … you … did … NOT! Sam?'

'Yes?'

'Maybe you could tell me about Las Vegas?'

'It's the best and worst place in the world. You can get everything there. Fine art and complete crap and …'

'And …?'

'And nothing really. I can't describe places like you. It has the Eiffel Tower, a pyramid, the Grand Canal, an Italian lake, the Statue of Liberty and Michelangelo's David. Everything and nothing. All fake, but sometimes so real you can't tell the difference. Fakes can be fascinating, but it's not real like Bubbleby.'

'Bubbleby isn't quite what it seems either, you know.'

We were nearing the foot of the hill, where the lane widened.

'Has it changed much – the pub?'

'I'll leave you to decide. Do you remember the locals? Stuart knew them all. They think most of our family are standoffish, but Stuart was a good mixer and he got on with them. They like me too. I worked there for a while. As a barmaid. They're always nice to me.'

'I must have met them, I guess, if they're the same locals, but I don't really remember any of them. It *has* been a long time.'

'Well, there's Bill Crofter, John Mason, Jake Baker and …'.

'… old Uncle Tom Cobleigh and all?'

'Could be. I'll leave you to decide.'

'No clues? No hints? I have to work everything out for myself?'

'Yes, I think so – for the moment.'

'They're all fine rustic names.'

'Names don't tell you much about character, unless people try to live up to them.'

We were crossing the green. Just in time, because a few drops of rain were starting to fall. As we approached the Hope, I could hear music inside. Van

Morrison, again. 'Have I told you lately that I love you?' If you can't beat 'em, join 'em. I began to hum and then sang the few words I could remember.

'No, you haven't told me lately, Sam. As a matter of fact I don't think you ever did. But I don't just mean me. I mean the whole family. You know what my favourite Van Morrison song is?'

'No?'

'"The Great Deception". The one about people living in a "world of lies"?'

'I don't know it.'

'Count yourself lucky, then. You've travelled, but you've led a sheltered life.' She smiled, wanly. And now, although she fascinated me, particularly because I felt the need to reconcile the Isabels I was encountering with the student Isabel, Stuart's sister, whom I'd known years before, I felt I was being patronized by someone, who despite her imaginative flights of fancy, had less experience of life than me. I didn't show it, but inwardly I was irritated.

She pushed open the door to the 'Bar' side of the Hope. It began to come back to me. There was the posh side with tables for dining, and then there was the Bar, with scarcely anywhere to sit – three or four stools and two benches, one on each side of the Bar's single table.

'I thought we were going to have lunch?'

'We are, Sam. We are. This side we get lunch and conversation. *Pazienza.* Everything comes to those who wait.'

I'm told patience is one of my virtues, but I was becoming increasingly frustrated by her evasiveness. After all, this was the same woman who had written 'NOW ISN'T SOON ENOUGH' earlier in the day. Still I wasn't going to make a scene in the pub.

The Hope Inn

The Hope Inn may or may not be the oldest pub in Lincolnshire. There are rival claimants, such as the King's Head in Tealby. But the Hope is certainly a plausible contender. Stuart had told me it was the oldest according to one criterion. Did he say it was the oldest pub, or the oldest building to house a pub, or the oldest building in continuous use as a pub? I think it may have been the last of these, because I remember him joking about the staying power of the drinkers. Something about continuous drinking for five hundred years, never once going home and being sustained in their longevity by their boozing. Not exactly binge drinkers or steady regular drinkers, but both. Men and women who had never abandoned Hope.

The Hope Inn certainly ministered to my image of what an 'oldest pub' might be. The floorboards creak, the thatched roof houses birds' nests, and the doorway is narrow and low – you stoop to go in, and people were shorter in the Middle Ages, weren't they? Inside the ceiling is almost as low; it has beams just above head height. Most of all, there are *legends* attached to the Hope. They say Sir Charles Cavendish bivouacked some of his troops there during the Civil War; they say John Wesley preached from a dais erected by the gabled lower windows (no record of whether he drank here, though!); they say Tennyson composed parts of *In Memoriam* in the Bar. So many stories! Impossible to get at the truth of them, but enough to convince everyone that the Hope Inn has played its part in history, even if most of the stories are apocryphal and Bubbleby is a backwater now.

As we entered the Bar, its present occupants looked as though they might have been there forever. I walked in just before Isabel and enquiring eyes turned towards me, not exactly making me feel unwelcome, but letting me know I was an outsider. Isabel was just behind me and as soon as the drinkers spied her, their reaction changed. You could tell that, despite the White family's reputation for being apart from the village, *she* was very welcome. It was harder to gauge her response to them, though she was charm personified.

'Hi Bill, hi Jake. Hello Harry and Ben. Do you remember Sam, Stuart's best friend? He used to come here sometimes with Stuart.'

There was no glint of recognition in their faces, but equally, if I'd met any of them before, I didn't remember them now. It had, after all, been quite a few years and I'd only been to the Hope a couple of times. Still they were relaxed with me now. Any friend of Stuart's and Isabel's, was, it seemed, a friend of … everyone's. Jake, a stocky cheerful man in his late forties, bought us a drink. Harry, a slightly younger, more serious 'bucolic' type, solicitously began to ask about every member of the White family, particularly dwelling on Uncle Wilf and Sherry, the family dog. Then he asked me if I'd seen Stuart lately and I confessed that it'd been years since I'd seen my 'best friend'. Afterwards I'd realise that one member of the White family hadn't been mentioned and that was Laura. Perhaps, though, they saw her often enough not to need to ask. It occurred to me that I'd never thought about whether she was gregarious. To my shame, I'd only seen her as Stuart and Isabel's mother. I'd never considered what personal and public worlds she might inhabit. Did she keep to herself on the hilltop at The Weavers, or was she a regular in the village store, the pub, the church?

'Are you staying long, Sam?', Bill, a man of about sixty with the physiognomy of a bloodhound, asked. I didn't know how to respond, so I looked to Isabel for an answer. She wasn't giving much away. 'For a while,' she replied.

And then the talk meandered into the commonplaces and clichés of country life. Just what I imagined conversation in a village like Bubbleby would be like.

'That Gerry Howden is a good lad, isn't he?'

'He certainly is. You know, after he finishes work this evening, he's off to cut grass at Paul Smith's farm near Louth, where they're having the sports day next Saturday.'

'Yes, he said he hoped Paul would have done most of it, so he'll just have to finish off. But he's never work shy. He'll do it all, if he has to.'

'There aren't too many good 'uns like him around now, are there?'

'There certainly aren't. You know Phil and Edith are having a lot of problems with their strawberries this year. They've got blight. You just don't know what's coming next these days, do you? All this ruddy global warming.'

'You never said a truer word. And the farmers up near the Top. The problems they're having! This year's drought is next year's flood. You just can't plan ahead anymore.'

'Well, not unless you plan for floods, gales and earthquakes', said Ben, the lugubrious barman. Isabel explained: there had been an earthquake, with its epicentre near Market Rasen, not too many miles away, the year before. Nonetheless I couldn't help thinking that extreme weather events were rare here.

The chatter continued: 'Did you hear that Mitch, the grocer, gave up his delivery round?' 'No, never! How long ago was that? I thought he'd be doing it till he dropped.' 'The price of petrol. We'll all be bankrupt if it goes on like this, won't we?' 'There's nothing to watch on the telly these evenings, is there?' 'Tell me about it.' 'It's enough to drive a man to drink.' 'As long as someone else is doing the driving. They even had extra police out to catch drinkers last Christmas, you know.' The voices droned on, merging into one another. To a wanderer like me, they were a chorus from a bygone era, an affirmative slice of rural life.

Isabel was asking Ben what was left from the lunchtime menu. 'Well, we had steak and kidney pud, Whitby scampi and vegetarian lasagne, but …'. He hesitated.

Jake chimed in, 'He always does this. Tells you what *was* on the menu. Not what's left.'

'What is left, Ben?' Isabel asked, affecting an ever-so, ever-so-polite manner that I remembered as one of her registers.

'Whitby scampi and chips.'

'Whitby scampi that's never been nearer Whitby than when they unloaded it at Grimsby from goodness knows where – Thailand or somewhere like that,' said Jake.

'Then I'd like Whitby scampi,' said Isabel, happy to join in the banter. I played my part too, 'Scampi for me as well, please.'

'Two scampis it is then. Sit yourselves down,' said Ben. 'It'll just be a few minutes.' We took our glasses – my red wine (not a man's drink?) and her cider to the table with the benches.

'This is nice,' I ventured. 'Nice to get away from it all.'

'That's what they think,' said Isabel.

'What do you mean?'

'They like to come here for an hour or two at lunch, if they can manage it. There's a group of about eight of them – always very busy – and it looks as though just these three made it here today.'

'But they all live nearby?'

'Oh yes, they all live in the village, but none of them work here. There's no work here anymore, except for Ben and his wife, the people in the store and the vicar, who has to run to two other churches anyway.'

'But there's farming?'

'Yes, I guess so, but you don't see many farmers here in the Hope. This lot like to play at being country bumpkins and they put on a special act for visitors. You should feel honoured. If you weren't here, they'd be talking about their stocks and shares, or their holidays in the Caribbean. Jake's an estate agent, Bill's a solicitor and Harry is a doctor.'

'Pity his poor patients, after he's left here.'

'Oh no, don't worry. He's very good. He knows just how much to drink to be on top form in the afternoons. Sober he's not great and drunk he's barely OK, but when he gets the balance right, and he nearly always does, he's the best doctor for miles around. People at death's door will wait days to see him rather than have someone else mess them up.'

'Is he your doctor?'

'Well, he's looked after the family sometimes. He's part of a practice. With all the trouble we've had these last few years, we've seen all of them … quite a bit. But yes, he comes to us and he's by far the best of the bunch.'

'All the trouble?'

'I think I need to visit the little girl's room,' and she was gone in an instant, through a door that was warped and rotting with age.

The scampi arrived. Ben put the plates down and asked if I'd like 'any sauces' ('Yes, Tartar, if you have it.' 'Yes', he did). Then he added, 'Take care of her, Sam. For all of us. Take care of her.' He looked towards Jake, who took this as his cue to come over to me. 'Ben's right. Do what you can for her, while you're here. She's been through a lot, all of them have, but especially her and Alice.'

'And Stuart? Where is Stuart?'

'We don't know. I don't know if any of them do either. He left fairly suddenly.'

At that moment Isabel re-emerged and Jake seamlessly switched back to the earlier small talk. 'That's what I always sez. Driving on these roads is bad enough without the bikers trying to pass you on the bends. Some of those lads need their heads examined. You need eyes in the back of your head to see them.'

Isabel sat down and stayed silent for a few moments. Then, 'Alice will be home with Alf in a couple of hours. I think you'll like him.'

'Alf? Who's Alf?'

'Her little boy. He's really cute. Bright as a button. Been going to school a while now.'

'How old is he?'

'About six. Yes, that's right. He just had a birthday. Yes, he *is* six.'

'And does he ...'

'No, he doesn't have a father. Alice always says she was too poor to get him one. But she's wonderful with him.'

'Does she work?'

'Yes, she's a dentist's receptionist. She has a good arrangement – with her hours. She drops him off at school, works through the day and then knocks off early, so she can pick him up. He's adorable. You'll love him. What do you think of the scampi?'

'Not bad, for the only food in town.'

'Bloody marvellous for last knockings, if you ask me. Pity about the chips!'

'Yes. Would you like some more Tartar Sauce? It helps to take away the taste.'

'OK, good idea, but I don't think I can go many more. You know you'll have to eat a big meal tonight, don't you?'

'I feared as much. Who does the cooking?'

'Mum. She who rules the kitchen rules the world.'

'And you and Alice, you don't ever?'

'Only bits and pieces, like Alice's scones and well, you know all about them.'

'Who could forget them?'

'So from that point of view it's a good thing that she doesn't get to cook. We've both tried, and so has Jules, but when Mum is in control, Mum is in control. The only one who can ever crack her is Uncle Wilf and he's losing a bit of his drive now.'

'That's a pity.'

'Yep, he could have been a great chef, if he'd put his mind to it.'

'Isabel, why am I here? Why did you summon me?' I put down my knife and fork, grabbed her hand and tried to get her to come to the point.

'Don't worry. I'm going to tell you, but not here in public – OK? Soon, I promise. You can look at Stuart's folders. It's for the best. Really. I promise you.'

'So it's all to do with Stuart? Not you?'

'Well, yes, Stuart, but not just Stuart. It's to do with all of us.'

Scampi had 'disappeared', further progress on the chips seemed impossible, Bill and Harry had left and Ben was beginning to look as though he was ready to close up for the afternoon.

Jake came across and said, 'I do remember you, Sam. You and Stuart brought Sherry here a couple of times. Ben only allows dogs in this side, not in with the fancy diners the other side. She was just a puppy then, but she was an instant hit with everyone. She still is, of course. It's good to see you back here. Will you come this evening?'

'This evening? Is that something special?' Jake nodded towards a poster on the wall: *Karaoke at the Hope. Join Us for Midsummer Madness. Monday July*

13th. Sir Charles Cavendish would be turning in his grave, assuming his ghost wasn't lurking in the innermost recesses of the Hope. No real Civil War is ever over. Who said that?

'It sounds great,' and looking towards Isabel, I added, 'I'll try to come.' She nodded.

'Don't forget to bring your voice. Everyone is expected to join in. We've got some stars of our own, but new talent is always welcome.' He was still being genial, but now the front he and his friends had been putting on was gone and his gaze was earnest. I realised he was trying to convey something more, trying to make sure I came back. I struggled to decode what his eyes were saying, but they gave nothing away. He nodded at Isabel, 'And make sure you bring her with you. Wilf, too, if you can get him to come. We don't see him as often as we used to.'

We walked back up the hill. The rain had held off and the distance seemed shorter than it had when we were coming down. Isabel talked a bit more about Alice and her brother Jules, who was working as a primary school teacher and would also be home soon. And she spoke fondly about Uncle Wilf, really her great uncle, who had been living at The Weavers as long as anyone could remember. He'd been out walking Sherry, the dog, when I arrived. Wilf hadn't worked for forty years. Back then, before we were born, Isabel's father had given up work in favour of a life of alcoholism. When he discovered that, Wilf decided to follow suit, but unlike his nephew he was a survivor.

We reached The Weavers. Sherry came running out to meet us, an elderly black-and-tan cross between a Jack Russell and a King Charles Spaniel. Despite her age, she still had all her terrier liveliness and her spaniel affectionateness. Ignoring Isabel, she rushed straight towards me, barking enthusiastically and licking my outstretched hand once she reached me. Her monochrome world had burst into technicolour with her joy at my arrival.

'Is she always like this with strangers?' I asked Isabel.

'Strangers? You're not a stranger. She remembers you. Have we forgotten you? You us? Course not – and she's got a head start over all of us, with her hyper-super, extra extraordinary sense of smell. And anyway, she's more intelligent than most people without that. And Uncle Wilf talks to her endlessly. So she's very well informed. He probably told her you're coming.'

'She remembers my name?'

'You'd better believe it.'

And there, a few steps behind her was Wilf, smiling and holding his arms out, as far apart as a person possibly could, to welcome me with an embrace. 'How are you, my champion? Come here quickly. I need an excuse to celebrate. This lot treat me like I'm senile and the last time I consulted my biography I was only eighty-seven years old.'

He had aged, but not greatly and it was hard to believe he could be eighty-seven. His short, untrimmed beard gave him a Santa Claus look, but this was outdone by his spectacles – ultramarine frames and large brown-tinted lenses. Amid all the hesitancies and the uncertainties I felt about meeting Isabel and the other members of the White family again, it was sheer uncomplicated delight to see Wilf. He was the grandfather I'd never had. He gave me a bear hug.

As we pulled apart he said, 'I plan to educate you while you're here, Samuel, but you need a rest, so we can delay your induction until tomorrow, provided you swear on all that's holy to you that you will be a good pupil and follow your lessons conscientiously. Is that a deal? If it is, we can drink now and start our tour of the – er, um – collections tomorrow.'

Wilf's joie de vivre was infectious. Without hesitation I became a bit-player in the drama that was his life. 'It's a deal, Uncle Wilf. I swear.'

'Wonderful! What's your salvation, great man? Johnny Walker, Chivas Regal, a John Smith's, a Disaronno, an Argentinian malbec or a white vin de pays d'Oc, alias first-class plonk.'

'I place myself in your hands, Uncle Wilf. My education starts here and now.'

'Then it's the malbec. 'And then winking, 'Disaronno is a digestive and so provided we get fed, which usually happens around here, we can see what you think of that afterwards. Today we eat, drink …'

'And be merry, for tomorrow we …?'

'Well perhaps, Samuel. There have been deaths in this family, you know, but I refuse to be intimidated. I come from a simple generation and my innocence is my redemption. I rejoice in being credulous, ingenuous, naïve, idiotic and just possibly even gullible. When I was young, we listened to the radio and my favourite of favourites was a programme called *Educating Archie*. Peter Brough and Archie Andrews. A ventriloquist and his dummy. I loved them, but I ask you. In all honesty. A radio ventriloquist! And I never questioned it! So who was the dummy? Q.E.D. I was, am and always will be an ignoramus.'

I wasn't sure whether he was under the influence. Then he suddenly ran away from me and hid himself behind an ancient oak tree. He was out of sight, but his voice was booming across The Weavers' drive. It took me a moment to realise he had taken on the role of a ventriloquist and was speaking in another voice. 'My lips don't move, but I can divulge secrets. "Oh no, not him, spare him. Take me instead." It didn't happen that way, though. She didn't let it happen that way. His mother wasn't there. So she couldn't have said that to her.'

And Wilf reappeared from behind the tree, himself again, beaming from ear to ear like the man in the moon, which was appropriate as he launched into a new repertoire … of moontalk. 'The wonders of modern technology, Samuel. Have you heard about the moonshot? In the West Country, they're planning to send a cheddar to the moon. It'll be the first cheese in space.' And, just as Isabel had reported, he began moonwalking, a superannuated Michael Jackson, collapsing the years between age and youth, reminding me of the ways in which Michael had eroded the shadow line between boyhood and middle age. And he began singing: 'It's a marvellous night for a moondance'.

I was lost for words. It was impossible not to warm to Wilf, but almost as impossible to read him. Was I being controlled and if so could Wilf, joyful, lovable Wilf, be involved? I blurted out, 'Do you like Van Morrison, Uncle Wilf?'

'Dan who? Never heard of him, but if you recommend him, that's good enough for me, my champion.'

'What exactly do you mean: they're trying to send a cheese to the moon? Who are they? The government?'

'No, no. *They* don't have that much imagination. It's a group of good people somewhere in the West Country. Their moonshot will come soon. Eat your heart out, Neil Armstrong. It's the fiftieth anniversary coming up and cheese will follow you. Cheddar will go where no cheese has gone before. One small step for cheddar, one giant leap for cheesekind.' And as Sherry came running up to us again, her tongue hanging out, he added, 'That's right, sweetheart, Laika was up there well before Yuri. That dog was a true pioneer. The first and the greatest of all. Where dogs lead, humans follow. And Sherry shall have cheese for tea.'

Was he descending into dementia? Was he drunk? Was he totally in control of his cascade of words? We walked towards the house and as we did so, his expression changed. His moonbeam grin gave way to a gentle, more serious smile. 'Alice and Alf will be here soon, Sam. And then Jules will come, and Laura and you and I and Isabel are all here already. It's all so exciting. What a wonderful reunion we will have! If only the others could be here too. But we must remember one thing, my shining star. There are lots of liars in these parts. Even in the family, I'm sorry to say. So take care, my friend. Take care, dear Samuel!'

Those words again. I didn't know where this was leading, but wanted to keep him on the subject. 'How can one tell the liars, Uncle Wilf?'

'By their toenails shall ye know them. But it's not easy. The liars have long toenails, but ask anyone if they have short toenails and they will say "yes". The liars lie; honest people tell the truth. Everyone says they have short toenails. It's a sad thing, but liars never own up and so all one can do is …'

'Pull off their shoes and their socks or their tights or whatever footwear they have on?'

'Yes, of course, my genius. You are so wise and you are half-way there in the blink of an eyelid. But it's not an easy matter. The liars won't ever let you see their unsocked feet and the truth-tellers take offence. It's not at all easy. So, great Samuel, what you have to do is get yourself a dog. Sherry doesn't wear shoes, but she is an expert smeller of toenails. She knows who can be trusted, but sad to say, she can also be bought. She can be a mercenary in the war to detect truth. She doesn't come cheap, but a little bit of Lincolnshire poacher and she's anybody's.'

'Uncle Wilf, I'm sure Sherry is a lady of impeccable virtue.'

'She is, my mastermind. She surely is. Just don't test that virtue with cheese.'

We were inside the hallway of the house now, going towards the lounge, and Wilf was chortling gleefully, '"Sam, Sam was a dirty old man/ Washed his face in a frying pan,/ Combed his hair with the leg of a chair,/ Sam, Sam was a dirty old man." Samuel was summoned from the dead by the witch of Endor and they say *she* was a great ventriloquist. Samuel, great man, you can be any Sam in the world, but please, please never be *Uncle* Sam. You will promise me that, won't you?'

'Yes, Uncle Wilf,' I said, 'I promise. Don't worry. I lived over there, you know, but I was never a convert, and I never will be.' I didn't have the heart to tell him that Sam wasn't my real name.

Wilf

We all have roles in the wooden O of family life, Sherry. Sometimes I think I should have left long ago, but I play my part, even though I'm in the seventh of the seven ages. I get tired but it's necessary. It's good that Sam has come. That's necessary too. I like the boy, but I shan't be the one to tell him. I always liked him. I'll just show him the collections. At my age, who could ask more of me? I care for them all. You too Sherry. Yes, you most of all. You never play a part do you? You are always just the same and you are very beautiful. Come here, my sweetheart. That's a good dog. And remember. Don't go near that horrible pond again. I know you like to swim, but not in that nasty pond. I'll tell you what we will do, if you are a good dog. We will write to the IOC. You know who they are? Yes, of course you do, because you are a very smart dog. Forgive me for even asking. We will write to them tomorrow and tell them that they must put the dog paddle into the Olympics. Then all the world will watch you swim and swim. And you will be a winner in the spaniel class and maybe in the terrier class too. Come onto my lap, dear soul. Well jumped! That's a clever girl. You are such a good jumper. As good a jumper as when you were a puppy. They don't make dogs like you anymore.

The Weavers

Alice arrived home in her smart-looking Vauxhall Astra just after four. And with her was her little boy, Alf, who was every bit as adorable as Isabel had said. Fair-haired, blue-eyed, smiling nervously at meeting a stranger, but excited to see a new arrival who would break the monotony of the house's routine. I didn't remember Alice well. She was a couple of years younger than Isabel and shyer. Dark-haired, five foot three, slimmer than either her mother or Isabel. Slim to the point of emaciation. Seemingly very normal. Not at all my idea of a single mother, but I was stereotyping, because I'd envisaged her as a stay-at-home dutiful daughter. I talked to her about the time we had gone to Woodhall Spa and complimented her on Alf. 'Thank you,' she said, 'I do my best. It's been hard since we lost Glen. He has nightmares sometimes, but he's getting better, thank goodness. Excuse me, will you, while I get out of these work clothes? I'll be back in a few minutes.'

And once she had disappeared upstairs, with Alf in tow, I raised my eyebrows to Isabel: 'Who's Glen? Who was Glen?'

'Oh, forgive me. I should have said. It's just that there's so much to tell. She had another little boy. He was younger than Alf and she lost him about two years ago.'

'Couldn't she afford a father for him either?'

'Sam, this isn't funny. This isn't the least bit funny. Glen is dead.' She turned on her heels and followed Alice upstairs. I was left with Uncle Wilf, who was snoozing in an armchair, Sherry, who was snoring in a corner, and Laura, who was very wide awake. She didn't say much, but I was fairly sure her antennae were picking up everything.

'A lot has happened,' I said to her.

'It's been a long time, Samuel. A lot always happens in families. Time doesn't stand still. It's only when you're away from a place that it seems like it does.'

'Have you been OK, Mrs White? I hope so.'

'Me? Yes, I'm fine. Nothing ever happens to me. Others come and go, but I stay put. Yes, I'm quite OK, thanks. I hope you're not too hungry. It'll be a while before we have dinner.'

'Oh no, I'm fine. Absolutely fine. We had food down at The Hope Inn.'

'I hope it was OK.'

I wondered if she disapproved of pub grub, but her perfect manners made it impossible to tell. 'Yes, it was fine. There wasn't much choice, but we had some scampi and that was quite OK.'

She smiled. 'I've got a few things to do in the kitchen. So please make yourself at home. It looks as though Isabel has deserted you for a few minutes. There are magazines to read, if you'd like to. This one is a good one. *Lincolnshire Life*.' I flicked through the pages of the magazine for a couple of minutes, but I couldn't concentrate and turned instead to the narratives of industry and idleness in the Hogarth prints on the wall of the lounge. Two opposed, but complementary lives. The apprentices in the prints seemed like twins who had travelled in different directions.

Jules arrived in a shabby 4x4 about an hour later. Tall, lanky and awkward. A tousled mop of ginger hair. Was he the youngest of Stuart's brothers and sisters, or was that Steve? It was hard to associate him with Stuart, or for that matter with Isabel. I remembered Stuart calling him 'the clever one in the family', or was *that* Steve? He was awkward with me at first, timid and defensive. Gradually, though, he began to relax as I fed him a few questions. He told me about his day at school, the problems he had teaching a mixed-ability class, with several Eastern European migrants who were often brighter than their Lincolnshire-born peers, but disadvantaged by their lack of fluency in English. He said he was a nervous driver and I sensed that the local roads were more of an ordeal for him than the day at school. Slowly, as he unwound, a variant of the White family charm broke through his reserve.

Laura came back to us. 'We'll be having dinner soon, so Jules, would you show Sam up to his room, please?' It was more an order than a question and Jules fell into line readily. I hadn't yet brought my bag in from the car, so I fetched that, accompanied by Sherry, who was eager to sniff through my belongings. Back inside, she settled quickly enough again and Jules took me upstairs to a large attic-like room under a sloping roof at the back of the top storey, the only bedroom on that floor. It was sparsely furnished, but one wall was lined with books and it had a large double bed and a wash basin. A single casement window in the wall opposite the bed opened outwards and there was a pine desk tucked away in a small alcove to the right of the bed. A strangely shaped room, not exactly a Gothic attic, but an odd room all the same. And it occurred to me that, although it showed no signs of having been occupied recently – no clothes in the single ancient wardrobe, no tell-tale traces of water or marks in the sink – it wasn't a guest room.

'Is this Stuart's room, Jules?'

And now he began to go back into his shell. 'No, not Stuart's.'

'But it *is* somebody's, isn't it?' Spoken as gently as I could manage, to avoid any impression of prying.

'It was Steve's.'

'And he's not here at the moment?'

'Yes, that's right. I mean, no, he's not here. He's been gone for quite a while now.'

I unpacked, freshened up in a bathroom along the hallway, one of several in The Weavers, and went back downstairs, where, thank goodness, Uncle Wilf had woken up and the atmosphere was more relaxed. Alice and Alf were with him. Laura was still cooking, and there was no sign of Isabel.

'Samuel, Samuel, Samuel, how can we thank you for coming to this poor benighted black hole in the cosmos to shower joy on us? I was just telling this young master of the universe' – he gestured towards Alf – 'that not every family has cabinets of curiosities and that if he behaves himself and eats his spinach and doesn't play with bad boys and girls, one day he shall have one of his own. And Sam, fear not, you will be inducted post haste. You shall hear the full history of cabinets of curiosities.' Alice's grimace was the facial equivalent of a groan. She clearly found Wilf's unquenchable exuberance difficult to stomach.

'The first thing you need to know is that curiosities may be housed in glass cabinets, but only if you don't have much space, because properly speaking the cabinets should be rooms. So here at The Weavers, after Alf's grand granddaddy passed on, we decided that his collection should be a room and I should have a room and everyone should have a room and each room would be a small wonder of the world.

'Each cabinet is a world in miniature, dear champion. It brings together objects from hither and thither; it mixes them up; it shuffles them. There is no purity in cabinets of curiosities. Collectors are mongrels ….'

'Like Sherry?' asked Alf.

'Yes and no. Like Sherry and not like Sherry. Sherry is a collection of two. She is a first-generation mongrel, and there are many more diversaratified dogs than Sherry, great master …'

'What's diversaratified, Uncle Wilf?'

Alice intervened, 'Please don't confuse him, Wilf.' And then to Alf, 'It's a word he made up, sweetheart. Don't worry about it.'

'As I was saying, the cabinets are mongrels. Collectors are no respecters of persons and they plunder, pillage and loot from all around the globe, until they have contained the world in a nutshell, with this rubbing shoulders with that, with like in bed with unlike and with rich bubbling away alongside poor. When the cabinets began, they were wonder-rooms. Mr Ripley – you know who I mean? Mr Ripley of the never-ending "Believe It or Nots?" – would never have believed it, since he was never more than a pale imitator of those pioneers. He has done no more than follow in their footsteps and his small feet have never filled the super-size shoes, in which they led the way.'

Laura was carrying plates through to the dining area at the far end of the room. 'Where is all this leading, Wilf?', she asked.

'It is leading nowhere and everywhere,' said Wilf. 'The important thing is that this young man understands that cabinets of curiosities are venerable – they have a provenance, a genealogy and a pedigree.'

'A mongrel pedigree?' I suggested, trying to enter into the spirit of his monologue.

'Quite so, great Sam, who sometimes reaches the finishing post before others have left the starting-blocks. So let me cut to the chase, make a long story short and even get to the point. The point is that we are continuing an honourable tradition. We are collectors all, and tomorrow and tomorrow and tomorrow I shall begin to escort Samuel on his tour of our worlds in miniature. The great collectors traversed the globe and brought everything home – the grand tourists brought paintings and statuary; others went further afield. Sir Joseph Banks, a Lincolnshire man himself, cooked, Kewed and botanized the world and many of those colonial heroes, let's be honest, brought home anything they could get their grubby little paws on. No offence, Sherry.' She wagged her tail at the mention of her name. 'None taken? That's good. Just go to the British Museum to see Sir Joe's spoils. He donated treasures to the nation and he became a national treasure. Of course, he was a bit of an exporter too. They say he was the one who decided this country should send its surplus convicts to Botany Bay. So he wasn't your average run-of-the-mill collector. But Sir Joe was only one of many. Others followed in his muddy footsteps. The Parthenon lost its marbles. Rosetta got stoned. And mummies lost their daddies. Anything and everything was up for grabs and many, many grabbables were grabbed. And those collectors who didn't travel purchased freaks of nature from those who sallied forth on their behalf.' It was hard to tell where Wilf's irony began and where it ended.

He whittled on, 'Of course, we latter-day initiates into this cosmopolitan society have no such good fortune, but we strive and struggle and strain to imitate the greatness of those whose shoes *we*, too, can never fill and … and … and, thanks to all our endeavourings, the White family has become unique in having so many collections. Sir John Soane managed a mummified cat and a progressing rake amid his many fine objects, but most of his booty is not curious. Burton Constable, not a million miles from here in Holderness, has a marvellous cabinet, replete with shells and fossils and instruments for measuring the weirdness of the world, in order to make it seem weirder still. Our wonders are housed on a more modest scale, but they are away from the public gaze and truly Samuel, my champion of champions, none of those collections is quite as curious as ours. Furthermore, theirs are singular; we are plural. Ours may be smaller in scope, but we outdo them all in our taste for the marvellous, the odd and, let's be honest … the downright ridiculous.'

I sympathised with Laura's response to this avalanche of words. Where *was* all this leading? Would the cabinets provide some kind of answer to the mysteries that seemed to engulf the White family? Or were they *just* oddities, arbitrary miscellanies of contingent objects? And Wilf? Was Wilf a seer or a windbag?

At this point, Isabel and Jules reappeared and Laura rescued us by saying dinner was ready. The table in the dining part of this large room could have seated ten and it occurred to me that perhaps it had once, without visitors: Uncle Wilf, Laura and her husband, Stuart, Isabel, Steve, Martin, Alice, Jules, Alf and Glen. That made eleven, but then all of them could never have been here at the same time. Tonight there were seven of us, and Sherry, from whom the years dropped away at the first sniff of food. Laura told Wilf not to feed her, but sitting across from him, I saw his hand dangle down several times and, although Sherry toured the table, casting her big brown begging eyes on all of us, she spent most of the meal within touching distance of Wilf.

He was less extravagant than before, possibly because he was focused on the serious business of eating and drinking, or perhaps because Laura's attention to the protocols of dining was keeping his excesses in check. He insisted on taking sole charge of the bottle of vin de pays d'Oc he had mentioned earlier, calling it the 'best doc for all ills' and staging a brief pantomime by producing a ruler from his pocket to measure out scrupulously equal amounts for the four of us who were drinking (Jules and Laura weren't). But he was more subdued than before and, when towards the end of the meal, he campaigned for a second bottle and Laura raised her eyebrows, he surrendered meekly.

Laura was a splendid cook and, as with almost everything about her, her table was immaculate. Cutlery, plates, serving spoons, dishes, napkins, wine glasses, drinking glasses, place mats, two lazy susans with silver salt and pepper shakers and a selection of sauces. Everything was unostentatiously in place. I'd been thinking of the White family as dysfunctional, but in Laura's presence this view was hard to sustain. Under her tutelage, everything and everyone seemed to function perfectly. She had that rare gift of bringing everything to a table perfectly cooked, at the right moment and with a minimal expenditure of effort.

Frustrated by Laura over the second bottle of wine, Wilf was swift to produce the bottle of Disaronno, while she and Alice were clearing the table. I remembered the taste. Amaretto. The almond-flavoured digestive. So much easier on the stomach than grappa. Isabel joined us, still saying very little, and now free from Laura's watchful eyes, Wilf was back on top form. He jollied us along with more news of the cheeseshot to the moon and stories of how the curiosities in the cabinets had come to the Weavers. Once or twice I saw Isabel looking at me out of the corner of her eye and, although I thought I could detect a question in her expression, I didn't know what it meant. Was she simply wondering whether I was a willing bit-player in Wilf's pantomime, or was she on the verge of asking me something else? Or, I hoped, hovering on the verge of *telling* me something more?

Wilf managed to pour us a second Disaronno before Laura and propriety returned. Eluding her glance for a second, he winked at me conspiratorially, as if to say that subversion was impossible in her presence, but there would be other opportunities. Alice took Alf to bed, Jules went off to mark papers, and then to my surprise, Isabel started to talk. I'd thought we would have to be alone before she would tell me anything, but now she began, with Wilf and her mother there, both of them keeping silent.

'It's not the same here, Sam. Not like before, when we were a big family. People have disappeared.'

She paused and, guessing that she was waiting to see whether Wilf and Laura would let her continue, I risked prompting her. 'Disappeared? Did Stuart disappear?'

'No, not exactly. He left. Just under two years ago.'

'And you don't know where he went? Where he is now?'

'He phoned me once. From France – about a month after he left. But nothing since then.' I was finally beginning to make a bit of progress. If she hadn't begun to open up a bit, I think I'd have been ready to jump in the car and head for home first thing the next morning.

'But why did he leave? Didn't he say? Has anyone else heard from him?'

She didn't answer. She became guarded again and I wondered if she had told me as much as she felt was permissible under the censorship of her mother and Uncle Wilf. I tried another question, as much to probe their attitude as to get an answer from Isabel.

'Stuart didn't say why he left then?'

And then Laura interceded. 'No, I think he just felt he needed a new challenge. There wasn't too much for him here. He seemed to want a complete break. For a while at least.'

I looked at Wilf, who put a hand to his eyes, then his ears and then his lips. Three wise monkeys.

'Do you think he'll come back?'

Laura shrugged, 'We really don't know.'

I turned back to Isabel. 'Stuart left, but others *disappeared*?'

'Yes, Steve and Martin disappeared.'

'And Glen?'

'No, Glen died. I told you. He drowned – in the pond just beyond the back garden. It was awful.'

'Alice must have been devastated.'

'Yes, she was. I mean, she is.'

'And Steve and Martin? When did they disappear?'

Laura interrupted again, looking towards me, but mainly directing her remark towards Isabel I felt. 'It's been very distressing. Isabel can tell you more tomorrow. You've had a long day, Samuel.'

'But it's not over yet, Mum. Sam and I are going back to the Hope. It's karaoke night.'

'Isabel, you're asking Sam to do too much in one day. He'll be exhausted.'

'It's fine, Mrs White. Really. I'll be OK, and we'll drive down this time.'

Isabel intervened. 'I'll drive, so he can have another drink. Don't worry, Mum. I'll look after him. And I'm quite sober.'

In the car I tried her with another question or two, but it seemed that her mother had silenced her again for the time being. I'd only been with her for a few hours, but it seemed like she'd left me hanging on for days.

Karaoke Night

I wasn't prepared for the scrum we encountered the instant we stepped inside the Hope – this time in the larger, posh side. We had to elbow our way to the bar, where Ben had two helpers in attendance. It was hard to order a drink above the din.

Karaoke night at the Hope has to be heard to be believed. There was a single governing principle: a well-known tune, a subversive set of lyrics. As we entered, a stout 'farmer-type' (by now I was beginning to think he was probably an accountant) was massacring an old Glen Campbell classic:

> *By the time I get to Dublin*
> *There'll be two of me ...*

And then, with a pretence of drunken staggering:

> *By the time I get to Albuquerque*
> *I'll be jerky...*

The mood was convivial, but manic. My vision of Bubbleby as a quiet backwater wasn't holding up too well. Anything seemed possible. If someone had offered me heroin, I wouldn't have been surprised. If I'd discovered that this was the nerve centre of MI5, I would have taken it in my stride. If I'd been told Martians had landed on the roof, I would have asked what they would they like to drink. I couldn't see Bill or Jake anywhere. Harry was down the far end of the bar. He waved. He might as well have been a hundred miles away.

'Shall we sit down, Sam? There are a couple of stools in the corner. We could pull them out.'

'OK.'

We inched our way towards the stools and as we did so, I inadvertently knocked the arm of a chubby middle-aged man, who *really* did look like a salt-of-the-earth 'local' type. It made him spill a drop of his beer.

'Hold on there, young man. There's some first-rate lager gone to floor and we can't have that, can we?' I thought I detected a Yorkshire accent. I assumed he was joking. Despite the hint of menace in his voice, I took this to be a playful piece of 'northern' theatre. I mumbled 'Sorry' and began to move away, only to find my arm held in a vice-like grip.

'Tha' needs to pay for it, laddie. I think another pint is in order.' He was genuinely threatening. And Isabel came to my rescue. Her hand gently took hold of *his* arm and saved me from the major 'scene' I was now imagining might develop. A bar-room brawl from an old Hollywood Western. But Isabel was soothing, placatory. She knew him and he knew her.

'It's OK, Rex. He doesn't mean any harm. He's not from around here, but he's our friend.' A short pause. Then, 'It's so good to see you after this long, and I was hoping I'd have the chance to buy you a drink soon.' And with a flashing smile, 'It's great that we bumped into you like this.' Isabel my rescuer.

'Oh, it's alright then, luvvie. If he's a friend of yours, it's all alright. You don't need to do that. A nice night, with the music an' all, eh?' And the moment was past. Again it seemed that any friend of Isabel's was a friend of everyone's. We reached the stools in the corner.

An overweight woman of fifty, wearing a low-cut scarlet dress, had taken the microphone. She had a vacant expression and to my shame, I said to Isabel that I thought she might be 'a spoon or two short of a full cutlery set'. I was wrong again. 'Tonight, ladies and gentlemen, I want to mend my ways, but I need a little help from my friends.' Her challenged look disappeared as she burst into song, with her own words for 'Help Me Make It through the Night'. Another Bubbleby surprise. Perfect pitch. A wonderful voice.

Yesterday was Fred and Ron

And tomorrow's Bill and Mike.

How I want to be alone!

Won't you help me buy a bike!

'Yes, folks, if you can just cough up a few quid, this poor much put-upon lady, who has had to sell her favours to pay the gas bill and keep the bailiffs from her door, could up sticks and ride away into the sunset on a lovely new bicycle, leaving all her troubles behind her.'

I don't care about this song,
Someone else can have this mike,
If I get three hundred quid,
I could buy a decent bike.

Yesterday was Fred and Ron
And tomorrow's Bill and Mike.
How I want to be alone!
Won't you help me buy a bike.

She got a round of 'encores'. I could hear Bill's voice yelling, 'It's not me. Not me. It's some other Bill.' Then, to change the subject, he started a chant, 'Do your Amy, Aggie! Do Amy!'

Aggie affected bashfulness for a few seconds, before surrendering to 'popular demand'. 'This is the tale of an elderly friend of mine, a dear old soul who wanted to stay put in her lovely little house in Skeggie, the one she had lived in ever since the war – and I do mean *the* War, not the Gulf or Iraq, or any of those shenanigans':

They tried to make me leave my prefab,
But I said no, no, no.
They said I had to pack, and not come back
I had to go, go, go.
I couldn't pay the rent
All my money was spent.

But when they said to leave my prefab
I just yelled no, no, no.

Yet more testimony of the power of 'home'.

'Aggie, Aggie, Aggie. More, more, more.' The chant was deafeningly loud, and I wondered how often the ancient timbers of the Hope had been subjected to this kind of assault. Aggie obliged with another chorus. Then she solemnly announced, 'She was forced to leave and, homeless as she was, the poor evictee went from bad to worse. She descended into the lowest depths of the NHS, down, down, down a greasy slope until she hit rock bottom, hooked on, yes folks, you know what it was – it's happened to all too many of us … prescription drugs. She began to sing again:

I've got pills,
They're multiplying
And I'm losing self-control …

When Aggie finally relinquished the microphone, to my surprise, Isabel was summoned to it. I imagined her declining, or singing a dirge about faraway places, human transience, or perhaps a folksy blues, but nothing of the kind. She picked her way through the crowd and gave a performance to rival Aggie's: an inimitable rendition of 'Annie's Song'. Her regular party piece or a one-night only special? Her voice lacked the strength and mellifluousness of Aggie's, but the mock pathos she injected into the song, holding her jaw as she sang, more than made up for an occasional missed note:

You look like my dentist
When she's doing a filling.
First she smiles sweetly,
But then she starts drilling.
She says, 'Let me fill you

And then fill you again …

As the evening wore on and lips and throats became increasingly lubricated, it was all downhill. Mostly songs from previous eras. Some good not-so-clean fun. There was a raucous 'Penis in Blue Jeans', which everyone enjoyed so much that they clamoured for more of the same and this opened the way for 'Penis, Goddess of Love that You Are' and 'I'm Your Penis, I'm Your Fire.'

After that the lyrics took a turn for the cleaner with a boisterous 'The First Time Ever I Washed My Face', which brought more than half the company to its feet. Then, just when I felt we had entered a time-warp, we were back to the present. I should have seen it coming, when the cries of 'Hen Song, Hen Song' went up:

If I just lay here
Would you lay with me …

'You must be tired,' Isabel suddenly realised. 'The long drive and now all of this.'

'Well, I'm not too bad, but maybe it's getting towards time to go.' I was remembering what Jake had said about bringing my voice with me and I knew that I couldn't compete with what I'd been hearing.

'Let's go then, Sam.'

As we made our way to the door, eggs remained to the fore. A cheerful woman on crutches had taken the microphone and was leading the drinkers in an ear-splitting reworking of 'The Lincolnshire Poacher':

When I first started cooking in famous Lincolnshire,
I found that I was frying for nigh on seven years,
But then I took up poaching as you shall quickly hear.
Oh, 'tis my delight on a shiny night in the season of the year. …

So my wish to find a rustic choir in Bubbleby was fulfilled just at the moment when we were leaving. It was a good note to end on. It had seemed like a long evening at the Hope Inn, but it was only ten thirty when we got back to The Weavers and everyone was still up.

'Did you have a nice evening?' Laura was as polite as ever.

'Yes, it was fun wasn't it, Sam?', said Isabel. A genuine questioning note in her voice. Unsure as to whether I'd enjoyed myself.

'We had a great time,' and then smiling at Laura to reassure her, 'and I'm not the least bit tired. In fact I think I need to unwind from such a busy day.'

This was meant to be Uncle Wilf's cue to offer me another drink. But it was Laura who replied, 'Physical exercise helps. Do you still play table tennis? I remember you used to be terrific.'

'Well, not lately? Why do you ask?'

'We have a table in the games room at the back of the house and the girls need some competition. I think it would be the perfect exercise to help you relax. Wilf, would you tell Alice to come down, so that Samuel can give her a lesson? Then Isabel can take her turn and after that we can have a nightcap.'

It was hard to tell whether she was being solicitous, nurturing or domineering, but it was clear that she controlled domestic life within The Weavers, though Wilf wasn't completely cowed into submission. He got up to do her bidding, muttering, 'Your wish is my command, my lady of the silver spoons. But this is on condition we all have a proper nightcap – none of that Horlicks muck – and Sherry shall be the arbiter of what is a real nightcap.'

Laura smiled.

Ten minutes later I was in the games room with Alice.

'Is Alf asleep OK?'

'Yes, he's fine, thanks. I read to him for a few minutes and he usually gets sleepy and then everything's alright. Thanks for asking.'

And we began an extraordinary game of ping pong. It was years since I'd played what had once been a favourite game with me, but it came back. Not exactly like riding a bicycle, but after about fifteen minutes I felt I was up to speed and Laura was right: I had been good at table tennis. She'd remembered that I'd been the best of the small group of us who played the game at college. Had I told her or had Stuart? But the extraordinariness of the game with Alice had nothing to do with my skill, skill marred only by my getting winded and sweaty after about fifteen minutes, nor Laura's memory. What was amazing was Alice's complete transformation as she played. The shy, almost anorexic woman I'd met again just a few hours before became a dervish, an astonishingly lithe athlete, who outclassed me in speed, skill and commitment. I lost three games to her in quick succession and I lost badly. We hardly spoke as we played and she was remorseless, clearly intent on beating me by as big a margin as possible. As she did so, a smile began to play around her lips and by the end of the three games, it was developing into a broad grin, which she made no effort to suppress. Laura's words about my giving Alice a lesson came back to me. Surely she must have known that her daughter would thrash me. Why, then, with her unfailingly good manners, would she have wanted to set me up like this?

'Would you like another game, or are you ready for my sister to beat you?', Alice half-smiled.

'One more then. You are very good, you know.'

'Well, I suppose I'm good at some things and not others. But you're right, when I'm good at something I'm usually very good and when I'm bad, I'm …'

I nearly interrupted to say 'horrid?', but restrained long enough to let her finish the sentence.

'… very bad. Not worth bothering with at all really.'

I'd known so little of Alice before, but now I recognised her as another obsessive member of the White family. The next game was over even more quickly and I lost even more ignominiously: 21-2. I was glad I wasn't competing with Alice at something for which I had no aptitude.

'Are you ready for Isabel now?'

'I guess so, but is she as good as you?'

'No, not at table tennis. But she can run rings around me in other ways.'

'I'm sure she can't.'

'Thank you for saying that, but yes, she can. She's very talented, you know.'

'And very upset too, I think?'

'Perhaps. Why don't you ask her yourself? I'll go and fetch her.' And she was gone.

Isabel, thank goodness, was, as Alice had said, a less accomplished table tennis player and we had three close games, of which I won two. We talked a bit while we played and I gleaned a bit more information from her. I found out that Martin, who was her eldest brother, had 'disappeared' about six years previously and Steve had left four years before.

'Both before Stuart left, then?' I asked.

'Yes, that's right. Stuart left just after Glen died.'

'Was he affected? Was that the reason?'

She put a finger to her lips and, walking to my end of the table to retrieve a ball I'd prodded into the net, she said loudly, '14 all', and then in an undertone, 'Walls have ears. I'll come to your room later – OK?'

'I didn't know what to make of your e-mails, you know?'

'I'm not sure I knew what to make of them myself, but I had to get you here, though it's not straightforward and Alice wasn't sure.'

'Can I ask you one very simple question now?'

'I guess so. As long as it *is* "simple".'

'Are you a Van Morrison fan?'

'Well, that's a harmless enough question. No, I'm not, but I've heard a lot of his music. He was a favourite of Stuart's.'

'Stuart's?'

'Uh-huh. What made you ask?'

'Everywhere I've been today he seems to be pursuing me. On the radio. At the pub. I've been hearing his songs all day.'

'Uh-huh? Must be a coincidence. Stuart's far away and it couldn't have anything to do with him … and no one here could be controlling the radio, could they? What channel were you listening to?'

'Radio 2.'

'I think that's the one Ben has on at the Hope. I guess it's time to be getting back to the others. I'll come to you later – OK?'

'OK.'

Perhaps then it had been Van Morrison day at the Beeb. Maybe I was looking for conspiracy, where there was only coincidence. I'd been slipping and sliding on the dark side of the road too long. Maybe I was the one with Van Morrison on my mind, though he'd never been a favourite of mine.

Back in the lounge, Sherry jumped up to welcome me back, licked me on the hand and then, unfailingly magnanimous with her favours, ran to make sure Isabel was greeted too. Uncle Wilf had been let off Laura's leash. He was holding forth on the joys of plastic. Jules and Alice seemed attentive, though it was hard to gauge whether their interest was feigned or genuine, and I still had the impression that Alice only tolerated him. Laura was smiling at him indulgently.

'… it's true that plastic cannot claim a looooooooooong (he spread his hands as he extended the word) history like gold and silver. Sad to say, it is a latecomer to the pantheon of the world's treasures. Nevertheless, even though I love gold and I like silver, I am hopelessly enamoured of plastic. I can still remember the day when I acquired my first Bakelite clock. A thing of plastic and a joy forever. *They* say di-ah-monds (he fractured the word into three distinct syllables) are forever and to be greatly revered, but then when *they* discover that some plastics last forever, *they* want to change the rules. *They* (he mouthed this pronoun with a marvellously contemptuous sneer) say some plastics are to be shunned, scorned and spurned, because they are non-bio-de-grad-able, but if they could only appreciate the preciousness of plastic, then no one on earth would want to de-grade it in the first place. Plastic should be universally loved, celebrated and curated. Tomorrow I shall wear my plastic horn-rims, so great Samuel will see plastic in all its glory and perhaps we can *up*-grade plastic.'

I began to wonder whether Wilf's cabinet was a collection of plastic.

'Would you like the nightcap now, Sam?' asked Laura. She seemed to be ready to see Wilf go to bed. I'd had plenty to drink and asked for a glass of water. The others had Horlicks or milk, and the moonbeam smile reappeared on Wilf's face when he was allowed to add rum to his milk.

I didn't settle immediately when I finally got to bed. It was around midnight. It had been a long day and, although I was supposed to have unwound playing table tennis, I hadn't. But I think I must have been dozing, when Isabel came. I didn't hear her enter the room and the first I knew she was sitting on the side of my bed, with her finger on her lips once again. She sat there silently for perhaps thirty seconds. Then she eased herself downwards to my face, kissed me on the cheek for three seconds and then very gently on the lips. I was half-asleep, but I found myself moving to pull her onto me. As I did so, she pushed me away.

'Don't. That wouldn't be right. Not now anyway.' She let her fingers run across my cheek with gentleness.

'OK, I don't understand, but that's OK. Whatever. I don't know why you called me to come up here, but everything is OK. Really.' Her brow furrowed and she didn't reply.

We were quiet for a moment and then I asked, as softly as possible, 'Are you ready to talk now?'

'There's not much to say really,' she whispered. 'But don't worry. Please don't worry. Tomorrow I'll show you Stuart's folders, after Uncle Wilf has finished with you.' And she was gone. I lay awake for quite a while after that. I'd misread the signals, but her tenderness had touched a chord in me and I was slightly less exasperated with her. I felt warm towards her in a way that I couldn't quite put my finger on. If she'd only open up, perhaps I'd understand that attraction. I didn't want to be left in the dark much longer.

Cabinets

I woke up early the next morning, when Sherry, more eager than ever to confirm her affection to a visitor who had proved his loyalty by staying overnight, jumped onto my bed. It was about 6.30 and, only half-awake, for a moment I thought Isabel had come back. I was relieved to discover it was Sherry, as I came to more fully. Licking my face and wagging her tail, she was altogether more straightforward than Isabel. Sherry stayed close by, while I shaved, showered and dressed, and then escorted me downstairs, panting as she eased her low-slung body down each of the steep stairs and looking up at me with brown-eyed love once we reached level ground. What would we do next? Might I be an additional donor of food aid to her personal charity?

Alice was in the kitchen, eating toast and fiddling with her mobile.

'Did you sleep well?'

'Pretty good, thanks,' I replied.

'Can I get you a coffee?'

'That'd be nice. Thank you.'

'Toast? Cereal? I can do eggs if you like.' My mind went back to the egg songs of the evening before. I was tempted to ask for poached, but refrained.

'Toast'd be great. Thanks. I thought your mother was the kitchen supremo.'

'Yes, she is, but when she doesn't get up early we're allowed to fend for ourselves.'

'I remember your scones.'

'Mmm, yes. They're a family joke. Isabel never lets me forget them, but I don't make them anymore. I think I could have perfected them with practice. That's where it'd be good if Mum gave us a free hand a bit more often.'

'Are you going to work early today?'

'No, I've a day off. But I was awake and so I thought I'd get up and have an hour to myself before Alf gets started. I'm taking him to a wildlife park.'

'Doesn't he have to go to school?'

'Mmm, well, seeing the animals will be very educational for him, though I'll have to explain that captivity isn't a good thing for most of them.'

Sherry was busy foraging for crumbs, but Alice wasn't helping her cause. She was careful with the toast and Laura hadn't left a speck of food from the night before.

'You could come with us, but I think Uncle Wilf has earmarked you for the collections.'

'Yes. He's extraordinary, isn't he?'

'Yes, he must be. I mean, yes he is, but we just don't notice, because he's always been here and he's always the same.'

'But he's eighty-seven now, or is that a pretence?'

'Yes, he must be. He was born in 1921 – December – and so, yes, he's eighty-seven.'

'He doesn't seem to change, though.'

Mmm, well if he does, we don't notice it. Not much, that's for sure. I think perhaps he's more enthusiastic than ever, but it's only a matter of degree. No real change.' She put two pieces of toast in front of me.

And once again I became the centre of Sherry's universe.

'Is she allowed toast?'

'Yes, but just very small bits. She begs from everyone.'

Alice was so different from her sister and yet equally unfathomable to me. I couldn't help thinking, thank goodness for Sherry. And Wilf. Never mind his layers of camouflage. I *knew* he was trustworthy. Alice went back to fiddling with her mobile, sending a succession of texts. She seemed the most remote of all the White family, but clearly she had plenty of outside contacts. Perhaps she was meeting a friend, or friends, when she took Alf to the wildlife park. Maybe that was why she had a day off work and wasn't taking him to school.

'You play a mean game of table tennis.'

She smiled, but didn't reply.

I ate my toast. There was no sign of Isabel or Laura, but Jules appeared, gulped a cup of coffee and apologised for having to rush off to work, saying he hoped we could 'do something together in a day or two. By the weekend at the latest.'

Alice deigned to notice me again. 'If you need to check your e-mails or anything like that, you're welcome to use my laptop while I'm out. It's in my room – my cabinet, I mean. It's wi-fi. Very straightforward and the broadband connection isn't too bad here. The room is the fifth one down the corridor.'

'Thanks, that'd be great. Are you sure?' I'd been checking my mobile for texts, but it would be good to have Internet access.

'Yes, it's fine,' and she was back in the world of *her* mobile again.

And then Uncle Wilf was with us. Warm, selfless Wilf, whose every waking moment was dedicated to being altruistic and agreeable, so that awkwardness was impossible in his presence. This morning he was wearing spectacular mauve-lensed, plastic horn-rimmed glasses, with upward-curling white fins.

'Good morning, great Samuel. Good morning, my darling Alice. And good morning to you, Princess Sherry. Have you all slept well, my dears? Sherry, I know you will answer for everyone.' And, transfixed by his gaze, Sherry wagged her tail.

'I take that as a yes. Samuel, Sammy, Sam, the hour is nigh and loins must be girded, as the task before us is an arduous one. I propose we embark forthwith and *tout de suite*, if our dear Alice will excuse us for leaving with unseemly haste.' Alice nodded, without raising her eyes from her mobile. 'And Sherry, if you should choose to accompany us on our mission as an auxiliary, rest assured you may return to this scene of consumption, when others descend for their morning nutrition. Samuel and I have a long campaign ahead of us in distant climes, but you have been, seen and conquered those realms many times before. So, Sherry, you must be the mistress of your own fate, but Samuel and I will be in thrall, and *en*thralled, with the cabinets.' Where he got his energy from at this time of the morning, goodness only knows. Alice's strategy for coping with him seemed to be to pay him as little attention as possible. Less accustomed to him, I was polite, but I had no need to feign good manners. I was genuinely charmed by his every word.

'Samuel, my hero. Here is my suggested plan of action. Shall we call it Plan A? It is a simple plan, but if you demur, disagree or, not to put too fine a point on it, can come up with a better plan, then we will call your plan Plan B. In that eventuality we will consult for a full three seconds and follow Plan B.'

'OK, Uncle Wilf. That sounds very fair.'

'Plan A is that we start at the beginning with the first cabinet, then move on to Room 2 and thereafter to 3 and 4. After which we could adjourn and complete our inspections another day.'

'I support Plan A. And if we see four rooms this morning, how far will we be?'

'That's the beauty of it, Samuel. We will be exactly halfway. So the second part of our task will be exactly the same in its extent, range and scope – not one iota more or less, my brave hero.'

'So which rooms will we visit today, Uncle Wilf?'

'Well, we will begin with my beloved nephew Desmond's cabinet. His was the first, a true original, and we come to it first. And this prioritizing will allow us to show proper respect to dear departed Desmond too. Then, proceeding down the corridor and taking the cabinets in order, we shall come to mine, then Steve's and then Martin's. If that doesn't tire us too much, it will mean four down and four to go.'

'I think it is an exemplary plan, Uncle Wilf. I'm looking forward to seeing your cabinet. Is it a collection of plastics?'

'All will be revealed, dear Sam. Very soon now. All will be revealed.' For a second I wondered if he meant he was about to unlock the mystery that Isabel had been dangling in front of me, but I didn't think so. Sherry accompanied us as far as the hallway on the left-hand side of the house and then turned tail and went back to Alice.

We went into Desmond's cabinet: a large square room off the main hallway, with just a single window. It was the only one in the main house. I remembered Isabel saying that there had once been just this single cabinet and that Wilf and Stuart had added to Desmond's collection, before later acquiring their own. The hallway had been extended at the back, so that it opened onto a narrow passageway that provided access to the remaining cabinets. The light in this first cabinet was poor and I started as I came face to face with the towering figure of a forbidding woman.

'No need to be alarmed, Samuel,' Wilf reassured me, as he switched on the light. 'This is Winifred Bayberry. The Suffolk giantess. Some say she was the tallest woman of the Victorian age.' And I realised I was staring at a seven-foot-high waxwork. Winifred was plump as well as tall, but her height enabled her to carry her weight well. I was still collecting myself, when Wilf introduced me to a second menacing figure.

'And this is her friend Arthur – Arthur Groat.' I hadn't noticed Arthur beside Winifred, because he was tiny.

'I know you're wondering, my champion. They're both life-size. Winifred was seven foot one and Arthur was two foot four. They toured together and they were inseparable.'

'Toured?'

'Yes, in their day they were great celebrities. They travelled the length and breadth of England, with forays into Wales and Scotland, and Desmond said they also went to France and Spain.'

My eyes were beginning to make out other objects in the room. 'They were circus performers, or some kind of entertainers?'

'Entertainers, yes. Circus performers, no. They were fairground attractions. Famous freaks in fabulous funfairs. Fairs were Desmond's passion. He was a showman himself. He loved fairs as a boy and when he grew up he travelled the country with a group of Irishmen and what we used to call diddycoys. He was a true cosmopolite and he knew people from almost every nation on the planet, my superhero. He knew folk from Russia and Italy, Egypt and India, Canada and

Brazil. Travelling people know no borders. But all that was before he met Laura. And after they married, he settled down here, only wandering once in a while when the urge came upon him. Settled here with a home of his own, he began to collect. First of all, minor ephemera. There was a coconut shy from Hull Fair. He brought it home, singing the song – you know the one? I know you know it: 'I've got a lovely bunch …'. I joined in to be sociable. 'Yes, that's the one. Then there was a test-your-strength machine from King's Lynn. You can see it over there. But these were just a prelude to his greatest acquisitions. He progressed backwards in time to collect true rarities like Winifred and Arthur. Then he bought a boxing booth. It's in that corner, disassembled. And music and rides and candy floss, but alas candy floss doesn't last and he learnt the sad truth that in life there are treasures that one has to part with. Do you like the horse, my megahero?'

And I realised that what looked like a rocking horse at an initial glance was in fact a fibreglass merry-go-round horse. 'When Steve and Martin were small, they loved to ride her. They never got anywhere, of course, but they loved to get in Rosy's saddle and imagine themselves as cowboys, riding the distant range.'

'So she's a filly, Rosy?'

'Now there's a question. It's short for Rosinante. I suggested Rosy to Desmond, so that his horse might bask in the reflected glory of that noble steed. But was Rosinante a stallion or a filly, or a horse of some altogether more dubious equine gender? If only the man of La Mancha was here to tell us.'

'You could be him. You could act the part, Uncle Wilf,' I suggested, once again pleased at the ease with which I was joining in his play-acting.

'I thank you, my champion. I'm truly flattered. I believe there is no greater hero in the annals of literature than the Don, but then what does an unlettered man like me know? Who can say what wonders I might have encountered, had I read more. But I shall seriously consider and inform you forthwith, soon and in about three, thirteen or twenty-one minutes whether I feel up to the role. Fear not. I shall not prevaricate. By the time we reach my cabinet, all will be revealed.

'First, though, we should complete our scrutiny of Desmond's cabinets. Here, prurience upon prurience, we have a 'What the Butler Saw' machine – one old penny and we could peer into its salacious interior. But I don't have one today and so, with your agreement, we shall remain uncorrupted. And there is an earlier-than-early cinematograph projector. I am sure you know, my unmatchable genius, that there was a time when folk went to the fair to watch motion pictures.'

'I didn't know, Uncle Wilf. When was that? What period?'

'Long, long ago, dear Samuel. After the freaks and before the roller coasters.'

'That's a big time-frame.'

'Well, let's just say before I was born then and not worry ourselves about the most precise of precisions for the very good reason that … I really haven't got a clue. Let's just say, it was back in days of yore. Shall we complete our tour of the cabinet? There are further fine waxworks in that corner and behind them there is Desmond's photo gallery.' The remaining waxworks were more predictable curiosities. A bearded lady, a centaur and a mermaid. In the photos on the wall there were conjoined twins, 'the fattest man in the world', an armless midget and a rhinoceros woman.

'*Lusi naturae*. Sports of nature, Samuel. I know you have a memory that stretches across eons of time and it was just last night I was telling you about collectors who crossed oceans to find them. Sports of nature. But Desmond found his nearer home, in the fairgrounds of dear old Albion. And before we became politically correct, Samuel, as I told you, they were the celebrities of their day. Regaled wherever they went. You know, Queen Victoria was entranced with Tom Thumb. She was a tad vertically challenged herself, of course, and I think that's why she was so attracted to Tom, though she could never compete with him in the dwarf stakes.'

'Really? What kind of man was Desmond, Uncle Wilf?'

'A lovely man. A great man, who ploughed his heart and soul into the happiness of this family. And the children loved this room. To them it was a playroom, never a museum.'

'But what exactly was Desmond like, Uncle Wilf, if it's OK to ask?' I wasn't exactly being disingenuous, but I was remembering what Isabel had said about Wilf giving up work, because her father had.

'Of course, you must ask, dear Samuel. You belong with this family and so you must see all of its cabinets and hear all of its histories. Desmond … Desmond was a *fine* man, a great and glorious drinking man, who was sadly taken before his time, my champion.' Wilf's gift for accentuating the positive remained uppermost, though there seemed to be an undercurrent now.

'How old was he?'

'Fifty-five. A mere lad. And it was sudden, very sudden. Completely out of the blue. He crashed his car. Went off the road and hit a tree. On a deserted road, near Horncastle.'

'Was anyone else hurt?'

'No, no. He was alone and no other car was involved.'

'Did they know what caused it?'

'*They* didn't, Samuel. *They* didn't, but what do *they* know? Sometimes *we* know more.'

'Do you know, Uncle Wilf?'

'Not in this instance. It is a true mystery. All I mean, great man, is that just because *they* didn't find a cause, it doesn't mean there wasn't one, but we truly believe it was an accident.'

'But he was a drinker?'

'Yes, a truly magnificent drinker. A drinker to be memorialized in *The Guinness Book of Records*. A man who achieved many mosts. I do believe he still holds the records for the most advocaats in sixty seconds and the most yards of ale in a single sitting. He was a nonpareil, rarer than anything in his collection: successful as a sprinter drinker *and* as a marvellous marathon imbiber. Truly stupendous. The rarest of rare combinations.'

'Was there any suggestion that he was drunk? When he had his accident, I mean.'

'*They* made suggestions. *They* thought he might be drunk, but when *they* tested him, my champion, there was not a drop of alcohol to be found in his blood. So then *they* examined the car and said there were no mechanical faults. *We* had to be sure, of course, so *we* had the car checked, and everything was OK.'

'Who was "we", Uncle Wilf?'

Well, Laura organised it, but I was by her side and the boys were nearby. Rest assured, my defender, no stone was left unturned, no avenue was unexplored and nothing seemed untoward.'

'So it was just an accident. I don't suppose anyone suggested suicide.'

'A horrible thought, Samuel. *They* suggested all manner of things, but why would a fine drinker like Desmond do such a thing, with so much undrunk liquor in the world and a collection such as this to complete his bliss. No, this is a suggestion to be buried deep and never disinterred. I'll be honest, great man, it is a thought that flitted into my mind for a zillionth of a second, but I dispelled it in the next zillionth and I have never allowed it to re-enter.'

And Wilf had become a sphinx whose garrulousness reminded me of the diversionary manoeuvre of the dove I had seen flying out of the hedgerow, while driving towards Bubbleby the day before. I wondered whether he, too, might be protecting his young. I looked at Desmond's curiosities again and saw them as darker. Winifred had become a Gothic apparition; and Rosy, the merry-go-round horse, seemed to be leering at me.

'Shall we go on to the next cabinet, my superstar?'

'Your own?'

'Yes, precisely. My very own.'

In the corridor that led to the extension, Wilf grabbed my shoulders and turned me towards him, so that we were face to face, our mouths less than a foot apart. If I'd been with any man other than Wilf, I think I would have been troubled by the closeness, but despite his inscrutability, I trusted him. 'I have decided, great Samuel, to accept the challenge. Thanks to your inspiration, I shall be the greatest knight that ever graced the plains of Spain and as soon as we step over my threshold, I shall inform you of the true gender of Rosy.' It seemed he had known all along. Was he an ingenuous Don Quixote, or a wily Sancho Panza? As we entered his room, he seized a curtain pole that was standing upright in a corner, brandished it high in the air and, unabashed by the lack of windmills to tilt at, declaimed magnanimously, 'Rosy was a male horse. We are told at the outset of the world's finest epic that *he* was the greatest of all hacks.' I was beginning to see why Alice found him wearisome!

By now I was prepared for his cabinet to contain a collection of plastics, a library of Cervantes' works, or an assortment of exhibits illustrating the history of alcohol through the ages. What I wasn't prepared for was … teapots. It would be hard to say how many teapots there were in that room, but there must have been at least three hundred. Teapots of every shape and size. Plain teapots and ornate teapots. Tiny teapots and huge teapots. Teapots with short spouts and teapots with elephantine trunks. Teapots with Oriental motifs and teapots depicting English idylls. Teapots on shelves. Teapots hanging by their handles from wall fixtures. Teapots in glass cases. An enormous teapot on a wooden plinth in the middle of the room and beside it a table set up for tea. There was clearly fine china – Wedgwood, the best Satsuma and Royal Worcester among it – and there was, yes, a cheap plastic teapot in a corner. Wilf was as good as his word. He didn't discriminate. Plastic rubbed shoulders with bone china. He said nothing for a moment, waiting it seemed for me to express my awe at his wonders.

'It's a marvellous collection.'

'Thank you, my colossus. Only a true connoisseur can appreciate such gems. Would you like the full tour or the edited highlights only?'

I managed to curb my initial impulse to plump for the latter option in time to reply, 'Well perhaps some editing would be advisable, Uncle Wilf, as there are other cabinets ahead, but I do want to see *all* the highlights.'

'And of those there are many, but let us suffice ourselves with the earliest, the finest and my favourites. The earliest is this little lady. You may think she's a geisha, because she looks Asian and exotic and she's designed to please, but she's from Meissen and she's elderly now – nearly three hundred years old.'

'She must be very valuable.'

'It's of no consequence, my enlightened one. We should never concern ourselves with the pecuniary or mercenary, let alone, God forbid, the venal, when dealing in affairs of the heart and she is greatly loved. But, of course, I love them all equally. I love my plastic one as much as this, and I love Humpty Dumpty, who as you can see has been put together again, and I broadcast my love of my radio to all the world each and every day.' Humpty Dumpty was a squat yellow teapot with the nursery rhyme figure, who did look as though he'd had a fall and been repaired, sitting on top and the radio was a flat elongated pot with a cocked high spout that suggested it was primed to be pressed into action at any moment.

'And here, my giant-killer, is my collection of one-cup dunkers. I know what you are thinking. You are thinking that these are not really pots at all, but they too have played their part in the service of tea. Turning to the right' (was he parodying the patter of a tour guide?), 'we see another esteemed member of my egalitarian community. This, great Samuel, is a genuine replica of the marvellous teapot of Dr Sam Johnson. A great teapot for another great Samuel. A glorious multi-cupper for a man who was a true devotee of tea, in both quantity and quality. Ah, but I see your gaze is wandering elsewhere.'

Wilf had said nothing about what was clearly the *pièce de resistance* of his cabinet, but my eyes had turned towards the table laid for a tea party in the middle of the room. 'Have some tea?' he squeaked in a high-pitched rabbit-like voice. There were several seats around the table, but only three were occupied – by large latex puppets: the Mad Hatter, the March Hare and the Dormouse.

'Sit down, King Samuel, and taste some tea. It's always teatime here.' And he duly poured some 'tea' into one of the Royal Albert cups that were on the table. But this wasn't *Alice in Wonderland* and the 'tea' was wine, as in the best prohibition-era movies. Wilf was in full flight. 'It happened like this, Sir Sam. The day Alice was born I decided to dedicate myself to tea and to make sure she would have the most wonderful, maddest tea parties in the world. Every day of her life, if they could only make her happy.'

'Did they make her happy, Uncle Wilf?'

'They did, Sam, they did for a long while. We would come here when she was a tiny tot – from about two years old – we would come every day until she was about twelve and then, alas, it happens to the best of us, she grew up. We had one marvellous tea party when she became eighteen – just those of us here present, you understand – but after that she turned sane and she doesn't come here anymore. So now the Dormouse, the Hare, the Hatter and I observe the rites of tea most days and to console ourselves we sup a strong brew. Will you join us in a cup, my champion?'

He filled five cups with wine and quickly drank his own and those he had poured for the three dummies, and then he disappeared under the table. It took me a second to realise that the high-pitched sound that was filling the room was his thrown, ventriloquist voice.

'It's oh so easy when they can't see your lips. Anyone can do it. It wasn't just Archie you know. It was the same across the pond with Charlie McArthy. Another radio dummy. My lips don't move, but she speaks through me.' And then the voice seemed to become female. '"Not another one? Let it not be him. This is confusing me. Please let it not be him." We used to have such lovely tea parties, didn't we? "I think you might do something better with the time than waste it asking riddles with no answers".'

By now I should have been thinking that he was madder than the Hatter, crazier than the Hare, but I didn't. He had the gift of making me see the world as he saw it and I found myself looking at the three tea party puppets to try to work out which of them was the ventriloquist's dummy. None seemed right for the role. The voice seemed to be coming from one of the unoccupied chairs. Might it be Alice's?

He re-emerged after a minute, poured more wine and reverted to his own sonorous voice. 'A dilemma faces us, my guardian of the faith. If we continue to take tea, we may be unable to complete our itinerary for this morning, but if we stay, we can continue to sup to our hearts' content.'

'It's a bit early in the day for me, Uncle Wilf, but I can sit here with you, if you like. We can talk and there will be other days for our tour.'

'Well said, great man. We'll stay a while then.'

'Were you and Alice the only ones who came to the tea parties, Uncle Wilf?'

'By and large. More or less. But there were always extra chairs for passing guests. Occasionally some stopped by, as you have today.'

'Who else stopped by?'

'Oh, many creatures: Farfel the Dog, Orville the Duck, and more recently, after Alice had left us, Winston the mock turtle. And there were others, too.'

'Some of them were dummies, weren't they?'

'*All* of them were dummies.'

'And did you have to give them all voices or were there humans with them?'

'No – no humans, as far as I can remember, my braveheart.'

'So just you and Alice and these puppets came? No other people, Uncle Wilf?'

'Not that I can remember. But I have a secret to tell you. Can you keep a secret, my one and only hero?'

'My lips are sealed.'

'Well, it's this,' and he dropped his voice to a whisper. 'When a man gets to eighty-something and drinks a few cups of tea, then occasionally, only very occasionally mind you, he doesn't remember absolutely everything.'

'That may be true in some cases, but never in yours, Uncle Wilf.'

'Flattery will get you everywhere, my master orator, but truth to tell, I have my lapses.'

I doubted I would get any more out of him, but remembering his banter from the day before, I made one further attempt.

'How long are your toenails, Uncle Wilf?' He didn't reply immediately, but ceremoniously stooped down and took off his shoes and socks, the same brown suede shoes and yellow socks that he had been wearing the day before. He put his feet on the chair beside him. His toenails were short.

'Perhaps I could leave you here with the tea for a while, Uncle. I've just remembered I should have been in touch with someone. I'll be back soon.'

This wasn't exactly true, but the tea party had made me burningly curious to see what Alice's room had in store and I remembered her invitation to use her laptop, which gave me the perfect pretext. I left Wilf and made my way further down the corridor in the extension to Alice's room If it contained mysteries, I wasn't to find them that day, because virtually everything in her room was shrouded under dustsheets. One exception was the laptop, on a small Davenport desk by the window, and Isabel was there, using it. Today she was 'normal'.

'Hi, Sam. Did you sleep OK?' Virtually the same words as her sister's, but she flashed me a smile and seemed pleased to see me. I wondered how long this mood would last.

'Yes, OK, thanks. How about you? You left in a hurry last night.'

'Yep, I guess that's me. I came in a hurry and I left in a hurry, too, didn't I? Alice said you might be using her laptop, if you managed to get away from Uncle Wilf. Looks like you did.'

'Well, we only got halfway through what he'd planned, but then I think he got more interested in the wine in his teapot.'

'Uh-huh, that's been known to happen.'

'Is he very drunk most of the time? He says some pretty strange stuff and I just can't tell if it's the alcohol talking.'

'Yep, that's right. I mean you've got it in one. We spend all our time with him and we can't tell either. By the way, I've just been writing to Lilith and I gave her your e-mail. Just in case she wants to be in touch. Since you mentioned her, I thought you might like that after all these years. I'll be through in another minute and then the machine's all yours.'

'Don't you have your own?'

'Yep, but the bloody thing keeps playing up and so Alice lets me use hers when she's not here.'

'So, when you were writing to me, was that on this laptop?'

'Mmm, sometimes. Does it make any difference?'

'No, of course not. I just wondered.'

'There. Finished. All yours.'

'And this afternoon you're going to show me Stuart's folders?'

'Yep, if that's alright with you. We can leave it till tomorrow if you like.'

'This afternoon is good.'

'After lunch then?'

'OK.'

'I'll make us something and then we can look at it together. Everybody is out, except you, me and Uncle Wilf … and Sherry, of course.'

She got up from the desk, where the laptop was perched a bit precariously. Davenports weren't designed for this and I realised that the front had books under it to tilt it backwards and make the desk surface flatter.

'See you in a while, Sam.' And she was gone, almost as quickly as the night before.

I logged on. There was the usual advertising and spam. My former colleague was in Greece, and had managed to find a connection in 'this idyllic spot in the Peloponnese, untouched by civilization'. My uncle had had his colonoscopy and didn't seem pleased with the results, though he was cagey about what they were. My ex-wife had written (a rare event), mainly about money matters and with little news. And there was a message from Lilith, earnest Lily, who couldn't be crazy if she tried, and who, according to Isabel, was now 'with' Spike, who couldn't be serious if *he* tried. It was blunt and to the point – more like a text message. 'Urgent, Sam. Phone me ASAP', and there was her number.

I was dumbstruck. I'd known her less well than I'd known Isabel. Hardly at all. So this peremptory message was even odder than Isabel's. But I knew Lilith had to be taken seriously. I called her on my mobile. After a perfunctory 'hello', verging on rudeness, she spoke in a grave tone.

'Isabel said you're at the Weavers. It's not safe. Get out as quickly as possible.'

'What?'

'Just leave. Now if possible.'

'What about Isabel?'

'What about her? Oh, no, don't worry, she'll be OK – more or less. I mean she's not in danger.'

'And I am?'

'You may be. I don't know, but you may be. Can you come to see us now?'

'Now? Did you say "now"?'

'Yes, that'd be best. Let me give you the address. Have you got a pen?' I put Alice's laptop on the floor, lifted the lid of her Davenport, found a pen, fished an old credit card slip out of my pocket and wrote down where Spike and Lilith lived in Lincoln.

'I was supposed to have lunch – with Isabel.'

'Who else is in the house?'

'Just Isabel and Uncle Wilf.'

'I think that's OK then, but it's still better if you come right away. Is that alright?'

'Well, yes. I suppose so. But what about Isabel? What should I tell her?'

'The truth. Just tell her you're coming to see Spike and me. She'll understand.'

'And I can't bring her with me?'

'Noooooooooo. Just come, quickly. Phone when you get near. And you can stay overnight. OK?'

Five minutes later I'd spoken to Isabel, who was less than pleased, but seemed to understand, and I was on my way to Lincoln. As I drove, one image kept returning to my mind: the combat knife that I'd seen lying alongside the pens and pencils when I opened Alice's Davenport.

Lincoln

I'd never been to Lincoln before. My travels weren't quite as extensive as I sometimes let people believe, but I'd been to many places around the world and comparatively few in England. Lincoln, I soon discovered, is really two towns: one at the foot of the hill, where the main shops are, and the other, historic Lincoln, at the top, clustered around the cathedral. And then, of course, there are suburbs, swelling the old city into a typical contemporary sprawl. Lilith and Spike lived at the bottom of the hill, in a street close to the centre.

I didn't have many memories of Lilith. Mostly I remembered her as Isabel's excessively serious friend, but one recollection that had engraved itself in my mind was a conversation I'd had with her about names. It was in Tony's café on a rare occasion when I'd been alone with her. She'd explained that her parents had called her after Adam's first wife, because that Lilith had lived before Eden and was therefore exempt from the Fall. I'd commented on the strangeness of this choice and asked her whether they were staunch Christians. She'd replied that they weren't. In fact they were confirmed agnostics, who believed in the power of names and had thought 'Lilith' might help her to grow up without guilt. So I'd playfully asked whether it had worked and she came as close to smiling as I'd ever seen her and said perhaps it had. At the very least it had freed her from some of 'Eve's burdens'. She'd said then that she felt unhampered by either guilt or innocence. Lilith was humourless, dark and forbidding, with scary Mephistophelean eyebrows. Unfailingly calm and completely reliable. And thinking back to that conversation in Tony's, I remembered that we'd been there together, finishing a coffee after others had left, and my recollection was that Tony's wife Milly was the only other person in the café at that moment. Now I wondered whether time might have played tricks with my mind. Could I be associating Lily with Milly – rhyming names – and in retrospect be imagining that Milly was there? But my memory told me that Milly had been hovering by the doorway into the kitchen, eavesdropping, interested to hear what we were saying. True or false, it was a puzzling memory, since Milly invariably kept herself aloof from the absurdities of 'stoooo-dents'.

As I parked the car and walked towards Spike and Lilith's door, I was thinking about the oddity of their being together. I found it hard to imagine two people with such conflicting responses to life complementing one another. But if

I worried about Lilith's gravitas, I felt sure that Spike's perennial lunacy would compensate. When I arrived, Lilith was home and Spike was out. Her hair was dyed black and she was wearing Goth clothing and make-up that intensified her natural sombreness. No piercings, though. More like Morticia Addams than later Goth icons. It occurred to me that I hadn't seen anyone dressed like this in London or the South-East for quite a while. Was Goth dress another byway of the 'real' Lincolnshire of today? But then neither she nor Spike was Lincolnshire born and bred. I couldn't remember where she'd come from – was it somewhere on the south coast? – and Spike was a Londoner.

'Hello David,' she said, extending a polite hand. No kisses on the cheek with Lily. I was taken aback by her greeting for an instant, but then I remembered. She was the only person at college to whom I'd ever confided my other name. That conversation in Tony's had continued and, as if to complete my side of an exchange of confidences, I'd talked about my names. She'd asked me if my parents had named me after the Biblical David and I'd said I didn't think so and I certainly wasn't up for fighting any Goliaths. I can't remember whether she asked me why I called myself Sam. If she did, I doubt that I would have, or could have, explained. I'd learnt concealment early.

She didn't take long to come to the point. 'Isabel told me you're staying with them. How come, after so long?' She'd cocked her head on one side.

'She invited me. Out of the blue. I'd not been in touch with Stuart or her for years and she e-mailed me. She sounds upset.'

'She is. I don't know the full story, but there's something very wrong there.'

'You have some idea, though?'

'Well, she was here recently, talking a lot and not making much sense, but she kept on talking about "the men" and "the boys".'

'You mean, she's having a bad time with men, or boys?'

Her head moved from side to side and then she shrugged her shoulders. 'That's what I thought at first, but it's not that. She's worried about them. Worried what may happen to them. She said *they* got her Dad and Glen and made Steve and Martin leave and then *they* drove Stuart away. Now she's worried about the other men and Alf.'

I was hesitant. I stuttered, something I hadn't done in a long while. 'I know sh-she says St-stuart disappeared, but did he leave voluntarily?'

'I just don't know. She was babbling. She was a bit incoherent. So I asked her if she was in some sort of danger and she said "No, only the men", but I don't really know. And then she started talking about "the others" being in danger too.'

'Who are they?'

'I don't know, but I think she must have meant visitors. That's why I had to get you here, to warn you. I think you may be in danger.'

'Don't you think this may all be in the imagination?'

'I don't imagine things, David.' Lilith was at her most severe.

'No, I didn't mean you. I meant in Isabel's imagination. Her father is supposed to have died in something that could only have been an accident …'.

'Who told you that?'

'Wilf.'

'Well, I don't know, but at the time there were rumours of brake failure. And the little boy, Glen's, death. That's supposed to have been an accident, but who knows?'

'Do you think Isabel could be the s-source of the danger?'

'No. She's mixed up, but she wouldn't hurt a fly, though with that family you can never be sure.'

At that moment, Spike's key turned in the lock and he was home from work. The atmosphere changed. 'Sam, Sam, Sam. You're here. It's great to see you, you old fart. Long, long time!' He gave me a hug.

'Good to see you too. What have you been doing all these years?'

'Oh, a bit of this and a bit of that. Ducking and diving.' He feigned a punch. 'Mostly misbehaving. Marrying Lily, getting divorced from Lily and then getting back with Lily again.'

I looked at her, but the grin on his face wasn't reflected on hers.

'Well you know how it is, Sam. She couldn't stand to live with me, but then we split up and she couldn't stand to live without me. So I swallowed my pride and came back and everything is wicked again.'

Lilith still wasn't smiling.

'Only thing is she won't marry me again. Once smitten, twice shy. I don't know if you could put in a good word for me, mate.'

'Well, I can try. It's so good to see the two of you again. And together. That's even better.'

'I asked him to come over, because he's staying at The Weavers.'

'Oh shit,' said Spike. 'Put on the armour plating, bolt your room door at night and keep garlic and a crucifix handy.'

'Spike, there aren't any vampires at The Weavers. Don't scare David any more than necessary. It's bad enough as it is.'

'Well, you have your opinion, love, and I'll have mine. You know what I think we should do. I think we should take Sam and David with us to collect Annie.'

Lilith explained, 'Annie is our daughter.'

'She didn't tell you about Annie! The greatest thing that ever happened to us. And she didn't tell you!'

'David only got here ten minutes before you.'

'But you had time to talk about the bloodsucking White family, and you didn't mention Annie!'

'I thought he should be warned.'

'Consider yourself duly warned. And come and meet Annie. If we leave now, we could take our time and go up Steep Hill, and we could show you the sights. Did you ever hear the one about the Irishman, the Scotsman, the Welshman, the Englishman and the stateless person? …'

Lilith cut him off.

Ten minutes later we were walking across the High Bridge over the river in the middle of Lincoln's pedestrianized shopping area and towards the Stonebow, the arch built into the ancient Guildhall. Lincoln seemed to contain more architectural layers than most English towns and Lilith was a mine of information. 'This is Tudor, but as we go uphill, we get into medieval and when we come to the top, we'll see the cathedral and the Roman remains.'

Spike interrupted, 'And on your left, please observe Marks & Sparks, which brings more visitors to Lincoln than the cathedral, the castle and the Roman remains put together. House of Fraser lies ahead and there's also a Poundland and a Pizza Express.'

She glowered at him. 'David can see these in any high street.'

'But probably not in the same constellation. And the stateless person said…'

'Spike!'

We went under the Stonebow and Lilith continued. 'There's an uphill quarter and a downhill Lincoln, but it's as if it's archaeologically inverted. The really old layers are at the top, the medieval layer is on the way up Steep Hill and downhill is modern.'

'So, please take note, Sam, you have to dig upwards: bottom is new, top is old and the further you go, the older it gets. But you know what? I think M & S was here before Pizza Express and Mr Marks and Mr Sparks are on the level, despite any rumours to the contrary. Don't quote me on that, though. I could be wrong, the way the economy is going these days.'

Lilith was ignoring him. 'It's an extraordinary city, and it must have been even more so centuries ago. You can see the cathedral from miles away and it's supposed to have been the tallest building in the world once.'

'A major visitor attraction. Can't you just hear what the pilgrims who were seeing it for the first time were saying, "Holy shit!" And Lincoln is also the city where they built the first tanks, Sam. I may not know much, but this I do know. Art, architecture and culture, bullshit! This county is the home of modern warfare, and the damn dam-busting World War II raids started from here. Don't be fooled. Agriculture and arty-farty culture it has in spades, but it also has a helluva lot to answer for in other respects.'

And as we walked up first the Strait, an incline that leads to Steep Hill, and then the hill itself, they continued in the same vein, a discordant, atonal duet, two people who seemed to be poles apart and yet umbilically linked. I wondered what it was that had led them to come together again after divorcing. Maybe it was Annie. I wondered what she would be like. A cherub, a gamine, or just plain ordinary?

Steep Hill was cobbled and lived up to its name. I watched older people struggling to get up sections of the hill, while others, clinging onto a handrail, found that coming down posed its own set of problems.

'Do you remember reading *Sons and Lovers* at college, Sam? Well, this is where Paul Morel was wishing a man could have a young mother.'

'A prize arsehole, if you ask me,' Spike chipped in. 'Uphill may be older than downhill, but when sons and mothers get mixed up, that is seriously out of line.'

'This is the Norman House. Some people call it Aaron the Jew's House. There are two of these houses here. From the twelfth century probably. Supposedly built by Jewish financiers, I think. Or at least they say one was. They built in stone, when everyone else was building in wood. That's why the houses have survived, and they're among the oldest in England.'

'What she's not telling you is that that was before they kicked all the Jews out of Lincoln. Don't be fooled by the butter-wouldn't-melt-in-their-mouth looks of the good people of Lincoln. They could be right little Hitlers too.'

If Lilith had joined in with his sparring, they would have made a great double act, but she mostly kept herself apart, refusing to disagree with him or dispute his mood. So their talk followed two parallel routes, straight lines that kept close together without converging.

We were getting near the top of the hill.

'And this is the Wig and Mitre. It's a famous pub.'

'So called because a bald bishop spent most of his time here, blind drunk, instead of being in the cathedral up there. He was a believer in the saying that God helps those who help themselves. So he left the congregation to save themselves and he helped himself to the ale here. Wouldn't mind betting he got kickbacks too.'

She was drawn to respond. A minor victory for him? 'It wasn't a pub in the past, Spike.'

'Then it must be named after one of the modern bishops. They're a pretty dodgy lot too, if you ask me.'

'Is there time to go in the cathedral?', I asked.

'Not really, Annie gets out of school in fifteen minutes, and then we should get her home. She doesn't really like the cathedral, apart from the Imp', Lilith answered.

'The Imp? I remember hearing about it, but I think I've forgotten what it is.'

'The Lincoln Imp. It's a kind of small gargoyle. I think the medieval clergy thought it was better to have all these things inside a church, rather than outside. The cathedral was a kind of encyclopaedia of knowledge, as well as a holy place.'

'Well, if Annie likes gargoyles, maybe Sam should take her back to The Weavers with him. Don't worry. Only joking, my love. I don't want our little angel going there again.'

'Spike, enough. First the Whites are vampires. Now they're gargoyles. What next?'

'Well, I'm working on it, but remember you're the one who brought Sam here to warn him. I think we should keep him here to save him from those what-d'you-call-ems – you know what I mean – their Chambers of Horrors?'

'Cabinets of curiosities.'

'Same thing. I bet Sam would be scared by those ghoulish waxworks.'

'I saw some of the cabinets this morning. Uncle Wilf showed me. They've certainly got some odd stuff.'

'There you are, Lily. Sam thinks they're odd and he's very polite too! Those cabinets are a rocky horror show, collected by the Munsters. Frankensteins, complete with monsters – the whole lot of them, if you ask me.'

Again Lilith didn't answer, nor allow a flicker of emotion to cross her face. Spike might be performing for my benefit, but she certainly wasn't. We walked past the cathedral and it was then that I remembered that strange rumour about Lilith having committed suicide in a cathedral close. Where had I heard it? Soon we were waiting outside the gate of Annie's primary school. Five minutes later, she ran out amid a bevy of excited eight-year-olds. A straw-haired girl with enormous blue eyes, wearing an unkempt school uniform, which I guessed had been spick-and-span that morning.

'We're here, Little Orphan Annie. Come to your Dad.'

And Annie obliged, running, laughing, and saying, 'But I'm not an orphan, Daddy, am I?'

'No, sweetheart, of course you're not. You have a Daddy who loves you very very much, and the most wonderful Mummy in the world. All we need is for your Mummy to marry your Daddy again and we will be the most perfectest family there ever could be. And this is your Uncle Sam, who has come all the way to Lincoln just to see us, and who has been saying he wants to meet you, he wants to meet you, he wants to meet you.'

Spike winked at me and I joined in his clowning. 'I want to meet you, I want to meet you, I want to meet you. Hello Annie. I *am* very very very pleased to meet you.'

Her smile spread even wider. 'Would you like to meet Tennyson too, Uncle Sam?'

'Tennyson?'

Lilith explained, 'She means the Tennyson statue at the back of the cathedral. It's a favourite of hers.'

'Then I would love to meet Tennyson. Will you show us the way?'

She nodded, but became slightly shyer, simply pointing to let me know what direction we'd be going in. We walked back along a few streets in this older part of the town, and found Tennyson on a lawn behind the cathedral. Now we were with Annie, I *knew* my guess was right. She was the indissoluble bond between Lilith and Spike.

'Can you tell Uncle Sam who Tennyson was, Annie?'

'Yes, Daddy, he was a very famous poet.'

So I asked, 'And do you know any of his poems?'

She put a finger in her mouth, thought for a moment and nodded. ''Tis better to have loved and lost than to have ever, ever …'

Spike nodded rapidly, inanely, to encourage her.

'… to have ever, ever loved at all.'

But Lilith had to have it right, 'Never, dear, not ever.'

'I like Annie's version better,' said Spike.

'Did Tennyson really write those lines?', I turned to Lilith.

'Yes, he did. In *In Memoriam.* There was a lot of passion there. More than he's sometimes given credit for.'

And Annie ran towards the statue, turned to face us, curtseyed and declaimed, 'I shall ever ever love and never never love and lost.' I was surprised at how much this moved me. First Alf, now Annie. What was it about these angelic Lincolnshire children that was touching such a chord in me? Inured to feeling as I thought I'd been for several years, I was putty in their hands.

'Can we take Uncle Sam to our house for tea?'

And now Lilith and Spike collaborated, by hesitating. It was hard to imagine Lilith teasing anyone, but this was surely what she was doing.

'Pleeeeeeeeeeeeeeease!'

'OK, darling, take your Daddy's hand and we'll all go for tea.'

Annie's grin spread wider as she said demurely, 'I have two hands, Mummy.' And she held them both out towards her parents, one each side.

And together we retraced out steps back down the hill, past the shops and over a level crossing, before stopping at a baker's to buy cake, because Annie said that would make it a 'proper tea'. And that's what it was. No Mad Hatter's tea party. Just a happy occasion, with sandwiches and cake. Annie's magnetism held her parents together and momentarily at least engulfed me in its field as well. After tea, she was allowed to watch two TV programmes and play with her games console, before Lilith told her she had to go to bed, saying to me as she moved towards the stairs, 'Don't forget you're staying here tonight. Spike will find you anything you need.'

Spike grinned and saluted, but as soon as she disappeared, the smile left his face.

'Do you know why she's so worried about me being at The Weavers?'

'Search me, mate. She gets ideas in her head sometimes, but she's pretty much on the ball and so she may have a point. Her instincts are nearly always right and besides this time I think she knows a bit about what's going on. And the White family. All joking aside, they are a bunch of weirdoes.'

'I guess so. I just don't know what to make of them.'

'Anyway, you must stay here tonight. She'll let me loose long enough to take you for a pint and by the time we get back she should be more relaxed. I still don't understand her after all these years, but I watch and learn, and I can more or less read her moods. Around about nine, she usually unbuttons a bit.'

'I'd better phone Isabel and explain.'

'She's another lady of secrets, isn't she? But yeah, good idea. You know you can stay as long as you like, you old fart. I'm glad you're here, you do know that, don't you? Lily is wonderful, but being with her all the time can get a man down sometimes.'

I called Isabel and she was silent on the other end of the phone.

'Are you annoyed with me for staying over?'

'I thought you wanted to see Stuart's folders.'

'Well, you did say we could leave it till tomorrow.'

'Yes, that's right. OK. See you when I see you, best wishes Sam.' She cut me off. The Isabel of the e-mails had returned.

'Are you OK, pal? Ready for that pint?'

'Sure. Great.'

Spike called up the stairs. 'Sam and I are just going down the pub for a quick drink, love. We won't be long.'

'Be sure you're not.' Lilith's tone sounded more accommodating.

'Would you bring me some cripps, Daddy?'

And I could just hear Lilith saying, 'No more junk food for a while, darling.'

And Spike, who had heard this, 'Next time, Annie get your gun. Crisps next time. Sleep well. See you in the morning, when the day is dawning.'

'Night, Daddy.'

'Night night, my angel.'

The pub wasn't crowded, since it was still early, and it had none of the character of The Hope Inn. This was city life, though not big city life. Spike was refreshingly easy to talk to.

'What happened between you and Lily? What was so bad?'

'The age-old story, Sam. An affair. Not much of an affair really. More of a fling.'

'I see. And I guess Lily is the last person in the world to forgive easily.'

'No, I mean, yes. But I think you've got hold of the wrong end of the stick, matey. She had the affair, the fling. Me? Never. I wouldn't dare!' His smile was ironic, but I realised he'd been very hurt.

'So you divorced her and now she won't marry you again.'

'No, *she* divorced me and now she won't marry me again.'

'Because she feels guilty?'

'Well, who knows what lurketh in the mind of a Lilith, but she says not. She says she had to divorce me, because she couldn't feel guilt and she thought she ought to. So that was the best way she could do the right thing. She says she's got no conscience. She says there's something missing in her.'

'I heard a crazy rumour – that she'd committed suicide.'

'Not so crazy, Sam. There's a lot going on beneath her Goth disguise. She had a go at herself up by the cathedral. Now she always wears those long black sleeves, but if you get a chance take a gander at her wrists. I think it was serious, not just a cry for help, but anyway, if she was, she didn't do the job well enough and the County Hospital isn't far away. They got her to A & E quickly.'

'That's hard to believe. No guilt, and she did that?'

'Well, yeah. That's what I used to think, but that's what she says, and now I've been around her for so long, I believe her. No guilt trips.'

'But she's OK now?'

'Well, according to Lily, Lily has always been OK. That day when she tried to do herself in, she said it was the logical thing to do.'

'And afterwards?'

'Afterwards she said it *wasn't* logical any longer, but divorce was logical and then a while later she decided she should be with me again and said everything was OK.'

'But in the meantime, she'd divorced you and now she won't marry you again?'

'Yeah, that's about right. She divorced me after her fling. It was with a fellow-Goth. After a few weeks she found she had nothing in common with him, except the black dye and The Sisters of Mercy. Then, a while after that, she tried to do herself in, and then she decided everything was logical and OK. Well, more or less. She just says there's no logic to our being married, because she's not good enough for me.'

'But she doesn't feel guilt?'

'Yeah, that's what she says.'

'And she's miserable around you?'

'No, that's not quite right. Not always, and never when Annie's there. So life can be great with her still. But this is getting a bit morbid. Ready for another pint?'

'A half'll do me. Uncle Wilf has been plying me with drinks.'

He was back from the bar a couple of minutes later.

'What's going on at The Weavers, Spike? Why is Lily so worried?'

'Search me. I told you, I don't know. Seriously, that lot were always a mystery to me. Maybe Lily will be able to tell you, you old fart.'

'Anyway, now we're on our own, I can tell you how it ends.'

'How what ends?'

'The one about the stateless person. It ends up with him saying, "Well, if only I could be a stereotype too." Can I ask you something, Sam? Something really serious?'

'Of course. Go ahead.'

'Are you still a West Ham fan?'

'Yes, though I haven't always kept up with them when I've been abroad.'

'Thank God! Thank God, twice over! Thank God you haven't defected and thank God you've been away and been spared some of the torture, you lucky bugger. High five, fellow masochist!'

We brushed palms and for the next fifteen minutes Spike continued to be Spike and I tried hard to be a stereotype. Then we went back to their house. Lilith was downstairs now, waiting.

Lilith

Lilith had been watching TV in the sitting room, but she switched it off and we talked, while Spike busied himself in the kitchen.

'Is Annie, asleep?'

'Yes, she dropped off quickly, clutching Horncastle.'

'Horncastle?'

'Yes, her bear. She calls him that because she bought him there.'

'Isn't that where Desmond died?'

'Yes, right. At least I think so. Somewhere near there. But no connection.'

'I'm not sure what's connected and what isn't around here.'

Lilith smiled for once, 'Just assume everything is connected and you'll be right most of the time.'

'But not all?'

'Probably not.'

'Annie's a sweetheart.'

'She is. I know I'm biased, because I'm her mother, but Annie is unique.'

'Did you ever take her to The Weavers?'

'Just a couple of times. Usually when I've gone there, she's stayed with Spike. But I don't worry about taking her, if that's what you mean. Isabel is fine with me. Mixed up, I guess, but I dunno. Sometimes I think she's going to tell me what's really bothering her. She throws out hints, but just when you think she'll tell you everything, she clams up again.'

'That's how she's been with me. She seems to be leading up to something, but yes, when you think she's going to open up, she steps back. But you must know more than me. You wanted to warn me.'

'Yes, David.'

'But I still don't get it. What's the danger? What's happened there?'

'I dunno, but as I said, it's men and boys that are at risk, from what Isabel said.'

'Yes, you said. Have you seen much of her over the years?'

'On and off. We've always kept in touch, but sometimes more than others. She was terrific when Spike and I split up. I went through a very bad period. I saw a lot of her then. She was my rock, but that's not how we generally are together. Usually I feel *I'm* supporting *her*, protecting her against I dunno what.'

I dunno, I don't know. The words were littering her remarks and seemed to sum up everything that I was being told about the Whites, The Weavers and Bubbleby. But then *I* didn't seem to know much about anything anymore.

'What happened when you and Spike split up?'

'It was hell. He was so goddam decent about everything and I just wished he could have made me feel guilty. But he didn't and I couldn't feel it, when he was so understanding and gentle. So I told myself I was a selfish bitch, but …'

'But?'

'Well, we kept on seeing one another. Annie was with me most of the time, but with him some of the time, and when I saw how her eyes lit up every time she saw him – and sometimes there were tears in his – then I knew we had to be together. The three of us.'

'You just called yourself a selfish bitch. It sounds like you felt guilty?'

'I know. I should have, but I just didn't. I kept telling myself I was a worthless bitch, messing around with a nobody for no reason, but that was an objective judgement. Inside myself I didn't believe I was guilty. I knew I should be seeing it like that, but I didn't. I just felt it was something that happened, not a great moral betrayal or anything like that. And then I got angry with him for not rubbing my nose in it.'

'And the feller you "messed around" with?'

'Oh, it was nothing, nowhere. He was a waste of space. That's what made it all so stupid. He's long gone and I never cared much for him anyway and I don't think he cared for me either. It just happened.'

'And now you stay home and look after Annie, and Spike goes out to work and brings home the bacon and everything is OK, except you can't feel guilty?'

'Well, things are sort of OK. He gets peeved because I won't marry him again. Says it's because I'm not committed, bless him. And he likes to look after Annie whenever he's not working. He dotes on her. And I do work you know – from home.'

'Oh, right. What do you do?'

'Well I used to have a good job in Internet security, but I gave that up when I went through my bad spell. Now I do bits and pieces of consultancy work from home. I'm still in demand and I make good money. So, keep it to yourself, I'm the main breadwinner in the family.'

'You just get consulted once in a while, for big assignments? As a kind of trouble-shooter?'

'That's one way of putting it, but not exactly. Actually, and this is strictly between you and me too, I do less work keeping networks secure than hacking into them.'

'So who are your clients? Who do you work for?'

'No, *that* would be telling. I've told you too much already. Let's just say sometimes I work for big organizations and sometimes for ordinary individuals, who need to know something.'

'And you charge high fees, I guess?'

'Well, it depends. It's not exactly an ethical profession, but I only do what I think is right and I charge what I think is right. Very little sometimes, if I think it's a job that needs to be done and the client can't afford much. Anyway, let me tell you what I know about Isabel and the Whites.'

'Yes, it's about time someone did. Tell me everything.' I smiled. 'Have you hacked into them?'

'No. I wish I could tell you everything. I only know what I've been told by Isabel, but maybe it'll help. I dunno. Let me get you a drink first.'

'Water would be great.' Lilith disappeared into the kitchen and was gone for about ten minutes, before emerging with two glasses of water.

It was a long July evening and the sun was only now beginning to go down, its rays striping lines across the room. As Lilith talked, time and place vanished. In another age she might have been a tribal storyteller, passing on shared communal wisdom at dusk, but the tale she told was a very individual one with no obvious moral or resolution. I interrupted once or twice, but for the most part I just listened. When she finished, I realised I'd forgotten about Spike and that he must have gone upstairs.

'You remember Isabel dropping out of college fairly suddenly?' I nodded.

'She got an emergency summons from her mother. So she went home in a hurry and her father died. He was alive when she got there. It hadn't happened then, but he died shortly afterwards.'

'Afterwards? After she got there? So what was the emergency then?'

'Well, that's where the mystery began. I dunno. Remember I was down in London and we didn't have mobiles then, did we? They were just coming in. In fact, we didn't even have a landline in our flat and so I was calling her from phone boxes and only getting bits and pieces of information. But it seems her mother was very distraught and said she should come home right away.

'Her father died, was killed in a car accident, or whatever it was that happened, the night she got home, and she's never been the same since. Stuart didn't go home, not even for the funeral, but I guess you were with him and so you know that.' I nodded. 'There was a delay before the funeral. They held it about ten days later, but he never went. I didn't know Stuart very well, but he was odd when he did come back to The Weavers. That was quite a while later. I was up here by then and I'd go over there to see Isabel about once a fortnight and it seemed he was avoiding me. But maybe he wasn't really so odd. I mean he was odd with me, but then I'd never known him well. So maybe he wasn't so odd really. I dunno.

'He was usually around until a couple of years ago. That's when he left. Then Isabel got really upset. She was bad before, but she became much worse then.'

'Any idea why?'

And Lilith embarked on a slow drawling monologue. A sibyl who spoke in oracular tones, but provided few answers. 'She was never the same after her father died. There was talk of suicide or foul play, but no evidence to prove it was anything other than an accident. The police spent a while investigating where it happened, but I don't think they saw it as a crime scene or anything like that. I think there may have been a coroner's inquest too. But if there was, well, it came to nothing. Laura and Uncle Wilf had tests done. They had the car checked out, I think, but there weren't any mechanical faults. Steve and Martin were upset. Alice was beside herself, but Isabel took it worst of all. She didn't make a lot of sense when she talked to me. She refused to accept it. She said her father should have lived forever, whatever he'd done. I think she wanted Stuart home. She'd always been closer to him than the others. I think that's why she had followed him to London when he suggested it. To our college, I mean. She was interested in geography, with her imagination and all that, but she wasn't really academic. I think she'd come to be near Stuart. Stuart and her Dad were the centre of her universe.

'Anyway, Stuart stayed away for a while. Life went on. She worked at different jobs. Didn't really stick at anything. She was a waitress and she had a brief spell as a barmaid at The Hope Inn. They all love her there, like she's their own daughter. She even worked down at Butlin's in Skegness one summer, God forbid! After Stuart graduated, he worked in London for a while and then eventually he came home and she seemed a bit better. But she took it badly when Martin left. He just disappeared into thin air. Gone overnight. And then something similar happened with Steve a couple of years later.

'I asked her about them – Martin and Steve – at different times and she said she had been completely out of touch with Martin since he disappeared, but Steve had got a good job somewhere nearby and he was OK. But she mainly felt things were OK, or at least she seemed to cope, because she had Stuart; and I think she got closer to Alice and, of course, she loves Uncle Wilf, but then everyone loves Uncle Wilf.

'It's just these last couple of years that she's been as weird as she is now. When Stuart left, she went off the rails. She'd phone me sobbing in the middle of the night, talking about Glen's death and saying she was frightened. You know, sometimes when I think of The Weavers, what comes to mind most is the funerals. I went to Glen's funeral. There was no talk of foul play that day, but well, the police had been there and I wondered. Nothing much was said, but I wondered. Isabel was pale as a ghost. Alice was worse, like death warmed up. Even Uncle Wilf wasn't himself.'

'And Stuart?'

'Yes, he was there, at *that* funeral, and he seemed very upset. He talked more than usual. He talked to me a bit, that time. He was saying that they needed to stick together, to stay close. Isabel always talks about faraway places and that day, it was like he was saying the opposite. I mean he was talking a lot about Bubbleby and The Weavers. Not exactly disagreeing with her, but talking about home and how important it is and all that kind of stuff, and saying it for her more than anyone else, I think. A kind of mantra. Saying the same thing over and over again to try to bring it into being. I don't think he quite believed it himself, but I'm not sure. Even when he was talking to me, it seemed he was trying to say something to her. Maybe he was thinking I could persuade her. I dunno. He wasn't making a lot of sense, but he was saying that Lincolnshire was "real" and they needed to stick together in the house. He said a lot of things like that. It didn't seem very specific and it didn't make much sense, but it was as if he was trying to persuade Isabel that she was wrong, as if he was telling her to stop fantasizing about faraway places. He was very close to Alice too and he felt they should be bonding to help her live with what had happened to Glen.

'And then, of course, he was the one who left and she's still here. I dunno. Maybe he persuaded her through what he was saying, but he didn't convince himself. Isabel doesn't make too much sense. Sometimes she rambles and sometimes she's very lucid. She talks about Stuart and Glen a lot. Sometimes Martin and Steve. And she seems very worried about Jules, and little Alf. The men and boys. I think she's worried about Stuart, too, though she doesn't say much. Yes, I'm sure she is. I think she's worried about Uncle Wilf, but well, I'm not sure. I dunno.'

She was speaking more and more hesitantly, contemplatively, scrupulously, as if trying to make sure that every word she said was entirely accurate. I dunno, I dunno.

'She's very worried for the ones who have stayed … I think. I don't know what happened with Stuart. I'm fairly sure he just took off unexpectedly, though. I don't think it was planned. I'd seen them about a week before and there was no mention of his leaving and then suddenly he was gone. He had a good job here, you know, working for the Council, like Spike, but not here in Lincoln. Their local Council, down there. I think he was pretty well paid. He always seemed to be flush with money and there was no talk of him having another job to go to.'

I'd refrained from interrupting her, though it occurred to me that there was something missing in her narrative, and now I asked, 'Did they never have relationships? Did Isabel never have boyfriends?'

'Oh yes, she's had scores. Most weren't serious. She jokes about how awful the men she's seen are when she talks to me. She used to be very funny on the subject of men. A couple of them may have been more serious, but it doesn't seem she can stick with anyone. Dunno. Maybe her standards are too high. You know, lately she's been talking about you.' I raised my eyebrows, but she didn't expand. 'She's lovely, but she can find fault with people over the tiniest things, you know? She dropped one of her boyfriends, because he wouldn't eat curly kale.'

'I know the feeling. Can't stand it myself.'

'Then watch out, if she gets anywhere near you.'

'She has. I mean she did for a moment, but I don't think she meant anything by it.' Lilith raised *her* eyebrows, but didn't probe me on this.

'And Stuart? Did he have relationships?'

'Well, I don't know too much about who he might have been seeing. Only what Isabel told me, but I think Stuart had "friends". Maybe he finally ran off to one of them. I doubt that, though.'

'And what about Steve and Martin?'

'Well Steve definitely had boyfriends. He led a fairly secret life. I guess it's not always easy, being gay in this part of the world, but he seemed to be a together sort of person and I think he went off to one of his friends. And Martin was seeing Margie for as long as I can remember. She's still somewhere around. In Louth, I think. Goodness knows what she thought when he suddenly vanished off the face of the earth. And then there's Alice. She used to be – how should I put it? – spontaneous. She'd go with anybody. Complete strangers. But after she lost Glen, she changed. Isabel says she doesn't go anywhere now and she hardly lets Alf out of her sight. She says she's a wonderful mother to him. There's no doubt about it. The Weavers is an open prison and some of them have walked, but Alice and Isabel stay.'

'And Jules?'

'Yes, Jules too. He's hard to read, but I don't think he'll leave.'

'Well, perhaps it's not so odd that several of them have gone. It's natural to leave home sooner or later.' I was trying not to be sarcastic.

'OK, yes, I know, but I don't think it's usual to have so many siblings leaving so abruptly, without explanation. Two maybe, but three – that's more than a coincidence.'

'Three have stayed.'

'Yes. Three gone. Three still there. Maybe you're right.'

'You know why I'm here?'

'You said that Isabel summoned you, out of the blue.'

'Yes, but she said that I should come, because Stuart had left some stuff for me to read.'

'It almost sounds like you're being called on as a kind of executor, for a living person.'

'Maybe, but are you sure he's alive? When she first wrote to me, she was very ambiguous and I thought she was saying he was dead.'

'I suppose anything is possible with the White family, but Isabel certainly thinks he's alive and I'd be surprised if she's wrong. I don't think she has a clue where he is, but she feels he's tied to her, and she would know, intuitively, if something was wrong with him. Like there's telepathy between them. She feels more linked to him than any of the others. And you know something else that's strange?'

'What's that?'

'The last time she was here she was talking about you in the same way. She didn't say it clearly, but she kept bringing you into the conversation in a way that suggested she felt equally close. Well, maybe not in the same way, but very close in some way. I dunno.'

'That's bizarre. I've not seen them in years.'

'Yes, I know. What have you been doing all these years, David? Is it a secret? Or are we allowed to ask.'

And I found myself saying, '*You* are allowed to ask, Lily.' Her directness made me able to confide in her in a way, I realised, that I never could have with Spike, for all his cheerfulness and camaraderie. So we swapped roles. I became the storyteller and I told her something of what had happened to me in the years since I'd left college. Not everything, but a brief review of my 'life'. I never lie, but I've learnt to live inside myself and I don't volunteer information if I can avoid it.

She was a good listener and I found myself disclosing things to her, just as I had that day in Tony's café. I edited my story to avoid tedium, but it was still a lengthy tale. By the time I finished, evening shadows had given way to darkness and I couldn't see her face any longer. Neither of us had moved to put a light on and Spike had stayed upstairs. I can't remember everything I said that night, but I told her how as a small boy I'd had wonderful parents in Somerset, parents who wanted to do everything for me and who were everything to me. Then, when they thought I was old enough to understand, their decency obliged them to tell me that I wasn't really their son, nor my 'sister's' brother. They tried to reassure me that, although I was adopted, they would always be my 'Mum and Dad' and they loved me just as much as they loved my sister, who was their 'own child'. They were the most sincere and principled people I've ever met, but from that moment I knew that they were just kindly guardians, liberal do-gooders who were incapable of giving me real love, unconditional love. I spent long hours alone in my room, watching sci-fi movies and feeling I was an alien in their house until the time arrived when I would put their world behind me. It came when I left school. I spent a year backpacking around Europe, my first taste of life as a nomad. Spain, the Midi, Italy, Slovenia, Croatia, Greece and Turkey. It was good to be near the Med in winter and it felt right to be travelling. Having decided that I had no 'home', I loved the sensation of being 'away'.

I had school grades that were just about good enough to get me into some kind of college, but I hadn't applied. I was drifting, happy in my wandering, and with no real thoughts about the future. It was only during the second summer after I finished school that I found a college place, through clearing. That was thanks to Stuart. I met Stuart on the beach at Weston-Super-Mare. We bonded almost immediately. I can't remember how we started talking, but I think he asked me the time and we fell into casual conversation. We were exact contemporaries and we seemed to be travelling similar roads. We'd both left school a year before. He told me about the college and said if I was still looking for a place, maybe I should try it. He had a place lined up there and he thought it was a decent enough Uni, with the advantage of being in London. It wasn't in the top flight and he felt sure there would be places available through clearing. He was right. I applied, got accepted and that was how we became close friends. Following his suggestion, I'd phoned the college's clearing hotline, wanting to do English and Psychology and I'd ended up being offered a place to do English with a bit of Philosophy and History thrown in. So, I told Lilith, meeting Stuart had been a chance coincidence, but it was one of those serendipitous coming togethers that changes lives. Well, at least it was a defining moment in my life. I couldn't be sure Stuart had felt the same, but our lives had become intertwined in the years we were at college.

Lilith intervened. 'I think Stuart may have felt something similar, though of course he never said much to me. But he did once tell me about how he'd met you. It was just like you said, only the way he put it, well, it was almost as though he'd gone there looking for you … or someone like you.'

I carried on with my story, skipping some chunks of my past and glossing over other bits. I told Lilith about my years in college and how it was then that I'd decided to be Sam and not David. When I was about ten, my parents had informed me that I was called Sam, when I first came to them, and *they* had decided to christen me David, claiming me as their own by renaming me. I grew up as David, but when I met Stuart that day on the beach, I told him my name was Sam. I couldn't have said why at the time, but afterwards I realised I was looking for a new identity and I suppose I thought reverting to 'Sam' might give me that. Anyway, I became 'Sam' at college and I'd been Sam ever since, with everyone except Lilith.

After I left college and I couldn't find a decent job in Britain, I'd gone first to Thailand, and later to the Caribbean – to Aruba – to teach English. I got some bits of freelance journalism work there and when I moved to the States a couple of years later, my CV was just good enough to land me a job on a small-town newspaper in Arizona. I told Lilith about my short-lived marriage. We'd got married on impulse after a night when we'd drunk too much and we parted fairly amicably when we realised it had been a silly mistake. The main problem was the bother of getting divorced. But even that wasn't too bad. A quickie Nevada divorce to end a quickie Nevada marriage. After that I thought maybe it was time to try England again. I'd come back, not found it much better than before, made a few new friends – not many – and not really tried to re-establish contact with my old ones. I suppose I was still drifting, but that was me. A nomad, not keen to talk about myself. Keeping quiet helps you avoid being pinned down. It allows you to be multiple. It's a kind of travelling.

Back in the UK, I'd found a bit of freelance work in London, but not enough to live on, when I heard that my 'mother' had died. She'd been a widow for ten years – my parents were in their forties when they adopted me. I'd never been back, but I went to the funeral in Wells, saw my 'sister' for what I knew would be the last time and found out that 'Mum' had left me half her worldly wealth. She was scrupulously fair. I didn't inherit a fortune – they hadn't been rich – but she had the house and, after my 'sister' sold that, I had more than enough for the down-payment on the house in Essex. That's the barebones of the life-story I told Lily. There were lots of excisions and a few embellishments. I didn't let on that I was censoring details here and there, but Lilith could see through me.

'It's OK, David. You don't need to tell me more. I know it's difficult for you.'

And at that moment I could hear music drifting down the stairs. Indistinct, but very definitely Van Morrison singing 'Someone Like You'.

'Does Spike like Van Morrison, Lily?'

'I'm not too sure, but he's been playing that lately. Isabel gave me one of Stuart's DVDs and Spike has been playing it a bit.'

'I heard Stuart was a Van Morrison fan?'

'Dunno. I guess so, if he had the DVD.'

'It's weird. Van Morrison seemed to be everywhere on the radio yesterday. It was like he was accompanying me up here.'

She smiled, again, 'Maybe that was Stuart summoning you.'

'Exactly.'

'No, I didn't mean that. I was being ironic. Stuart always had a way of making us feel he was the centre of attention, but no, David, that's just coincidence.'

I wasn't convinced. 'What's the statistical likelihood of my hearing Van Morrison ten times in a couple of days. One in a million?'

'Dunno, but if something is a one in a million chance, I guess we never notice the million minus one happenings that could have coincided on a given day, but didn't.'

'Yes, I don't know, though. Isabel thought maybe the BBC were having a Van Morrison day. I think they have days like this, but now Spike is playing *Stuart's* Van Morrison DVD.'

'David, lighten up. If someone is out to get you, I don't think they would do it this way. Why Van Morrison? Why on earth, would they? It's about as likely as the idea that there are vampires at The Weavers.' But then she changed tack and added, 'But the words are good, aren't they? Maybe Stuart was looking for someone like you, when he met you on the beach. You know, I'm sure he did say something like that.' And this time she was at her most serious. There was no 'dunno' to distance herself from what she'd said.

Beth

During the night, I had troubled dreams about eating fish and chips in Tony's café, which seemed to have relocated itself in Calabria or Sicily. Outside enormous crows were flying overhead, in search of carrion; and crowds of children were clamouring for my attention. They appeared to be the crows' prospective prey, because they were begging me to save them. Then the café became a taverna on a Greek island and an Orthodox priest came in to tell me I should choose one of the children. Tony's wife, Milly, dressed as a fearsome Goth, was hovering by the kitchen door, watching my every move. She seemed far away, but I called to ask her for advice as to which child I should choose. She put a silencing finger to her lips and turned away. The crows were swooping down now, coming closer and closer towards the children. A phone rang in the inner recesses of the taverna, distracting me from the children for an instant. I moved to answer it and as I did so I came to. I'd left my mobile on, so its alarm could wake me up. The phone was rousing me, but it was a call, not the alarm. I reached out just in time to answer it on the sixth or seventh ring. It was Isabel.

'Please come home, Sam. Sorry about last night. I just didn't think you should have decided to take off like that yesterday. Come back now, and everything will be fine.'

I was barely awake, struggling to find words. 'OK, I'll be with you in a w-while. Are you OK? Is everything alright?'

'Well no, not exactly. I mean yes, I'm fine today, but I'm worried.'

'What about?'

'Oh, lots of things. But particularly about Uncle Wilf. So come when you can. I'm not saying it's urgent like before, but well, it is. So come back soon, please.' And this time there was an element of almost pathetic pleading in her voice.

'OK, Spike and Lily have been really kind and I thought I would stay a bit longer, but I'll be with you later today. Don't worry.'

'They're good people, but come, Sam. Soon, please. I need you. *We* need you.'

'Yes, OK. I'll be there. Take care.'

'Can I call you again? I mean in a couple of hours, if you're not here.'

'Yes, that's fine. Take good, good care.'

'I will. Bye, Sam. But Sam?'

'Yes?'

'You will come soon, won't you?' She was speaking with the innocence of a child.

'Yes, I will. Don't worry.'

'And I'll show you the folders that Stuart left for you.'

'OK, that'll be good. Bye now then.'

'Bye, Sam. Bye bye. Bye again.'

I staggered to the bathroom and on the way back I met Annie, clutching her bear. Two more innocents.

I was awake enough to muster, 'This must be Horncastle.'

She nodded, very shy this morning, but smiling all the same.

'Would you introduce me to him?'

She nodded again. 'Horncastle, he is Uncle Sam, and Uncle Sam, he is Horncastle.'

'I'm very pleased to meet you, Horncastle. Is he a good bear, Annie? Is he well behaved?'

She nodded her head vigorously.

'And he is a gentleman bear or a lady bear?'

'He is a *teddy* bear.' She grinned. 'Mummy says it doesn't matter whether he is a man or a lady.' I could see Lilith was training her well.

'But *he* is a 'he'.'

'Yes, of course, he is,' and she gave me the kind of patronising look one gives to someone who is so idiotic that even the most obvious details have to be explained to them. Well, at least there was certainty here.

'Does he eat much?'

'No, he's a *teddy* bear. He doesn't eat, but he is allowed to come to breakfast and, and watch us eat, and, and …', she struggled to explain.

'Yes?'

'He has to have a cushion for his chair, because he isn't tall enough ovverwise and Mummy says he can't sit on the table.'

'Well, that's a shame, Annie, but your Mum is right and as long as he can come to breakfast, that's the main thing and if he doesn't eat much …'

And she finished the sentence for me, 'There's all the more for us. I like Rice Crippies for breakfast, but not every day.'

'What else do you like?'

'Sausage. I have it with egg sometimes, but I like my sausage more than my egg. Sometimes I get two, but usually I am only allowed one. I put butter on my sausage. In the middle.' She winked.

'That's a good way to have it. And what about your egg? How do you like that?'

'Well, I don't know. Any way. I have sojjers with my egg, you know.'

'Soldiers? For dunking?'

She hesitated, 'Yes, for dipping them in the egg.' She mimed to educate me in the art of dunking soldiers in eggs and carrying the yolk to one's mouth.

I hadn't realised Lilith was standing along the corridor, watching, but now she spoke. 'You're good with children, David. But you never had any, did you?'

'No. No, I didn't. I haven't.'

'Mummy, why do you call Uncle Sam "David"?'

'Well, that's a long story, sweetheart. He has two names, you see.'

Annie pondered for a couple of seconds. 'I don't think people should have two names, because if they did, we wouldn't know who they were, would we?' And she looked pleased with her observation.

'That's true, Annie. It's very true. So usually people have just one name, but sometimes it's more complicated than that. Anyway I will call David "Uncle Sam", and while he is with us, he will only have one name.'

'I will never have two names will I, Mummy?'

'No, my dear, not unless you choose to. Some women have a different name when they get married. Some choose that, some don't.'

'Mmm, maybe I *would* like to have two names. That would be fun. Will I get married, Mum?'

'Oh, I expect so.'

'I do have two penguins, don't I? Can I show Uncle Sam?'

'Later, dear. Now you have to go to school.'

'But I have to have my breakfast first, don't I?'

'Yes you do, sweetheart. Otherwise you won't grow up to be big and strong.'

'I *am* strong, Mum. Not big yet, but I am very very very strong.' And she swung Horncastle through a big arc and into my stomach.

'Ouch!' I feigned injury, grabbing my midriff and letting my knees buckle.

'What do you like to have for breakfast, David?', Lilith returned to adult-speak.

'Oh, anything really. Whatever you have. Maybe rice crispies or a sausage?' I winked at Annie, who enjoyed this and winked back. Co-conspirators.

'*Egg* and sausage?'

'OK, with "soldiers", please.'

'I can see you've been well briefed. Soldiers it is then. Tea or coffee?'

I looked to Annie for further guidance. 'Say tea,' she directed, 'and there's orange juice too.'

'A small orange juice and a tea then, please.' Entering Annie's world was a joy. For the moment The Weavers was banished from my mind.

Twenty minutes later at breakfast, Spike was in full flow. 'Oh you should see Lily first thing in the morning, Sam, before she scrubs up and puts on her funeral outfit. You know I love her any which way – never doubt that – but she's not a pretty sight first thing in the morning. Without her false teeth and before she puts on her make-up, she is a woman only a husband could love.'

'Daddy!', shrieked Annie.

'Without her fine Goth apparel and her earrings and all her other thing-a-me-what-nots, without her wooden leg and her false teeth and her glass eye, in those wee small hours of the morning, she needs a husband to love her.'

'Daddy!', shrieked Annie again.

'And here she has a ready-made, custom-built, state-of-the-art volunteer to hand. There's none so blind as them that can't see what's right in front of their noses.' I couldn't tell how much of this was being staged for my benefit, but try as he would, he wasn't managing to draw Lilith out.

She was getting ready to take Annie to school. I told her I'd be going back to The Weavers shortly and she urged caution once again. 'Don't stay there overnight, David. If you feel you need to be around for Isabel's sake, use us as a base. Visit them, but sleep here. The spare room is yours for as long as you like.' And unusually, she turned to Spike for confirmation, 'Tell him, Spike, it'd be for the best.'

'It is for the best, matey. Listen to the lady. Don't be fooled, just because she looks like she's kitted out for Halloween. It doesn't mean a thing. She's smart as hell and she has a heart of gold, and you never know, we prospectors may even find it one day, if we dig deep enough. And let's face it, *you* don't have to see her at the crack of dawn and so you get the best of her – and that can be pretty damn good – you get me as a drinking partner and on top of that you get to play with Annie get your gun. It's simple, a straight choice between us or the werewolves and witches. No contest, if you ask me.'

'Thanks, Spike. Thank you, too, Lily. Let's see. I'll go back to Isabel, but it's good to know I can come back. Old friends are the best friends.'

'Is Uncle Sam really going, Mummy? He only just came.'

'For a while, dear, but he will come to see us again soon. Don't worry. Now let's put your jacket on and then we can wave him goodbye as we walk up the street. Take care, David.'

'OK.'

'I mean *really* take care. Be very, very careful.'

'OK.'

They left, with Annie waving frantically until she was out of sight. Shortly afterwards Spike went off to work. Left alone, I realised that I'd been in Lincolnshire less than forty-eight hours, but it seemed like I'd always been there. I didn't think I'd be returning to Spike and Lilith that evening. They'd been wonderful company and it had been a relief to be with them, but The Weavers was pulling me back. Isabel fascinated me, Uncle Wilf was a once-in-a-lifetime experience, Laura and Jules had been pleasant and I needed to know more about Alice's combat knife.

Driving cross-country to go back to The Weavers was very different from my journey of two days before. My thoughts were too far away to worry about overtaking. I simply followed what was in front of me and when I got impatient drivers behind me, I decelerated to allow them to pass. I kept the radio off, to make sure no more messages could be beamed to me via Van the Man. I remembered what Lilith had said about men and boys being in danger and I imagined legions of Amazons lying in wait to ambush me: Valkyries descending from the skies, harpies hiding behind bushes, sirens seeking to lure me off the road to meet my end in a car crash, like the one that had killed Desmond. When a woman driver in an old MG sports overtook me, I braked to allow her to get a good distance ahead of me quickly. I kept thinking about the White sisters. I felt sure I could trust Isabel, despite all her mood swings. And it was hard to see Alice, reared on wonderland tea-parties, as a threat to anyone, despite the glimpse of the combat knife in her Davenport. Perhaps, after all, there was nothing untoward. Just a couple of accidents that had made Isabel paranoid. But then, if that was so, she had transmitted the syndrome to Lilith and Spike and, it seemed, the lunch-time clientele in the Hope Inn.

About ten miles from Bubbleby, I saw a hand carwash and tempted by its cheapness drove in. Three washers got to work on the car, sudsing, hosing and wiping with an industriousness that seemed distinctly un-English. As I paid, I asked the man taking the cash from me where they were from and the answer sounded like "Kazakhstan". I wondered what their visa status was. What kind of lives were they living in this remote part of Lincolnshire, waiting for the occasional car to stop in, to earn a pittance in English terms? When I got to Bubbleby, I saw the MG sports that had overtaken me parked outside The Hope Inn and on impulse decided to stop in there. I went in the Bar side. Ben was alone at this earlier hour, apart from a single woman I could see across the bar in the posher side of the pub.

'Hello, young man. What can I get you?' I grasped that 'young man' was a term Ben used for anyone under the age of eighty.

'A red wine. A large one, please. How are you?'

'Me? I'm OK thank you. Right as rain. All on your tod, today?'

'Yes, I'm just on my way back to The Weavers actually. Will you have one yourself?'

'No, you're alright. That's very kind, though, Sam. Much appreciated.'

'Can I ask you something?'

'Course you can.'

'Do Stuart's family come here much?'

'No, not these days. Isabel still comes and Wilf drops in once in a while. But Laura and the others, hardly ever. Well, Laura never did come in much. Alice and whatshisname used to be in more, but since their brothers left and the little boy had that dreadful accident, they've not come much at all. But then they're busy. They've got their own lives to lead.'

'Yes, but there's something wrong, isn't there? When I was here the other day, you told me to take care of Isabel.'

'We're all very fond of her. Her and Wilf and Sherry. We love them three.'

'What do you think about the accidents and the boys leaving?'

'Well, leaving is natural around here. There's not much work for the young folks. They mostly leave to get jobs.'

'And the accidents?'

'They're an unlucky family, aren't they? But it makes you worry that something else might happen. That's why we said, "Take care of Isabel." She deserves the best of everything.'

'Her friend doesn't think she's in danger. She says it's the men and boys who are in danger.'

'Oh, you mean, her friend, the lovely Lilith. Now *that's* somebody to be scared of, if you ask me.' But he was smiling as he said this. 'No, if an accident is going to happen, an accident is going to happen, unless you're very careful. And I never heard of accidents picking out men more than women, or anything like that. But then there are those that says the whole White family are an accident going somewhere to happen.'

Ben disappeared into a passageway behind the bar.

'Bloody bureaucracy!' The exclamation was from the woman on the other side. 'Red tape, red tape and then more bleeding bloody red tape.' I looked across at her. She was overweight and, if her two metal crutches and the awkwardness with which she was moving her arms were anything to judge by, semi-disabled. Then, after a few seconds I recognised her as the woman who had been singing 'The Lincolnshire Poacher' as we'd left the pub two nights before.

I was her only audience and so it seemed polite to say something back. 'S-sounds like you've got problems?'

'I should say so,' she barked hoarsely, and looking at her more closely as she spoke, I could see that she was virtually toothless. A rustic who sang local songs and might fulfil my vision of country life? 'You can't turn around without having to fill in forms in triplicate to meet the damn EU regulations and then you get the bloody inspectors coming to check everything. This used to be a free country.'

She didn't elaborate and so I resorted to more clichés to prompt her. 'Things aren't what they used to be. This government has a lot to answer for.'

'Tell me about it. You wouldn't believe how much trouble bleeding Defra is giving me over my chickens. Avian Influenza, Newcastle Disease. I'd never even heard of them a few years ago?'

I was beginning to warm to her. It didn't seem right that a challenged woman should have to suffer so much because she kept a few chickens. But again I was a babe in arms, and I was about to be enlightened.

'It's hard to make an honest living, and all you're doing is trying to help the economy through your exports. They do nothing to regulate the bloody bankers, but people like you and me can't do anything without dotting our "i's" and crossing our "t's", not to mention minding our "p's" and looking after our bloody "q's", whenever the inspectors come round.'

'You're in the export business then?'

She wasn't going to answer directly. 'It wouldn't be so bad if you had a decent broadband connection, but what do those shits in Whitehall care. North of Watford and they think you're an *untermensch*. And if you can't get around quite as quick as you used to (gesturing to the crutches) and you have a bit of extra weight, you've committed the cardinal sin of being O-B-E-S-E and they see you as the lowest of the low. You're scum in the eyes of all those cityfolk. You and me, sonny, they've got no time for the likes of you and me.' Another stopping-off point in my journey into darkest England. I was liking her more and more. But why did she think we had something in common? Or was she just being friendly?

At that moment my mobile rang. Isabel again. Not the pleading Isabel of earlier in the morning, but the histrionic, indignant Isabel of a couple of days before.

'Where on earth are you? You should be here by now.'

'I'm sorry. I'm in the Hope. Be with you in just a few minutes.'

'You're in the Hope?!' Incredulity personified. 'You should be here and you've stopped off for a drink, or three?'

'Well no, not three. But I don't know. I just stopped in, without thinking. For one drink. Nearly finished. I'll be with you right away, Isabel.'

'You're unbelievable!' And again she cut me off.

'Isabel? Isabel White?', said my new friend on the other side of the bar.

'Do you know her?'

'Yes, bless you. Course I do. We all know Isabel and Stuart, and all of that lot up there. You might say I'm a friend of the family. I've known Laura for years.'

I played dumb. 'What are they like, the White family?'

'Oh, a mixed bunch. Six of one and half a dozen of the other, like most families. But I dare say you know much more about them than me, Sam.'

'You know my name?' I said it gently and fairly quietly, though I still had to project my voice to be heard across the bar.

'I heard you talking to Ben. Hang on a mo. I'm coming round to see you.' She hoisted herself onto her crutches surprisingly swiftly and was out of the door, in through the one on the Bar side and on a stool beside me in fifteen seconds. So much for thinking of her as 'disabled'. Her hair was grey and straggly, her skin weather-beaten. She looked as though she was in her seventies, but it was hard to gauge. And I realised something else that I hadn't noticed before. Her ageing skin was brown. Not just weather-beaten or sun-tanned. She was racially mixed. 'My name is Beth – short for Lijsbeth.'

'Hello, Elizabeth. I'm Sam'

She smiled and raised her eyebrows, refraining from reminding me that she had just mentioned my name.

'Lijsbeth. Not Elizabeth. I'm Dutch. Born in Curacao, brought up in Rotterdam. I've lived here for twenty-five years and sometimes I even forget it myself, but I'm Dutch and it's Lijsbeth. I have to keep my name. You have to hang on to something from the past to know who you are. Especially when you're a woman alone. Been on my own since my husband died eight years ago.'

I should have been hurrying back to Isabel, but I was intrigued by the glimpse I was getting into Lijsbeth's life. I'd realised that her colloquial English had a slightly different ring to it and now I knew why. That apart, I could imagine her as one of the older mixed-race women I'd met while living in the Dutch Antilles. 'And you keep chickens. For the eggs?'

'Well I suppose you could say that. I export. I told you. I send chickens to Australia. That's why I have to be beholden to bloody Defra. Everything has to be just so to please them. You wouldn't believe the rules and regulations. And the bleeding Aussies aren't much better. They have some of the strictest health regulations in the world, you know. Island people, you see – like the English – but this island has always had to put up with us Europeans, and now it's got all the chickens that have come home to roost from its Empire. It's a bit more used to cross-breeding and impurities, though they say it's changing out there too. Did you know that many of your favourite flowers and veggies came from Holland? People here had never seen an orange carrot until you got some from us about three hundred years ago.'

'What colour were they before then?'

'Here? Here, people only had yellow carrots.'

'I never knew that. And you send chickens to Australia?'

'No, eggs.'

'Don't they have enough eggs of their own? A big country like that.'

Again she was kind enough not to treat me as an imbecile. 'I send fertilized eggs to Australia. A rare species of chicken. They can't get enough of my eggs out there. They hatch them out and everybody's happy, but I don't make money like the shitty city bankers, and the bloody British government doesn't give a monkey's about my contribution to the economy.'

First impressions. I'd seen Lijsbeth as a stereotype.

'If we only had decent broadband where I live, I'd be making twice the money. And my ISP keeps telling me it's super-fast. Another bunch of conmen, if you ask me.'

'Do you live in the village?'

'No, not far away, though. About four miles away. Up near the main road. The broadband is worse there than here. But none of us in this part of the world get good enough speeds, like those people down there who are making fortunes out of the likes of us.'

My mobile rang again. Beth smiled, 'That'll be Isabel.' I listened to a tirade on the other end of the phone. Beth could only hear my end of the conversation, but after the call ended, she said, 'She's a sweetie really, isn't she? Wouldn't hurt a fly'. (Lilith's exact words! Was this part of the shared discourse on Isabel?) I think you'd better go to her now, dear.' And in a flash she was off the barstool where she'd been sitting beside me, propelling herself across the floor on her crutches and opening the door for me, as if I was the one who was disabled and in need of help. Like me, she had to stoop to avoid hitting her head. 'Nice to meet you. Hope to see you again, while you're here. And …' (For the first time she hesitated), 'if you need me, call this number. Don't hesitate.' She handed me a card.

'Need you?'

'Well, you never know when you may need a friend when you're away from home. People like you and me have to stick together. If you have any trouble finding me, just ask for the egg lady.'

'Is that why you were doing "The Lincolnshire Poacher" the other night.'

'Could be, though some people seem to think my version is more scrambled than poached.'

There was no sign of the 'witches' by the green and driving up the hill, I only brushed the hedgerows once, when I had to swerve to avoid an oncoming Range Rover. The Weavers seemed quieter even than when I'd first arrived. Just one car outside. The Ford Focus in which Isabel had driven me to the Hope. And she was there, sitting on the doorstep, her head on one side, inquisitive but not as hostile as I'd expected. I thought she was in a better mood. I was wrong. As I got out of the car, she rushed towards me. Her face was ashen.

'You should have been here before, Sam. You really should have. It's Uncle Wilf.'

'What's happened?'

'I don't know. He didn't seem right first thing this morning, when I called you. Then, after breakfast, when the others had gone out, he went to lie down in his room. I went up to check on him and he said he was fine. But he didn't come down for hours and that's not like him. So I went up again and now he's not moving. He's breathing, but not moving.'

I rushed into the house and up the stairs. Wilf was lying on his bed, snoring very loudly. His mouth was wide open and his jaw had dropped. Isabel was just behind me.

'Maybe he's just sleeping deeply. Does he have any illnesses?'

'He suffers from sleep-apnoea. He doesn't complain much, but we know he doesn't get much good sleep and he often nods off in the day. For tiny amounts of time. Just seconds usually. He can drop off for ten seconds, wake up and say his power nap has done him the world of good, but I don't know whether it really does.'

'Maybe it's to do with that. Should we try to wake him? He seems to be dead to the world. Has he been like this long?'

'I don't know. I mean, yes, quite a while, but I don't know exactly. I found him like this half an hour ago, but he could have been like it for longer.'

'I don't think we should shake him. Let's just try talking to him and see if he wakes up' We both got close to his ears and shouted, 'Wilf! Uncle Wilf!', several times. Just when it looked as though he wasn't going to respond, Wilf opened his eyes, beaming more broadly than ever, but idiotically now, unaware of his surroundings, and yet keen to ingratiate himself with whoever might be near. Thirty seconds later he was with us again.

'Are you alright?' We said the words in unison.

'Never better, my children, but where am I?'

'In your room, Uncle. You came up here after breakfast.'

I saw a glass on his bedside table. 'Did you have a drink this morning, Wilf?'

'Well a man deserves a tiny tipple once in a while, great champion.' He was returning to normal. 'But that's just the left-overs of last night's milk, with a tiny top up this morning. Laura said I should have it, because I was looking a bit green around the gills.'

I was wondering how much of his 'milk' had been rum, when I noticed what looked like traces of a white powder in the bottom of the glass. I picked it up, thinking I'd tell Isabel as soon as we were out of the room, but she snatched it from me.

'Don't worry, I'll look after that. I'd better stay with him for a while. Why don't you go down? I got Stuart's folders out for you to read. There's one on a table in his cabinet, with a note for you.' I was being dismissed.

As I walked to the door, I heard myself saying, 'I met a woman called Beth in the Hope. That's why I was so long. I was talking to her. She seems to like you.'

She hesitated. Then, 'Beth, yes, she's a very nice woman.'

Stuart's Room

Stuart's room was the second one off the corridor in the extension. The table Isabel had mentioned was in the far right-hand corner, but before crossing to it, I gazed at the items in his cabinet. His collection was extensive, but more conventional than Desmond's or Wilf's. I'd imagined a farrago of surprising objects, but I was wrong … again. His collection told me nothing about him that I didn't know already.

When we'd been at college, one evening after a few beers, he'd waxed lyrical about becoming an engine driver. At first I'd assumed he was joking. Small boys dream of becoming engine drivers, but the journey into manhood transforms them into binmen, solicitors, IT technicians, warehousemen. Stuart's rite of passage seemed to have taken him in the opposite direction. His fascination with trains had, though, begun when he was young and that college evening he talked about his first train sets and train songs.

When I was small, I never thought of being a railway man. I did have train sets, though, and now *I would love to be an engine driver more than anything in the world. First of all I had a clockwork train that ran on a small oval. Then an electric set, with more rails, and sidings and points that sometimes caused derailments. I inherited that from my Dad. I think it may have been an antique even then, but that never occurred to me and it got some pretty rough treatment. Otherwise it would probably be worth a small fortune now. I grew up in the era of Hornby Hobbies, a great time for model railways, but I had a Triang train set from the 1950s. Not a Hornby Dublo. Uncle Wilf said that Hornby Dublo was the best you could get, but his friend worked for Triang. So he got a Triang set for Dad and I inherited it.*

I played and played with it, and I sang train songs while I played. I think I believed that the words would propel the engines around the track faster. 'Lonesome Whistle': 'All alone I bear the shame/ I'm a number not a name'. Country and Western? Train blues? I'd never heard of them. These were simply my *train set songs. After a while I imagined I'd written those words myself. 'Riding number nine'. When my trains came off the tracks, I'd stop singing – 'in Georgia doing time' – while I put them back*

And now Stuart's voice came back to haunt me in this, his holy of holies, his train collection cabinet. But it didn't fire my imagination. Like many such grails, it was a disappointment to the non-believer. There were several sets, which I surmised for the initiated would have chronicled the rivalries, takeovers and bankruptcies of the model railway companies that flourished and declined in the second half of the twentieth century. But all I saw were the gleaming surfaces of the newer models and the chipped paint on a Triang set, which I guessed was the one Stuart had played with as a boy.

The songs were more interesting. The walls were covered with sheet music and album covers that bore witness to various train journeys, literal and metaphorical, but all carrying their particular messages: coded references to the underground railroad, celebrations of the last spike, elegies for the blood, sweat and tears of men like John Henry. Stuart's collection was almost entirely American, though one wall had posters from God's Wonderful Railway and the London Tube's opening up the delights of Metroland. There were record players, various generations of speakers, cassette recorders, CD players, a Walkman, MP3 players, a gaggle of memory sticks and a shelf bowing under the weight of three laptops, piles of 45 records and neatly stacked CDs. And there was a single glass cabinet filled with vinyl Johnny Cash train songs: 'The Wabash Cannonball'; 'The Orange Blossom Special'; 'Hey Porter'; 'The Night They Drove Ol' Dixie Down'; 'The City of New Orleans'. Songs about crossing the Mason Dixon line and returning to the South. And *this* had captured Stuart's imagination. His train sets were an adult fantasy that was taking him back into childhood; the songs were anthems about journeys into an innocence that ignored the indelible scars of guilt and suffering. Testaments to an older America than the one I knew, but one that was cemented into a collective memory that didn't need the creative vision of an Isabel to bring it into being. In his absence I began to think of Stuart as more predictable than Isabel, less adventurous. But it was time to look at his folders. I crossed the room.

The note Isabel had mentioned was there on top of a red A4 folder, mundane and yet mysterious. For an instant I imagined I was being carried into a fable: a quester who travels into a strange land to uncover secret runes. But this was Bubbleby, safe secure Bubbleby and The Weavers. The note was a short introduction to the legacy that Stuart had left for me. I'd imagined I'd been summoned to play detective and to help Isabel and the family, but as I read his words, that assumption began to unravel.

Dear Sam,

I don't know when you will read the pages in these folders, but I know you will. There are three folders, three stories, but together they make one. I don't know where they will lead you, but I hope you will find belonging, and forgiveness. Forgiveness is all important. Please take care, my friend.

Stuart.

Three folders, but just one was here, and again those words: *Take care.* I opened the folder and began to read.

Travelling on that train, she was not sure what she would do when she got there. She had no doubt she was doing the right thing. She'd turned it over in her mind many times. Now, though, the difference between knowing what to do and knowing how to do it was paramount in her thoughts. Perhaps she'd leave the child on the doorstep.

The man in the seat opposite her was smoking and she wanted to tell him to stop, because of the child. She hated smoke herself, but today she wasn't thinking about herself. The child was all she could focus on. On another day she would have spoken up, but today she was timid. She was so sick of men. So sick of them, she didn't want to hear them, see them, smell them. All of them, except her husband. She didn't want conversation. If she could just get this over with. Then maybe she could get back to normal and no one need know. Smoke was definitely bad for babies, wasn't it, but exactly how bad? And was it worse when they were very, very small like this? He'd been premature and almost hadn't made it. When they said he would be alright, she hadn't known what to do at first. She'd gone away, back to her lonely room, the one she'd been in for those weeks, but that couldn't go on. She had to get back to her life and the child couldn't be part of it, though he was a marvellous little boy. She wished she could have loved him, but she couldn't drop her guard and allow herself to feel. She'd always wanted a child, but not this way, not this one.

She wasn't familiar with the part of this country she was travelling to. She was taking a journey into nowhere. There wasn't a station where she was going, but there must be taxis at the one where she would get off the train. As long as she didn't have to stand out in the rain with the baby. She hoped it would stop raining. Perhaps she should have waited until he was just a few days older.

Why did she have to be sitting across from a man? Why had he chosen to park himself there, when he could have sat anywhere on the train? But then perhaps there weren't many free seats in smoking carriages. She'd made a mistake coming into this one. She thought she was concealing her emotions, but she must have looked agitated, because the man leaned forwards and asked her if she was alright. She nodded, three times quickly, not wanting to speak, but then she looked at him more closely. He seemed harmless, apart from the cigarette, and so she asked him if he knew whether she could get a taxi at that station. He didn't. He wasn't from that part of the country either. Like her, he wasn't from any part of this country. He was going further, to a big town, somewhere further up the line. He was sorry he couldn't help her. He seemed to realise she was nervous.

They talked more and he told her about the friend he was going to meet, and when she realised that the friend was very special to him and he was gay, she felt more relaxed with him. She couldn't have coped with another predatory male. After a while they even began to joke a bit. He was Spanish and he told her a joke about the Falklands War, which they enjoyed, because neither of them was British. A man was walking along a street in London. He saw a legless beggar and pretended not to notice him, but out of the corner of his eye, he caught sight of the sign the beggar was holding: 'Falklands War Veteran'. He was moved, he changed direction and put a pound in the beggar's outstretched hand. 'Muchas gracias. Muchas gracias, señor. Hasta la vista.'

She had to take the baby to the toilet to change his nappy. The man said he would keep an eye on her bags. She wished she had someone like him to accompany her to her destination. A man who could simply be there, making no demands. As she changed the nappy, she thought this might be the last time she would ever do this. And he was so small, so perfect in his softness. His tiny fingers, his tiny toes. All so precious to her. He was being sent into the unknown and she hoped against hope that the future would be kind to him. The greyness of the day reflected her gloom, but this was only today, the present. The future must surely be better for both of them. It had to be. She told herself she was doing the right thing. If she said that to herself enough times, it would be so. She went back to her seat.

The man asked her the child's name. She told him that he wasn't christened yet and so she was just calling him 'baby'. The man was tactful enough not to ask whether the father had any say in the matter. Thank goodness. Perhaps he thought there was no father. But every child has a father, though some are never seen, and this one was going to his. Let him take care of the little boy.

The train reached her station. This town had the railway, but to her it was still nowhere. The man helped her, holding her bags while she manoeuvred herself, the child and his carrycot onto the platform. She wished she'd had a stroller, but then that would have been needed for this one journey only and the little boy was asleep and calm, not knowing what lay ahead.

The station was quiet. She made her way to the exit and there, in the ticket office, she found another helpful man. There were no taxis waiting, which was hardly surprising, since she had been the only person to get off the train. But this helpful man called her a taxi. It arrived in five minutes and she didn't have to worry about their getting wet. It was still overcast, but the rain had stopped now. The driver was kindly too. That must be a record. Three in one day! She had to give him directions for the last part of her destination, though he knew the village well enough. He chatted to her, aimlessly but cheerfully, as they drove there. The weather hadn't been good here either, but the forecast for tomorrow was better. The economy was bad, but there were still opportunities for those who wanted to work. It was a pity the Council didn't maintain some of these roads better.

She explained that she wanted him to wait and take her back to the station. It was no problem at all. He would not charge her for waiting, if it was only going to be a few minutes. Maybe even less, she told him. She asked if he knew the times of the trains for her return journey. He wasn't sure, but he thought that they were every hour at the weekend. He seemed to remember that they came through the station around a quarter past the hour. He'd dropped people off there a few minutes before that time more than once. If she wasn't going to be long at her destination, she would probably be back at the station around 8 o'clock. So she might be able to catch a train around 8.15. Did she have a return ticket? Yes, she did.

He told her a joke. A second man telling her a joke within the space of a few minutes! The joke was about a man who arrived at the gates of Heaven with the best of credentials and was welcomed by St Peter, but decided on balance he would prefer to go to the 'other place', because it was warmer. It was a long joke and somewhere during its telling, with her thoughts concentrated on the baby, her mind wandered and so she missed the point. But it reminded her of a joke she knew and so she told this to the driver, haltingly and with none of his fluency. Her joke wasn't really funny, but it suited her mood and now she was pleased to be talking. Her joke was more of a fable really.

A virtuous woman arrived at the Gates of Heaven. St Peter welcomed her and said she should be eligible for admission, but first she had to pass a simple spelling test. Salvation was becoming increasingly hard to come by and virtue alone wasn't enough nowadays. She was eager to gain entry, because she knew that many of those dear to her on earth would be there. She believed Heaven would be a perfected version of the world below, populated by those she had loved and purged of those she had hated. St Peter said the spelling test involved just one word. She had to spell the word 'love'. She replied immediately, 'L-O-V-E'. He embraced her and told her to enter. She was very welcome!

The woman flourished in Heaven, chosen among the chosen. She became a particular favourite of St Peter. So much so that after a few months, he asked her to be his assistant-in-chief. Even tireless St Peter needs help sometimes. So whenever he took a break and went higher into Heaven to enjoy blissful times among the blessed, playing the newest catchy hymns on his guitar and eating the latest spicy creations of the celestial chefs, the woman would deputise for him on the Gates.

One day a man arrived at the Gates. She recognised him immediately and she told him that they had known one another on earth. The man looked at her closely and replied, nonchalantly, that he was very sorry, but he did not recollect her. Still, he continued, this was not really surprising because one knows so many people in a life-time. She said nothing, but thought to herself that she had only known two men in her life-time: *her husband and this man. He said that although he didn't remember her, he was pleased to be coming to Heaven and it would be wonderful to get to know her. Might he come in? She told him about the spelling test. Just one word. The man said that should be easy then; he was a good speller. He asked her what the word was. She told him: 'floccinaucinihilipipification'. He frowned and asked what it meant. She explained that it meant considering something to be worthless. He began to spell it: 'f-l-o-x-e-n ...'. She raised her right index finger to her mouth to silence him. Then she said the word again and moved the finger to direct him downwards.*

The taxi driver smiled politely, but he was not really amused. She knew she had not told the joke well and perhaps it was not one that would appeal to many men anyway. However, she was pleased she had told it, not as she had heard it herself, but with variations to suit her mood. They were silent for a while and then they arrived at her destination. He was happy to wait, but did she have any idea exactly how long she might be? She was not sure, as she had said, but it would not be long. Probably just a minute or two.

She had planned to leave the child on the doorstep, but now she was there she knew she could not. His tiny fingers, his tiny toes. The weather was mild and the rain had stopped, but she knew she had to deliver the boy in person. She rang the bell. She shuddered. She was about to see that man again, for one last time. But she had been stupid. She had not been thinking straight and a woman came to the door. So it was all very different from what she had imagined. For a moment she was silent, unable to speak, and the woman was silent too. She had to say something. She mumbled the words, 'He belongs here, this baby. This is his home.' She kissed the child on its tiny forehead, thrust the carrycot into the unspeaking woman's arms and ran to the taxi. The driver had seen everything and now he too was mute. He said nothing all the way back to the station and then, after telling her the fare, asked if she was alright. He called her 'Miss'. She had taken her wedding ring off, but now her mission was complete, she could put it back on, once she was on the train. She could go back to her life. It was over.

And at the end of all this, Stuart had written: *It may not have happened like this. It may not have happened at all, but this is how I imagine it to have happened. This is my version. My story of how it may have occurred.*

I put the folder down, wondering where the other two were. There was no obvious sign of them. I went looking around the room, also wondering if I might find any evidence of Van Morrison, but there was no trace of him either. Just as I was thinking of going back upstairs, Isabel appeared.

'How is he now?'

'He's OK, I think. A nasty scare.'

I didn't know how to brooch the subject of the powder, but I had to say something. 'In his glass …'.

'I know, I know. Some powder. We need to watch him.'

'You mean, he may have been trying to …'.

'No, no, never. Not Uncle Wilf. It's either some kind of terrible mix-up or…'.

'Somebody else?'

'Well, yes. It's OK now, though. For the moment, anyway. There's just you and me here, but later I think we're going to have to keep watch.'

'Keep watch. You mean like take turns on sentry duty?'

'Well, yes. Something like that. Make sure nobody interferes with his drink, to start with.'

'That could be a full-time job!'

'Sam, don't joke. I think he's in real danger.'

'OK, so what do we do?'

'Well, if other people are around, one of us has to be near him all the time and we have to make sure no one gets near anything he drinks.'

'Or eats?'

'Yes, drinks or eats.'

'And at night?'

'One of us has to be awake, keeping watch.'

'Isabel, this is crazy. Seriously, if one of us is on duty with him and someone needs to watch his food and drink, this could be a full-time job for both of us, and I am being serious now.'

She was evasive. 'I know, I know. But just for a day or two. We'll do something.'

'What?'

'I don't know, I don't know. Take him somewhere else, just as soon as we're sure he's OK.'

'*Where*?'

'I don't know. Anywhere that's safe. Maybe to Lily and Spike. He'd be safe there, but first we have to be sure he's over this. He drank some of that powder, whatever it is. Maybe we can take the glass somewhere and get it analysed. Oh no, we can't. I washed it out.'

'Maybe we should call the police?'

'No, that's not necessary, and anyway I washed the glass out. I told you. We'd have nothing to show them. And they've been here before to investigate, and found no evidence. Now it's even less likely.'

'When Glen …'

'Yes, Glen.'

'So we just take turns guarding him?'

'Yes.'

'Tell me. Stuart mentioned three folders for me to read, but there's only one.'

'I know, I know. And there were three when I was writing to you, but then the others went missing. Since then.'

'Did you read them yourself?'

'Yes, more or less.'

'Tell me about them then. What you did read?'

'No, I don't think I can do that. You need to see them for yourself.'

'You know who took them, though, don't you?'

She turned her head away and walked to the far side of Stuart's room. She picked up a toy engine and started fiddling with it.

'Tell me, Isabel. If Wilf is in danger, you *have* to tell me.'

'Let's just go and check on him, Sam. We can make sure he's alright.'

'Even if we're not going to call the police, I think we should take him to A&E. Where's the nearest one?'

'No, we can't do that. No one must know.'

'Maybe we could get a doctor in to check on him. Maybe you could get Harry to come.'

'No, we can't do that either. It's impossible. Let's see how he is now.'

'So we can't call the police, we can't take him to A&E and we can't call a doctor?' She didn't answer.

As we walked back down the corridor, something prompted me to ask her if she'd had a job recently.

'No, I stay home, Sam. I used to do bits and pieces. I saved a bit and I don't spend much. I can get by without working and I don't claim benefits. I don't believe in it. I just prefer to be here most of the time. To be sure.'

'To be sure of *what*?'

'Oh, nothing in particular. Just to be sure things are safe … as safe as they can be.'

'You're staying home to look after Uncle Wilf, aren't you?'

'No, well not exactly, but yes, I suppose I am. I like to be here to do the best I can. To see that *everyone* is alright. Maybe if I'd been here, Glen's accident wouldn't have happened.'

'But it was just an accident.'

'Yes, yes. A nasty accident. But maybe if I'd been here all the time, I might have seen it coming and prevented it. You just can't know about things like that can you, but maybe it wouldn't have happened.' I didn't answer her.

We went up to Wilf's room, with Sherry who had been sleeping under the stairs beside us. She panted with the exertion that the climb put on her elderly heart, but once awake she was determined to be in the centre of events. Wilf already seemed fully recovered.

'Great man, can you ever forgive me for this indisposition? We should be completing our tour, but if it is not a terrible inconvenience, perhaps we could delay, procrastinate and generally postpone our explorations until tomorrow. I am beginning to fear that the quality of the rum being sold in our local emporia is on the decline.'

'Where do you buy your booze, Uncle Wilf? Or rather who buys it for you?'

'I buy it in an unmentionable place, my champion – unmentionable because it is a less-than-super supermarket that threatens the livelihoods of the proprietors of the shops I love and cherish. But needs perforce and costs must be considered and, sad to admit it, I can be a traitor to our beloved small shopkeepers.'

'So you buy your drink from a supermarket, Uncle?'

'I do, I do, my Hercules. I admit it. Guilty as charged and I alone am to blame. No one, no one else, not a living soul, ever buys it for me. I take total responsibility for affairs of the spirit and all things vinicultural.'

Isabel nodded. 'It's true. Whenever he knows one of us is going to a supermarket, he gets us to take him and he spends half an hour or so in the wine and spirits rows, while we do the rest of the shopping. Otherwise he likes to go shopping in Louth. There aren't any big supermarkets there, so the high street has flourished. It has small food outlets: butchers, bakers and a great cheese shop. And there are some speciality gift shops, too. Uncle Wilf prefers to shop there. He says that's the way shopping should be, but he can't resist the supermarket prices when it comes to his booze.'

Wilf hung his head in mock shame.

'Why don't you take a walk, Sam. I can look after Uncle Wilf for a while and you haven't yet seen all the changes to the garden at the back. You must see how it's come on. Oh, and Sam' – she touched my elbow and eased me into the passage, so Wilf wouldn't hear – 'I forgot to say, we can rely on Jules, too, you know. There will be three of us to look after Uncle Wilf. So it won't be quite as much of a strain as you must have thought.' I didn't know what to say, so I simply nodded. I'd better do as I was told.

Alf was in the bathroom washing his face. He had his own method of doing this. Instead of swashing a soapy flannel around his face, he held the flannel still and moved his face around it. He became self-conscious when he realised that I was watching and so I smiled at him.

'My mother says this isn't the usual way to wash a face. I know that, but I like to do it this way. I like my way better.'

'Then it's the best way for you. Mothers are wonderful and they usually know best, but sometimes a man has to branch out and do things his own way.' I was thinking of my 'mother' who had done her very best for me and yet had left me always wanting to do things my own way from a very early age.

'Yes!' said Alf, very affirmatively, and went back to his face-washing, moving his face around the flannel faster and faster.

The Pond

The Weavers' garden was large – around two acres – and it *had* changed. The extension had demarcated a line between the front drive and the garden itself. As I remembered it from my earlier visits, the garden had begun lackadaisically on the left-hand side of the house. Now it was firmly relegated to the rear and one had to detour around the extension to reach it. Its invisibility from the front of the Weavers lent it an added air of secrecy.

The lawn was still neatly cropped. The rockery appeared the same. The barbecue pit looked as though it hadn't been used for a long time, but the paved area that fronted it had obviously been swept recently. Several species of roses were in bloom. Had there been a rose garden before? Did the Whites have a gardener? If not, who looked after all of this? I guessed it might be Laura. And behind this part of the garden, there was still the uncultivated area, but now this seemed a contrived wilderness, of the kind that I knew had once been an important feature in certain types of classic landscape gardens. I reflected that Isabel with her sensitivity to the nuances of place could probably have given me a picturesque account of its evolution, but then maybe she wouldn't have been as alert to its transformations as a returning stranger like me. Gardens have always seemed to me curiously ambivalent places, midway between the enclosed spaces of houses and unmanaged wildernesses, both culture and nature. But the proportions vary and at The Weavers even the wilderness section of the garden now looked as though it was firmly domesticated. A controlled space. Little Alf swashing his face around his flannel came back into my mind and I thought how much I preferred his resistance to convention.

The garden was little changed, but something *was* very different. And then I realised what it was. The conifers had been allowed to grow unchecked and now they lined up like sentries, protecting an area at the back of the garden. Behind them there were apple trees and then the two willows (yes, there were two), overhanging a pond. I hadn't remembered the pond, though it must have always been there. The conifers screened it from view as one approached it from the house. Three stone steps led down to it and there were walls behind it and around its other two sides. So it was a separate sunken garden of its own. A sheltered, claustrophobic mini-underworld. Shaded by the trees and walls, it was an eerie isolated space that exuded dampness. It had been carefully enclosed, but it hadn't been as painstakingly maintained as the other sections of the garden. As I walked down the three steps, I saw some large seagulls that had journeyed inland at an unusual time of year and were fluttering above the pond, squawking noisily. And all I could think of was that this was where Glen had drowned. A little boy who had wandered into this spectral netherworld and met his death, away from the watchful eyes of his mother and the other adults in his family. But the water in the pond didn't seem very deep. It looked too shallow for anyone to drown in.

I decided to test it to find out just how deep it was. I didn't want to get my clothes soaked and, since no one could see me, I stripped off and waded in. The water was cool for the time of year, since the secluded pond wasn't getting much sun. I had to walk in about five yards before the water came up to my knees. It was only in the middle that it was deep enough for even a small boy to drown, unless perhaps he had been held down by force or rendered unconscious. Could Glen have come to grief while playing in the very centre? Might the water have been deeper when he had had his 'accident'? There was mud around the edge of the pond which suggested that it might sometimes be wider and deeper. I turned around to go back to the edge and get dressed and there facing me was Alice. She was smiling at my nakedness. I grabbed my clothes hastily, covering myself while still wet.

'Don't worry. I'm not seeing anything I haven't seen before. But what on earth were you doing in the water? No one ever goes swimming in that muck.'

I mumbled, 'Well I didn't know what it was like until I got in there. Local knowledge is a wonderful thing and I don't have too much of it, do I?'

'No, you don't, and you know you weren't exactly invisible here. The pond can be seen above the trees from the upstairs windows in the house. But then who would be that interested?' So Alice could tease. 'Izzy said you went to see Lily and Spike. How were they?'

'Oh they were fine, thanks. Great to see them after all this time, and Spike is as crazy as ever.'

She smiled weakly, unimpressed by craziness it seemed.

'Thanks for letting me use your laptop yesterday. That's how I came to go off. I had an e-mail from Lily.'

She nodded slowly. She didn't need to be told. It seemed that if Isabel knew something, then Alice knew it too. But then Isabel had said that we'd have an ally when Jules got home. She hadn't mentioned Alice.

'Where's Alf now?'

'Oh don't worry. He's with Izzy.'

'And Uncle Wilf?'

'Yes, they're together. The three of them.'

'Did she tell you what happened with Uncle Wilf?'

'No.' So perhaps they didn't share everything. 'What happened?'

'Well, he was taken very ill. Like he couldn't come round from a sleep, but it was scary. It seemed very serious for a moment.'

'He has sleep apnoea.'

'Yes, Isabel said. Maybe it was that.' And Alice had nothing more to say on the subject. By now I was fully dressed, though I'd not been able to dry myself properly. Not that that would have been easy, even if I'd still been alone.

'We can stay here a while if you like.'

'Do you come here often?'

She nodded. 'It's OK to mention Glen, you know. He's not a taboo subject. I come here to remember him. It helps a bit.'

'How did it happen?'

'No one quite knows. It was a Sunday morning and he came down here on his own.'

'Was everyone in the house?'

'Yes, pretty much. And the worse thing is that I was the only one who wasn't up. I'd had a late night and I was still in bed.'

'Who found him?'

'Me. It was terrible. As soon as I got up, I realised he wasn't there, with the others, and I came looking. And I found him here on the edge of the water. I tried everything. Mouth to mouth. Everything. But it was too late. I felt so guilty. I am guilty. I'll always be guilty. I should have been up and with him.'

'He was on the edge of the water?'

'Yes, just over there.' She pointed to a spot just below one of the willows. It seemed an unlikely place to drown.

'Was the water deeper then?'

'I don't know. Maybe. Yes, I think it was. We'd had a lot of rain. Do you remember the floods they had in Hull?'

'Well, not really. I heard something about them, but I wasn't living in England at that time. Did no one else notice Glen missing?'

'No. He'd had breakfast with them. Coco Pops, his favourite, and after that no one saw him. They don't know what happened. Stuart felt particularly bad about it.'

'More than the others?'

'Well, of course they felt dreadful too. We all did. But Stuart took it worst of all. As though he was somehow responsible, because he wasn't here. He wasn't around at that moment. He'd gone out to buy a newspaper.'

'So how long was Glen missing before anyone noticed?'

'Well, we couldn't be sure. He was there at breakfast and I came down about an hour after that, we think. Normally Uncle Wilf would have been keeping an eye on him, but he'd gone off to his cabinet with Sherry who might have given the alert, and no one was particularly thinking about Glen until I got up.'

'And you missed him right away?'

'Yes, of course.' The withering look she gave me said that she might have been delinquent some Saturday nights, but she *was* a devoted mother. 'And I went looking all through the house for him and then in the garden. Sherry came with me then and she ran to the back quickly, whimpering. So I knew he must have gone to the pond. He liked to make paper boats and try to sail them there.'

'Were there any paper boats that morning?'

'No, no sign of any at all. Sherry ran straight to him, crying. He was there, here, lifeless. I did everything I could. We all did. The paramedics came quickly, but it was no good. He was gone. I'll never forgive myself.'

'And Stuart left shortly afterwards?'

'Yes, first of all he was adamant that we should all stick together, but then he changed and he left.'

'Suddenly? Without any explanation?'

'Well, we heard him arguing with Uncle Wilf in his cabinet, but I don't have much idea of what it was about.'

'I can't imagine Wilf arguing with anyone.'

'Yes, well he wasn't exactly arguing. Stuart's voice was louder and he seemed angry. He was doing most of the talking, but I felt Uncle Wilf was the other side of an argument.'

'Did you hear what Stuart was saying?'

'Not really, but at one point I thought I heard, "You have to tell. This can't go on."'

'So Stuart knew something was hidden, something was wrong, but he wouldn't tell anyone himself?'

Alice shrugged. 'Who knows? And maybe I got it wrong. Maybe Uncle Wilf was saying that. He's said things like that when he's doing his ventriloquist act.'

'But you said you couldn't hear what he was saying?'

'No, I didn't say that. Just that Stuart was louder.' And she changed the subject. 'I didn't take you for the skinny-dipping type.'

'I didn't take myself for that either. I don't know what came over me. I just felt I had to test the water.'

'Would you like to test the water with me?' I was shocked. She was flirting and I hadn't expected it. Despite the talk of her promiscuity, I was still seeing her as the Alice of Tenniel's drawings. But perhaps she was just playing a game with me. Either way I was as shocked by the abruptness of her change of subject as by her change of tone. I smiled and looked away.

'Well, would you like to see my cabinet then?' and she batted her eyelashes. Remembering the combat knife I'd seen there, I was both curious and apprehensive, but I knew I wanted to see whatever she had to show me. We walked back.

Her room was different from the other cabinets I'd seen, because there were no curios on display. Everything remained under dustsheets except for the small Davenport on which her laptop was precariously lodged. She casually pulled up a dustsheet that was covering a large table. Beneath it there was a small arsenal of guns. Nothing state of the art as far as I could tell and, ignorant as I was of weaponry, nothing that I could identify. All I realised was that most of the guns were probably antiques and she confirmed this, when she told me that one was a Colt 45 and another a Winchester rifle. She named them all with the care of an expert taking pride in the minutiae of her subject, but the mythic Western guns were the only ones that meant anything to me and the only ones whose names left an imprint on my mind. I asked her how she'd acquired them. She explained that she used to go to sales, but more recently she'd been bidding on the Internet. One was a 'steal'. It was worth £4,000 and she'd bought it for £700. I was tempted to ask her whether she'd considered giving up the day job, but refrained. Weren't there regulations governing the sale of firearms? 'Yes,' she said and smiled equivocally.

She pulled off another dustsheet, this time revealing explosives and what I took to be bomb-making equipment: fuses, wires, switches, detonators. In another environment I would have thought I'd come across a terrorist. A third table contained arrows and a fearsome looking longbow. 'Just a replica', she said, 'but interesting to think something like this could have been used at Agincourt.' There were more modern bows as well.

'Do you practise archery?' I was wondering whether her interest was purely academic.

'Me? Oh no, I couldn't even hit a target at twenty feet. Not with an arrow, a bullet or a pea-shooter. These are just a collection. Everyone else in the house has a cabinet and so I thought I should have one too. So I decided on weapons. You never know.'

'You never know what?'

'I mean you never know when you might need them. For self-defence.'

'Where do you think an attack might come from?'

'Oh, anywhere. You just never know.'

And then I noticed a cabinet on the wall, without any cover over it. A cabinet within the cabinet. A medicine cabinet, full of small jars. I nodded towards it.

'They look interesting.'

'Yes, I'm quite proud of them. They're my poisons. Cyanide to kill people off fairly quickly. Arsenic for a slower painful death. So they say. The human mind can be very ingenious.'

'And *they're* all for self-defence?'

'Well, not exactly, I suppose. More like an insurance policy, for a pre-emptive strike, just in case it's ever necessary. There are thousands of ways to kill off enemies, aren't there?'

'If you say so.' Her flirtatious behaviour of a few minutes before was still in my mind, but now I was thinking that this was one member of the White family I wanted to keep at a distance.

She must have been reading my thoughts. 'Oh don't worry, I don't plan to use any of this stuff, ever. All it's really here for is to say "Keep off! Don't mess with me or mine!" So people will know. Just in case anyone is thinking of an attack.'

'But you've got it all covered up. Who would know you've got it?'

'Oh, I show it to selected weapons inspectors, like you. Then word gets around, even if no one is quite sure how much is real and how much is rumour. It's a deterrent, you see.' She sounded like a one-woman rogue state that might, or might not, be developing a nuclear capability, and was instilling fear just by raising the prospect. 'You'd be surprised how many people know. Ask them down at the Hope Inn. They don't know *exactly* what I've got, but they know enough not to meddle with me.' She nodded slowly, lending emphasis to her words.

'Is that where the attack is likely to come from then?'

'No, of course not. I just mean that people have an idea. Just enough for it to be a deterrent.'

Was she paranoid? I didn't think so. No more than Isabel anyway. 'So where exactly is the threat likely to come from?' And these words were a conversation-stopper. She didn't just not answer me, she turned on her heels and walked out of the room. Looking at the laptop on her Davenport reminded me of Lilith and I switched on my mobile. Sure enough, there was a message from her: 'R U OK?' I kept it simple and texted back, 'So far so good.' I could always phone her later.

I decided to check my e-mails on the laptop. My uncle was threatening to sue the hospital over his 'botched' colonoscopy. My ex-wife thought it was 'a bit rich' that I hadn't even answered her about the money that she knew I knew I owed her and my ex-colleague had discovered that the Peloponnese wasn't so idyllic after all, but had 'high hopes of Thessalonica'. There was a pile of advertising and spam in my inbox and buried in the middle of it, in danger of being deleted unread, was a message from Stuart.

No subject
Date: 15 July, 6.35 GMT
From: S.White@cabinet.com
To: SamWhoo39@gmail.com

Hi Sam,

I hope you've seen my folders. Isabel can show you them. And you can trust Uncle Wilf. He can tell you what's happened. Hope to see you again someday soon.

Bye for now,

Stuart.

How did he know I was at The Weavers? Who had told him? Isabel? Uncle Wilf? And with a start, I realised I hadn't thought about Wilf for a couple of hours, despite seeing all the poison in Alice's medicine cabinet. I rushed upstairs.

Isabel was by his bedside. Alf was on her lap, swinging his legs with pent-up nervous energy. Sherry was by her feet and looked up at me with wide-eyed love as I entered. 'He's fine, Sam. Nothing to worry about.'

'First-rate, my hero. Never better.'

Isabel nodded. 'It was a misunderstanding.'

'A misunderstanding?'

And Wilf chipped in. 'I got mixed up with my glasses. But I'm sure you'll agree that a man is allowed a few wobbles when he gets to eighty-seven.' He was tapping his head. 'This,' and he brandished the suspect glass magnanimously, 'is a totally innocent receptacle, my knight in shining armour. Well, an almost innocent receptacle. Guilty only of not having seen alcohol for days. My wobbles were collywobbles and this fine glass was the vessel in which I mixed two splendid Alka-Seltzers. Sad to say, sometimes a man of a certain age has to resort to such drastic remedies once in a while, to settle his inner turbulence.'

Isabel nodded again. 'What we saw was the dregs of some Alka-Seltzers that hadn't fully dissolved.' I beckoned her to the doorway, so we could speak just out of earshot from Wilf.

'So this was all a false alarm?'

'It looks like it, but I still feel we should keep watch. I'm sure something is up.'

'But why, if all that happened is he took some Alka-Seltzers?'

'I know, I know, I know. But he's covering something up.'

'You know Stuart just sent me a message?'

'*Stuart* just sent you a message?'

'Yes.'

'Well, what did he say? Where is he?'

'I've no idea where he is and he didn't say much. Just that you would show me the folders and I could trust Uncle Wilf.'

'Well, that's a fat lot of good. That tells us nothing. The only strange thing is he knew that I'd asked you to come up here.'

'Yes, exactly. You didn't tell him?'

'No, nothing. A while back I kept trying to phone him and text him, but I didn't get through, and all my e-mails were bounced. What address did he write to you from?'

'A cabinet.com one like you.'

'Right, that's our own ISP. Mum set it up – with a friend, a computer buff in Mablethorpe, I think.'

'She has friends in I.T.'

'Mum? Yes, she has all kinds of friends. That's why she's out a lot. Visiting here, there and everywhere. Coffee mornings, Council meetings, the Women's Institute. She has lots of professional contacts and friends in just about every field. So she's very well looked after for anything she can't do herself. I mean *we're* very well looked after. Anything she can't do herself, she has someone who can do it for us.'

'And how about Bubbleby? Does she have friends here?'

'Yes, yes, of course. She's got friends everywhere. But I suppose she spends more time outside Bubbleby than she spends here. She's friendly with the vicar and his wife and she's on good terms with the people in the village store. I don't think she goes in The Hope very often now though.'

'Why not? Did she used to?'

'Yes, a bit, but I think she's too busy for that now and she never was much of a drinker. She used to see her friend Beth there, but Beth comes up here to see her now, once in a while.'

'Where is she today by the way?'

'No idea. But she'll be back in time to cook dinner. She always is, unless she phones. And Jules will be home soon. That's a relief.'

'Should one of us take a turn here now then?'

'Yes, I think we should. You first? I'll feed Sherry. Alf, come with me, dear. It's time to give Sherry her doggie dinner.'

Back in the room with Wilf, I wasn't exactly feeling relieved. Why all this need to protect him, if all that was wrong was that he'd taken a couple of Alka-Seltzers because of an upset stomach? Before I'd felt sure he wasn't involved in any kind of deception and just a few minutes before I'd seen Stuart saying he was to be trusted. Nevertheless the thought was occurring to me that perhaps he and Isabel had concocted the Alka-Seltzer story to conceal what had really happened. The sides of the glass had looked as though it had contained milk, and who would take Alka-Seltzers in milk? But perhaps I was wrong. Perhaps I'd simply 'seen' milk, because Wilf had referred to it as such. And now the glass was gone. Isabel had made sure there was no evidence to examine. Yet she still seemed worried about his safety.

Then I saw it. On a shelf on the far side of the room. A second red folder.

Wilf was dozing now and so I moved quickly across the room and grabbed the folder. I took it into my bedroom, eager to read it right away, but there, following me into the room was Jules, back from school. Looking nervy, but eager to talk.

'Long day?'

'It wasn't too bad, but it's good to be home. Isabel said Uncle Wilf had a bit of a turn.'

'Yes, it seemed so, but maybe it was a false alarm.'

He nodded, non-committally. 'So he's alright now?'

'It seems so. I hope so.' I was thinking maybe I should still be with Wilf. In my haste to read what was in the folder, I'd left him alone. 'I heard from your brother.'

'Stuart, or one of the others?' It was impossible to tell whether he was surprised or not.

'Yes, Stuart. I never really knew the others.'

'I miss them all, you know, especially Steve. What did Stuart have to say?'

'Nothing much. He just mentioned some folders he'd left for me to read.'

'Do you have them? Have you read them yet?'

'I've not really looked at them yet.'

He smiled, a shy quiet smile that might have been self-deprecatory in another context, but had a look of knowingness about it. 'It's OK, Sam. I understand. I'm a suspect too, from your point of view.'

'Perhaps, but what is it I have to be suspicious about?'

'Oh, I don't know. Nothing as far as I can see. Everything is OK, but my sisters have some funny ideas, you know. It can be a bit boring around here sometimes, but everything is fine. There's never any drama. Just the same old routine. I go to work, Alice goes to work and looks after Alf. Uncle Wilf talks. Sherry looks for food.'

'And Isabel?'

'Isabel, yes she's different, I suppose. Isabel … imagines. She imagines glamorous, faraway places, but she can't go to them and that's why she has to make things seem more exciting here than they really are. She imagines conspiracies. But life isn't like that. At least not here. It's just humdrum. Maybe it's different in big cities. You must know. You've been places. But here one day follows another and nothing really happens.'

'Glen's death must have been a dreadful shock, though. And your Dad …'

'My Dad died years ago.' And that, he implied, was that. He wasn't going to say anything about Glen or his father. 'Isabel has such a wonderful imagination, though. Who needs to travel when you've got an Isabel? Who needs to read fiction with someone like her around? I thought of asking her to talk to my kids at school about the wonders of the world, but I don't think the Head would approve. She's too much of a loose cannon. You mustn't take everything she says seriously, you know.'

I tried another tack. 'Was Stuart like that too? Did he write fiction?'

He was smarter than I'd realised. 'Do his folders seem like that then?'

'Well, yes, or at least one of them. Are they fiction?'

'So you have been reading them.' He raised his eyebrows. I've no idea if they're fiction. I haven't seen them myself. I know nothing about them, except what Isabel has told me, and she has decided that they are specially for you. She imagines all sorts of things, you know.'

'I've read one and I just found a second one in Uncle Wilf's room, and there's another one that's missing.'

'Ask Isabel then. Maybe she's drip feeding you with whatever's in them, fact or fiction.'

'Do you think Uncle Wilf might have taken it up there, the second one, to hide it from me?'

And now he was getting exasperated. 'Oh sure, and he has a headless ogre in his wardrobe to make sure no one gets near his underwear, so that they can't discover it's full of blood and gore. And the C.I.A. have had this place under surveillance ever since they found out about Alice's weapons' cache. And Sherry is bugged with a device planted by Apple to try to steal Microsoft's secrets, because I'm really their leading secret programmer. Honestly, Sam. There's no conspiracy. Nothing out of the ordinary happens here. This is Bubbleby. *Nothing* happens here. Never did. Never will. It's a cul de sac. Ask Alice, if you like. She's in cahoots with Isabel and knows everything she knows, but she'll tell you the same as me. Everything is ordinary.'

I'd come to Lincolnshire looking for ordinariness and not found it, but now I was with someone who believed in it and I'd become the sceptic. There was no further to go with Jules. *Our conversation* had turned into a cul de sac. He moved to leave the room. 'Don't forget we're going to do something soon. This weekend, at the latest. Agreed?'

'OK.'

Then he changed his mind. 'But you know, we can do something now. I can show you my cabinet if you're in the mood. If Wilf's going to be out of commission for a while, you may need another tour guide. My stuff is nothing special, but you can see it now if you like. I can show you Martin and Steve's first. They're pretty humdrum too.'

I was thinking I should be on guard duty in Wilf's room, but something told me I might find out more from Jules. 'That'd be good. Thanks.'

He took me into the extension, where the three brothers had rooms at the far end. There were musty odours in both Martin and Steve's cabinets: Martin's was airless; Steve's smelt positively mouldy. Rooms on which doors had been closed too long, like memories that hadn't been allowed to breathe. I said as much to Jules and he replied, 'Well, that's a poetic way of putting it, but I see what you mean. There are things we don't talk about too much, but nothing out of the ordinary. I do miss Steve you know.'

Martin's cabinet was home to a collection of maps and globes. It reeked of staleness, the yellowing leaves of books that hadn't been opened in a very long time, and although I was wondering if its contents might unlock some of the Whites' closed doors, I found myself wanting to view its contents as quickly as possible. One could tell from a single glance that an orderly mind had been at work. Closer inspection revealed a series of exhibits that offered an encyclopaedic history of cartography through the ages, arranged in a satisfyingly linear form. There were reproductions of ancient maps from all four corners of the globe, along with more recent 'originals' – atlases, navigational charts, books about cartography and various map-related objects, including a large coffee-table with an inlaid reproduction of a seventeenth-century Dutch *'Nova Totium Terrarum Orbis Geographica Hydrographica Tabula'* and a set of place maps and coasters that offered snapshots of the expansion of Georgian London. There were photos of Babylonian maps carved on stone tablets, representing the world as Mesopotamians knew it, a disc of land surrounded by sea; and there were reproductions of Pharaonic plans of funeral processions and sarcophagi. Later in the sequence there were framed prints of Ptolemaic maps; there were extracts from the marvellous medieval *Book of Roger*, and Islamic maps that led on to Mercator and his projection. And there were more modern maps: several from the Ordnance Survey, an early version of the London tube diagram looking for all the world like an electronic circuit, and an axonometric map of New York. There were maps that asserted European claims to the ownership of distant places and maps that corrected the biases of Eurocentric cartography. There were physical maps, climate maps, political maps, demographic maps and an apparently famous map that had unlocked the mystery of how cholera had spread in Victorian London. Maps of every shape, size and hue. And what struck me most about the narrative that Martin had put together was that few, if any, of the maps were innocent. They were all laden with agendas. There were early maps which *knew* that Babylon, Jerusalem or Rome was the centre of the world. There were nineteenth-century maps that had firmly instated the zero meridian in Western Europe, with London, Paris, Copenhagen and Cadiz and a number of other places among the favoured candidates for its location, and a particularly wonderful world projection that had the small Atlantic island of Ferro as the prime meridian. Beneath the legend on this map there were two sentences explaining this: Ferro had been chosen by Cardinal Richelieu, who had decided it should be point zero to comply with the Ptolemaic belief that the meridian should be located at the westernmost point of the known world.

There was an exquisitely framed triptych on the far wall of the room. The left-hand panel was devoted to a short account of 'The European Prehistory of the Antipodes' in Gothic script. The right-hand panel held a twentieth-century map. And between them there was a reproduction of an Aboriginal rock painting that mapped part of the territory of the Nyoongah people of Western Australia, a wonderful splash of colours inventing a geography that transcended 'logic', but who could prefer 'logic' in the face of this? The text in the left-hand section told of how in Ptolemy's day, there was a belief that anyone living below the equator might melt from the heat. In the medieval period, people had been burnt at the stake for asserting that a southern continent might exist; this had been seen as a heresy that flew in the face of Christian geographical beliefs. Then, when European navigators and explorers first travelled 'down under', they imagined Australia as Paradise. When it failed to match their preconceptions, they speedily reinvented it as Purgatory or Hell, because everything there was morally inverted. It was summer in January, winter in July. There were enormous birds that couldn't fly and hopping animals that sped across the ground with their young in pockets. Even the swans were black. And then, understandably, given that eighteenth-century prisons were 'hell', the British decided to export their surplus convict population to Botany Bay. The map in the right-hand panel of the triptych was a redemptive corrective. It relocated Australia dead centre in the top half of a 'revised' projection of the world, genially pointing out that *terra australis* was no longer *incognita* and was now being reinstated in its rightful place in the middle of the upper hemisphere.

Then there was a New Zealand map that reduced Australia to Lilliputian size by rendering it as a small island off the coast of the north and south islands of Aotearoa. So many maps, so many agendas. But again and again there was a claim to centrality. Jerusalem or Rome, London or Paris. President Sukarno had decreed that Jakarta should be the prime meridian long after the general consensus had fixed on Greenwich. Meanwhile, of course, Islam had always known that all prayers turn to Mecca. Everyone, it seemed, wanted their home, their religion or their seat of power as the centre. Yet, as I looked at all these maps, I realised that I didn't share this craving. I had no centre. I'd never felt settled anywhere and, confronted with this battery of evidence, I began to wonder if I was a mutant, a deviant unable to feel a seemingly universal human desire.

Martin clearly had a gift for narrative. I wondered what had prompted his devotion to maps. Had he shared Isabel's flair for imagining places and inventing geographies? Had he perhaps even inspired his younger sister? Or did his collection stem from an altogether different impulse, a desire to codify the world, to make it manageable? I asked Jules, whose answer was as prosaic as ever.

'I never really thought about that. He was always interested in maps, as long as I can remember, but no, he wasn't like Isabel. She's different. She likes to dream up places. When she was a little girl, she'd do drawings with Never Never

Land next to Switzerland. She didn't need to get things right like Martin. She has a different kind of temperament. She's always had her vivid imagination.'

I pointed to a three-tiered Christian map, in which the earth was sunk beneath the waters of the Great Flood, Noah's Ark rode the waves and at the top a benevolent God looked down on the animals and the single family he'd chosen to save from His deluge. Jules was unimpressed. 'That's not even a map at all!' So I tried again. 'Look at this one then! It's a medieval *Mappa Mundi*. It gets everything in.' I hoped its conflation of geography and theology might convince him. A Last Judgement divided the damned and the saved above the known world around the Mediterranean, and beyond this in the outer reaches of the map, in territory as yet unidentified as Africa or Asia, lay fiery beasts, two-headed peoples stranger than any of Desmond's fairgrounds freaks, and half-human species with tails, fins, wings. I told Jules that to the medieval cartographers who had drawn this map, Heaven and Hell were as real as Rome, Cordoba or Athens. I added, 'Humanity has always imagined worlds into being. Isabel is in good company. These maps are just as valid.'

He wasn't impressed. 'Well, the way I see it is this: if you're making a map you want it to be accurate. If my sat nav started imagining, it would be no use at all, would it?' He was almost sneering. 'I'd bin it right away.' There was no arguing with his logic, but I was thinking less about him and more about the contrast between Isabel's imaginative flights and Martin's apparent desire to encapsulate and manage the whole world in his cabinet. Martin seemed to have had the true collector's instinct. Jules went on, 'Maybe Isabel's view is OK from an artistic point of view, but there aren't many people around here who see things that way, you know. People have their feet on the ground in these parts.' I'd come to Lincolnshire half-expecting this kind of common sense, but nothing I'd seen so far had supported his view that Bubbleby was 'ordinary'. Jules was different from the others.

'So do you think this is the back of beyond here? Off the map?'

'Course not. We're just like everyone else. No dragons or hobgoblins here. We've got our own spot on the map, though you need a detailed one to get us in, I suppose. Nothing grand, but we have our place. And with digital mapping we may not be so tucked away as we used to be. I mean anyone can find us now, if they're interested.'

'What's in your own cabinet, Jules?'

'Oh, it's nothing special. I'll show you in a minute. Let's look at Steve's collection first.' We went into the next room.

I was in for another surprise. After hearing Steve was gay, I'd not expected to see a collection of erotica, celebrating naked *female* bodies. Most of his pieces were tasteful, but some verged on pornography. I asked Jules about Steve's response to women and he said drily, 'Well, nobody worries about that too much when someone like Botticelli is involved, do they? They say he was gay, but it seems as though he had a thing going with his model for *The Birth of Venus*. Steve is complex. I don't think he ever had that kind of relationship with women, but who knows? As you can see, he had an eye for collecting women. But lots of people collect these kinds of paintings, don't they? Nothing unusual. It's been in vogue for centuries.' And I suppose he was right. We were in more conventional collector's territory: an art archive devoted to the female nude.

And so we went on to Jules's room and, after what he'd said about ordinariness, I was expecting that his cabinet would be an oasis of normality amid the White family curiosities. It took me a minute or two to make out what was in the room. It had dark blinds that were pulled and he made no move to open them. He switched on a light as we entered, but then turned it down with a dimmer switch, so that it was hard to see anything at all. 'Careful. Don't trip over Sherry.' I hadn't seen her follow us into the room.

I peered into the near-darkness and gradually my eyes managed to discern what the room contained. Jules's collection was the embodiment of everything that Spike had jokingly suggested might be at The Weavers. I was among more waxworks: life-size models of vampires, ghosts and succubi. There was a replica of the cinema's Frankenstein, the monster who had usurped his inventor's name in virtually every celluloid version of the story; and, half-hidden behind him, a truly terrifying Dracula, leering over a sleeping maiden, blood dripping from his lips. A minute after we entered a screen started playing a film. I knew it. It took me a few seconds, but then I recognized it as Werner Herzog's *Nosferatu*, the creepiest movie about the Transylvanian count that I'd ever seen. 'It switches on when someone comes in the door,' Jules explained, 'We can watch it all if you like. It's not that long a film.'

'That sounds great, but maybe another time.' Satanism and blasphemy were particularly to the fore. There were film posters of *Rosemary's Baby*, *The Exorcist* and *The Devils*. I wondered for a second if this display might be parody. As such it might have been ordinary, funny even, but as my eyes grew accustomed to the dark and I could see Jules' face more clearly, I realised there was no hint of humour there. He took his collection very seriously. He stopped the movie, flicked another switch and a voice intoned, 'There's a man who walks the streets of London late at night / The Ripper, Jack The Ripper.' Surely this had to be over-the-top camp, but Jules gave no indication that he saw anything amusing. I tried to probe him, while remaining tactful.

'You take your collection pretty seriously?'

'*Deadly* serious.' The emphasis he put on 'deadly', accompanied with a snarling lip, had effected a transformation in him. Was he imagining himself as a vampire, a werewolf or a zombie? Isabel had said he was an ally, but I was beginning to have my doubts.

'Uncle Wilf was planning to show me the collections. Perhaps it would be good to let him take me through what's left just as soon as he's up to it. I wouldn't like to upset him.'

'Good idea, and there's just one cabinet you've not seen. So if he shows you that, you'll have seen the lot and one more shouldn't be too much of a strain for him.' It was only a while later that it occurred to me that there should have been two, Isabel's and Laura's, but then perhaps Jules hadn't listened carefully when I'd told him what I'd seen already.

I went upstairs with the second folder in my hand and Sherry following me loyally. Wilf was sound asleep again, but this time breathing normally. So I stood in the doorway of his room, keeping an eye on him, while reading the folder. The contents of Jules' cabinet had made me edgy. I was prepared to be shocked by the folder, but I wasn't.

Stuart had written:

This is how I imagine the story continued.

She was in a state of shock after the woman handed the child to her. She couldn't invent a story that might make meaning out of it. There was just the isolated moment, minutes ago but already distant in time, when the woman had passed the baby to her. She had taken him inside, where the older man, so hard to surprise, looked astonished, but wisely said nothing. One of her own children was newly born, like this boy, and for an instant the new arrival had seemed possible to her, because she could make a connection between the two children and she had almost everything that this baby might need. Almost, but not quite. She was breast feeding her child and she knew she was unable to suckle a second child. How did women manage who had twins? But that didn't matter. She hadn't had twins. This child wasn't hers. He was an invader. The older man, who usually spoke so many words, stayed silent. He loved children, but he was mute. Darkness was entering her world. Her soul was in danger of being conscripted to despair. She understood nothing; she had no narrative to explain why this child was in her living room, in her arms. But the woman at the door had said that he belonged in her house and that woman's troubled countenance had carried the look of truth.

And the child. So small, like her own, but darker-skinned than her new son. They could never have been twins, although they had been born at the same time. In the same month, perhaps in the same week, possibly even on the same day. Her own son was asleep upstairs. She must go to him. She must make sure his rest was untroubled and perfect. He must remain unaware of this second child. His place must not be usurped. Yes, now she knew. That was why the dark woman at the door had brought him here. So that he could take her son's place. That was the reason, but the usurper would not be allowed to take a scrap of what belonged to her new son. Not one morsel. And the lives of her other children must not be disturbed. She would go upstairs to her own son. She looked towards the older man and, as so often, he was reading her mind. He was not a blood relative, but he understood her better than anyone. Better than her own parents had. Better than her own small children. Better than her husband. The husband who was not here, but would return. She looked towards the door and the older man nodded. He understood. She should go to her own baby. He took the usurper from her, cradled him in his arms, trying to reassure her that there was no threat to her life, her home, her children. He placed the usurper back in his carrycot and put that on an armchair. Then she was gone from the room. Upstairs her new son was sleeping soundly, not needing to be fed at that moment. She went along the corridor to the bedroom where her other two sons were sleeping. Older, but still very small. They were at peace too. The arrival of the usurper had done nothing to upset the balance of her family. It must not, it never would, it never could. She would make sure of that. Her mind was numb, but she knew one thing. She would do whatever was necessary.

Downstairs the older man looked at the child in his arms, thinking that in their first weeks of life all children are the same, amoeba waiting to take shape, but all blessed with the unfathomable marvel of new life. The child deserved an equal chance. No more, no less. Such a small mite. Unable to fend for himself and so he had to be taken care of. He had to think quickly, before the woman came down, before her husband came home, though that might be some time. The boy had been asleep, but now he opened his eyes and stared at him. He smiled, but then, as if sensing that he had been abandoned and was unwanted, he began to cry. The older man began a lullaby he had sung to the other children: 'Hush little baby, don't you cry.' He gently rocked the child until it was calm again and then he placed it back in the carrycot. He did not know who could give this baby care and love, but he would take it where this could be so. All his mother's trials, now over. And for him, so much to think of, so unexpectedly. To have to determine a human being's life in minutes. A human being starting out on life's travels, but as yet, so unformed and embryonic, he could do nothing but cry to attract attention. She would be down soon. He knew the child could never be safe in this house. Not today, not any day. There was danger now and there would be more, when the husband returned. Yesterday and yesterday and yesterday. If only the clock could be turned back. And in that moment he put on the mask that he would wear for the rest of his life. He became an alchemist of oratory. He had always been a talker, but in that instant he assumed the extravagantly garrulous persona that would be with him for the rest of his life, insulating his inner self, so as to defend those dear to him from harm.

She would be down soon and he had to find words to deflect attention from the infant in the cot. She came and he spoke of the way the rains had raised the level of the water table, the micro-climate in which they lived, the danger of rats coming into the house if their habitats were changing. He spoke of a lunar eclipse. He told sad tales of the death of crows. He told her that the Bard and not the Bible had a saying for every occasion. And he spoke of pity having the power of a naked new-born babe, and, though her mind was far away, she understood what his verbosity was attempting. She was an animal in another country, but she listened silently to his cascade of words, as he told her that he would take the child where it would be safe from harm. He should go quickly, before her husband came home. She was crouching now, on her haunches in the corner of the room and she began to whimper. He had one eye for her and one for the infant. He knew it would be dangerous for her to be near the child alone. Risky for both of them. He spoke to her gently, explaining that he was taking the child, so she need not worry. Afterwards, this would seem like a moment out of time. She would not forget it quickly, but forget it she should. He could not be sure how long he would be gone, but he would return as soon as possible. She must look after the other children. She must protect them, and protect herself. He stroked her hair. He kissed her forehead. He gave her his hand and she raised herself from the corner, no longer a cowering animal, but still silent and remote from the human world. Would her husband be home soon? He did not know, but she should not worry. Her own baby was safe and so were all her other children. Those unborn as well as those born. There was nothing to worry about. Nothing at all. No, she did not have twins. And yes, it was very unlikely that she would ever have twins. He was sure that all her children would be singular.

He left, carrying the cot. He had seen the piece of pink paper by the baby's feet. Now he read it. There was a name and there was a place. And underneath that were the three simple words: 'Returned to sender'. The woman who had brought him must have been as distraught as the woman in the house, but she was gone and he could do nothing to help her. He had not even seen her, but there was the name. Perhaps he would find her some day in the future, but there was no time to think of her now. This was more urgent. He had to protect those close to him and he had to save the child. He closed the door behind him soundlessly, quietly placed the child on the back seat of the car and turned the key in the ignition. Now, gods, stand up for bastards!

And at the end Stuart had written: *I can't be sure, but it must have happened something like this. The older man would tell me about it many years afterwards, but with no details. Just the bare fact of the coming and the going of the child on that day. He said nothing about what happened afterwards, but I learnt more later. When the nightmare began for all of us, but for her I think it started on that day.*

Standing there in the doorway, reading Stuart's words, I was immersed in his imagined past and I hadn't realised Wilf had woken up and was staring at me intently. For once he was silent and for an instant his expression seemed faintly menacing. In that moment I felt sure he had removed the folder, so that I wouldn't see it and now he knew I'd read it. Then he spoke and he was his usual self again.

'Samuel, Samuel, how I regret this cursed indisposition that has laid me low like this. We should be travelling in the realms of gold, investigating cabinets together, but alas and alack, woe is me, I fear a whole day's delay has been thrust upon us. My sins have found me out, though rest assured, I am a man more sinned against than sinning. Tippling is a grave misdemeanour, though not the worst I'll have committed before I shuffle off this mortal coil. But to cut to the chase and get to the nub and hug the hub and rub the rub of things, I think it will be tomorrow and tomorrow and tomorrow before we can continue our explorations of the cabinets. Can you ever forgive me for this outbreak of neurasthenia, my defender of the faith?'

'It's OK, Uncle, really. Don't worry.' I wasn't finding it easy to join in his game any longer. 'But I'll stay with you a while if that's alright. Perhaps we can make plans for what we'll do tomorrow.'

And I remained with him for an hour or so, while he talked about marmalade, whippets, toboggans, aluminium, bakeries, atolls and a host of other things. A world of contingent detail leading nowhere. Sherry came to inspect us once, stayed for five minutes and then, reassured we were alright and had no titbits to offer, went back downstairs where the pickings were likely to be better. At the end of that hour, Jules arrived saying Isabel had sent him up to 'have a chat with Uncle Wilf'. So my watch was over and there was no doubt that Isabel trusted Jules. I went downstairs, still wondering how Stuart knew I was at The Weavers. Isabel had summoned me, but unless she was a better actress than I thought, she hadn't been in touch with him.

I avoided the lounge and kitchen and went out the front door. Isabel's Ford, Laura's Mercedes, Jules's Range Rover and Alice's Vauxhall: all four cars were there, along with another one. An MG sports. The same one that I'd seen twice earlier in the day? I put on my mobile and was about to make a call, but then I decided it would be better to go round the back of the house. Then – was *I* becoming paranoid? – I imagined I could hear the sound of Van Morrison's 'I'm Alabamy Bound'. Another train song. It was issuing from one of the cabinet rooms at the side of the house. Was it Stuart's? Or was it playing itself in my head, because I'd seen the lyrics in Stuart's room?

I needed to be further away to make my call and so I walked towards the lower garden by the pond. It had been raining and two blackbirds were pecking at the grass in search of worms. There were bees zigzagging among the flowers, pollinating them. A magpie was at the bottom of the three steps by the pond. It flew off as I approached them. I dialled Lilith's number. Please pick up, Lilith, pick up, pick up, pick up. She did, as humourless as ever.

'Yes?'

'Lily, it's me. Do you think you might be able to help me?'

'Dunno, but yes, what is it?'

'Stuart sent me a message. He knows I'm here and it seems that Isabel didn't tell him. I'm wondering if you could find out who told him.'

'You mean hack into their computers?'

'Yes, could you do that?'

'I could, but do you know how Stuart found out? Did someone tell him?'

'I don't know, but I'm guessing so. I don't think anyone phoned him or texted him. No one seems to have been making secret calls.'

'Well, I think maybe you are, David?'

'Right, yes. I see what you mean. Secret calls are …. I wouldn't know.'

'Exactly.'

And now I was feeling like a babe in arms again, not just in the tech savvy world that Lilith inhabited, but also where common sense was involved.

'Do they all have laptops?'

'Well, not Uncle Wilf. I don't think he knows how to use a computer.'

'But all the rest of them?'

'I'm pretty sure. I don't know about Laura though. I haven't seen her with one. But Alice and Jules and Isabel have all laptops.'

'All wi-fi?'

'I think so. I'm not s-sure.'

'Find out – OK? And let me know.'

'And do any of them share?'

'Well, I know Isabel was using Alice's laptop. And I was too.'

'Well, that doesn't matter too much, you klutz. I'm not investigating you. You're my client.'

'That's nice, to be your client. Are you going to charge me ethical rates?'

'No, don't be silly. This needs sorting out. Find out what you can. Look around and see if you can see any desktops. See if you can get the number off their router and text it to me. And ask Isabel what ISPs they use and what e-mail accounts they have. She won't lie to you. She may not tell you much, but anything she does say will be reliable.'

'Oh, I've just remembered. They have their own ISP: cabinet.com. Stuart wrote to me from that and Isabel certainly uses it.'

'Yes, of course. I should have remembered. Isabel has mailed me from that.'

'And I've just remembered something else.'

'Yes?'

'Isabel just told me. Her mother set it up with a computer expert in Mablethorpe.'

'OK, that's good to know. And in that case, I think we can be fairly sure that Laura is computer literate.' Lilith's manner didn't allow sarcasm, but her words had a ring of irony to them all the same.

'That's true.'

'I'll see what I can do from here. I may come down and eavesdrop. It's easy to listen in to wireless, if people aren't properly set up and you know a little bit about what you're doing.'

'Eavesdrop?'

'Listen in nearer the router. Let's see. Bye for now, David.'

'Bye.'

Someone behind me coughed. It was Isabel. 'I heard what you said, Sam. Sorry. I didn't mean to be earwigging, but I was here and I couldn't help it. I didn't know you'd be calling anyone. I just wanted to get a break from the others and … to be close to you.'

'I was talking to Lilith.'

'Yes, I realised. You get on well with her, don't you?' She almost sounded jealous.

'I s-spose I do. I hadn't really thought about it, but I spose I do.'

'She's great. Wonderful with everybody, except herself.'

'I think she gives Spike a hard time.'

'Yes, she does. And he's great too. Two of the nicest people you could ever hope to meet.'

'So different, though. Chalk and cheese.'

'Yes, but they are perfect for one another really.'

'Spike thinks so, but Lily doesn't seem too sure.'

'You know, I think she knows it. In her heart. Her problems are with herself more than him.'

'She was telling me how she got her name.'

'Really? She never told me that.'

'Her parents named her after Adam's first wife?'

'Ohmigod! No?'

'Yes.'

'Imagine that. I'm surprised she didn't want to change it.'

'Why did you want me here, Isabel?'

'I just thought it would be nice to see you again. To have you near, and Stuart had sent you those folders.' She wasn't looking me in the eye.

'Are they really from Stuart?'

'Well that's pretty much what he knew. He heard some of that stuff from Uncle Wilf and so it's his too in a way, and you could say that Alice and I are involved, as we had a conflab about whether I should ask you to come. She wasn't as keen as me, though of course she likes you very very much too.'

'But I hardly knew her before.'

'Maybe not, but anyway we talked it over and I was the one who thought you should be here. I was pretty sure it was the right thing to do.'

'You didn't exactly sound sure when you were sending those messages. You seemed to be changing your mind a lot.'

'Yes, I suppose I was. Yep, I was, but well no, not exactly. It was more like I was having my mind changed for me. Alice thought you shouldn't come and Uncle Wilf kept changing *his* mind and that affected me. First, he said yes and then he said no. He thought it was the right thing to do, though.'

'So you and Alice discussed it with him?'

'Yep.'

'But not with your Mum or Jules, or Stuart?'

'I told you. I'm not in touch with Stuart. I don't know where he is.'

'OK, but not with your Mum or Jules?'

'No, not with them.'

'It seemed like you wanted me up here to play detective, or something like that? Was it to help you solve the mystery?'

'You mean Glen's death?'

'I guess so, but not just that. Your father's accident and whatever else it is that's been happening with the family. What led your brothers to leave in a hurry? Everything. Did you want me up here to help with all that?'

'Well, nope, not exactly.'

'Not exactly?'

'Well, it wasn't that I wanted you to play detective. More like I wanted you to be detected, I suppose.'

I'd realised that she'd ducked the question, when I asked if the folders were really from Stuart and now I felt my heart beating faster. '*Be* detected. What on earth does that mean? What the hell do I have to do with the things that have happened here? I was Stuart's friend, OK, and I like you, but I'm completely in the dark about all this other stuff. You're playing games with me.' At that moment a seagull defecated on my arm. It was opportune, because it broke my mood. I looked at the birdshit and smiled.

She smiled back and said very gently. 'I'm not playing games, Sam, honestly. You're here because I love you. And not just me. Alice loves you too and so does Uncle Wilf. And Stuart would tell you the same, if he was here. I know he would.'

And that was the last thing I remembered.

Hospital

My head was buzzing and Isabel was leaning over me. 'You're awake. Thank goodness.'

'Where am I? What happened?'

'You're in Lincoln County.'

'Lincoln County?'

'Lincoln County Hospital. Don't worry. You're going to be alright. It grazed the side of your head.'

'What did?'

'The bullet. Someone tried to shoot you, kill you. It was close, but it could have been much worse.' There was a dressing on my head.

'Don't worry, Sam. It's OK. You didn't even lose any blood. The ambulance came quickly. And the paramedics were great. They checked you over and got you here fast. They said you probably passed out from the shock and the doctors think so too. You've just got a low side parting in your hair.'

'But who? What happened?'

'Someone took a potshot at you, probably from the house. With one of Alice's rifles.'

'Alice?'

'No, not Alice. One of her rifles. Someone else. You have to forgive me. For getting you to come up here. I shouldn't have done it. I should have known it was too dangerous.'

'Is that why you were changing your mind so much? And Alice thought I shouldn't come.'

She nodded.

'I don't remember what happened.'

'We were by the pond, talking, and someone tried to shoot you. They found the bullet. The police took it away and the ballistics people have it now. They said it's probably from a rifle, an old rifle. So it looks like one of Alice's. They'll know more in a while.'

'The police?'

'Yes. The police came and now ballistics have the bullet'

'And what did they say?'

'What I told you. They need to be sure. That's all I know. I came with you in the ambulance. I phoned it first.'

'But you know the police found the bullet? And you told me what they think.'

'Yes, yes. Jules phoned and said that. You've been unconscious for a while.'

'It's more than a graze, isn't it?'

'No, it's not. You mustn't worry. You're going to be fine. For sure. They've done a scan and they say everything is OK. They're just keeping you here for observation. I'm not sure how long.'

'And I thought Uncle Wilf was the one who might have to come to A&E. Is he OK?'

'Yes, yes. He's fine. Jules is taking care of him. Round the clock. We can trust Jules. His Gothic stuff is just his fun. He is … normal. And he's sent Lily the info' she was asking you for about our router and the computers, especially Alice's laptop. We've all been using that.'

'You were eavesdropping?'

'Well, yep. We're all in this together. And there's no time for shilly-shallying around now, if someone's tried to kill you.'

'And do they know who …?'

'No, they're investigating.'

'Do you know?'

'Let's leave it to the police. The nurses said I could sit here till you came to, but they think you should rest now. I'll tell Lily and Spike you'll talk to them later.'

At that moment a nurse came in and told Isabel she should leave. She nodded and got up.

'Before you go, just one thing. Do you know what happened to the third folder?'

She hesitated. 'Yes, you can read it as soon as you're well enough. Uncle Wilf and I took it. We thought it was for the best. It seemed like the right thing to do, but maybe it wasn't. I mean, now it's pretty clear we were wrong. I was wrong.'

'So first you got me up here to read the folders and then you started taking them away?'

'Well, yes. Uncle Wilf thought it was better you didn't see them, after all, and he's usually right. But he'd had the opposite view a while before. By then you'd seen the first one anyway.'

'Isabel?'

'Yes?'

'Do you have a cabinet?'

'Course I do. Why did you ask?'

'Well, after Uncle Wilf showed me some, I saw Stuart's and Alice's and then three with Jules, and he said there was one more to see.'

'So?'

'Well, it seemed to me that there should be two more. Yours and your Mum's.'

'Gotcha. No, Mum doesn't have one. Everyone else does, but not Mum. She was never interested in having one.'

'That explains it then.' But I felt it explained everything and nothing.

'Her only real hobby is keeping bees, but they're outside. She doesn't have a cabinet.'

'Bees? I didn't see them. Only a few buzzing by the flowers.'

'You wouldn't see them, unless you went down the right-hand side of the house. The hive is there.'

The nurse was frowning and tilting her head towards the door. Southeast Asian. Probably a Filipina, but hard to be sure.

'I'll be back later, Sam. Don't worry. Oh, and when they let you go, I think it's best you go to Lily and Spike. But I'll be here during regular visiting hours this afternoon.'

'What time is it now then?'

'It's about 10.'

'A.m.?'

'Yes, morning. 'Fraid you missed out on last night.' She turned to the nurse, 'Will they keep him in overnight?'

'The doctor will be doing his rounds in a while.'

Isabel left and the nurse was very attentive. She *was* from the Philippines. I think maybe I was getting a bit delirious and I asked her what Manila was like. 'Wonderful,' she said. 'It's my home. My happy place. My happiest place on earth.' She was only in England for the money she earned, but she liked it 'OK'. Her husband was a steward on a North Sea ferry that made nightly crossings from Hull to Zeebrugge, and back from Zeebrugge to Hull. Sometimes he didn't get off the boat for three months at a time. But they were lucky. When he had leave, she took leave and so they could be together here then and sometimes they went back home together for vacations. Some of her friends were working as maids in Hong Kong and had husbands who had had to go to the Gulf to get jobs. I remembered an Iranian friend I'd had in the States who told me it was the *Persian* Gulf and so

I corrected the nurse. 'That sounds nicer,' she said. 'Persia sounds nice, but most of the men from the Philippines who go there work on the other side, in the Emirates.' She spoke about the hardships endured by couples who had to live their lives apart like this, but then when they got into middle age, they usually had enough money to go home, build a house and make sure their children got a good college education. I asked who looked after the children while they were working abroad. It varied, but it was usually the grandparents. She had a daughter and her mother was bringing her up. She and her husband were 'lucky, luckier than many people'. Then she became more insistent that it was time for me to rest.

So many, many people away from 'home', but she wasn't a nomad like me. She had a sure sense of where she belonged, and even her husband had regularity in his life, criss-crossing the sea, repeating the same journey again and again, with a home away from home on the boat. I went to sleep, contemplating how many different kinds of orphans there were in the world. I dreamt of winning a fortune in Vegas and squandering it on a trip to Bubbleby, though I'm not sure exactly what I managed to spend it on! It seemed I wanted to set up an orphanage in the village, but the money was already gone and I was frantically hoping to recoup it, playing slot machines in the Hope Inn. There were children everywhere in my dreams. Alf and Annie, who metamorphosed into Stuart and Isabel. Then they were being chased by a skeletal foundling, asking for more, though he didn't seem to be Oliver. I had a shuddering thought that he might be the drowned Glen, come back to haunt his killer and beg for another life, but then his identity also shifted and he was no longer a starving waif, but Annie's bear, Horncastle – plump and comforting.

I woke up to find a young British Asian doctor stooping over me, peering intently but saying little. This time I knew where I was and my watch said it was 4 p.m. I couldn't believe I'd slept so long.

'How do you feel?' He was restrained, but sounded genuinely concerned.

'Not too bad. Am I going to be OK?'

'Yes, yes. Nothing too much wrong. The scan was perfectly normal. How does your head feel?'

'Sore.'

'Any pains? Any headache?'

'No. It's just sore on the outside.'

'Yes, that will be there for a while, but I think we can discharge you. Blood pressure is normal. Everything seems good. So you can go home. As long as you have someone to look after you tonight. The nurse will see everything is OK.' He scribbled some notes rapidly, filled in a form, pulled back the curtain around my bed and moved on to his next patient. Beds must be in very short supply, if even a gunshot injury didn't merit more time.

The nurse's expression was impenetrable. I guessed that she was thinking I should have been kept in longer, but it was impossible to tell. She plumped up my pillows, brought me water and a pill and said she could arrange transport to take me home, if I needed it. I told her my friend would be back soon and it shouldn't be necessary. 'Your friends are waiting to see you now,' she said. 'They were here before the doctor came in, while you were sleeping, and they had a word with him. They're waiting outside now.'

Friends, plural! Not Isabel. It was Lilith and Spike. Spike was as irrepressible as ever.

'Well, look at you, you crazy son of a bitch. Fancy getting yourself shot! You should have been quicker on the draw. Always sit with your back to the wall, shoot first and ask questions afterwards. That's my philosophy. But anyway, how are you feeling, you silly bugger?'

'I think I'm OK. Not too sure really. A bit shook up, but I think I'm OK.'

Lilith was hovering behind him. Her Goth appearance was attracting attention from other patients in the ward, but she was studiously ignoring them. 'Isabel told us everything that happened. She wanted to stay and come back in with us to see you now, but I told her I thought it was better not to. You're coming home with us tonight.'

'The nurse said something about transport.'

'No need,' said Lilith. 'We didn't come up in our car – I was walking up to collect Annie from school when Isabel rang and Spike raced up here from work – but we can get a taxi. Just as long as you feel up to it. I don't think they should be letting you out this quickly, but I suppose they know what they're doing.'

And Spike, too, went into practical mode. 'They probably need the bed. Let's just make sure you're alright on your feet, though, you old fart.' He helped me out of bed and walked to the end of the ward and back with me. 'You seem fine to me, but how about the head?'

'I think it's OK. I feel a bit strange, but I think I'm OK.'

'Then let's get you home as soon as possible.' And as he said it, I couldn't think of anywhere in the world that would be more like home than Lilith and Spike's house. Maybe I was luckier than my nurse who was far from home, but she had a surer sense of belonging than I had ever known. She came back after a couple of minutes and gave me some pills and a form with some do's and don'ts. Discharged. Like the rifle that had shot me.

'Where are we here? At the top of the hill or the bottom of the hill?'

Spike explained, 'Well, we're at the top. Not exactly in the top, top-hole, fancy fancy, des. res. part of the top. We're a bit away from the cathedral quarter here. But still up, not down. And there's something else you need to know.' He came close to my ear to whisper. 'We're right opposite the prison and so I think we need to get you out of *this* jail pronto just in case they have second thoughts and try to clap you in that one. Once these authorities get their hands on you, you never know what'll happen next. I kid you not. It could be nearly as bad as being in the clink at The Weavers and even worse than being taken over by that lot up in the cathedral close and that's saying something. And by the way, I think they are going to have quite a few coppers snooping around The Weavers now. They're going to have a hard time passing this one off as an accident. So it'll be good for you to be with us.'

Lilith was saying very little, but I knew that she would tell me more than Spike before long.

'Annie? Where's Annie?' I turned to Lilith to ask.

'Don't worry, she's being well looked after. One of her friends' mothers picked her up from school. Spike will fetch her as soon as we get home. She'll be eager to see you again.'

'Does she know I've been … shot?'

'Well, not exactly. But we believe in always telling her the truth (I wondered if Spike altogether agreed with this, but now *he* was keeping quiet) and so we will. We'll tell her it wasn't serious.'

'No, not serious. Just that someone tried to kill me.'

Lilith gave me a withering smile. 'Yes, of course, but Annie doesn't need to know all the details, now we know you're OK. Let's get you home.'

'Close your eyes and duck down as we drive by the jail, matey. Remember what I said. You've just got out of two pokeys. Too soon to get banged up in another one. Up the Hammers!' He began singing 'I'm Forever Blowing Bubbles.'

An hour later we were 'home' and I was drinking camomile tea with Lilith, and Spike had gone to fetch Annie.

'Do you know who it was, Lily? Who tried to kill me?'

'No, I could hazard a guess, but what do *you* think? Do you have any idea?'

'Not Isabel for sure. She was with me, and the shot was fired from a rifle. Isabel said it was probably from the house.'

'It seems so.'

'And not Alice, because she's a lousy shot.'

'Who told you that?'

'Well, Alice.'

Lilith raised her eyebrows. I took her point, remembering what Uncle Wilf had said about toenails.

'And not Uncle Wilf, because he was poorly and someone had just tried to poison him.'

'Isabel thinks that too, but if so, the poison clearly didn't work and he certainly got over it pretty quickly. And she says he reckons he only had an Alka-Seltzer.'

'But Isabel thinks he's in danger.'

'Yes, and she's probably right. That's why she wanted us to look after you. So she could go back and look after him with Jules. He's not like the rest of her brothers. He's stayed home.'

'Why?'

'Dunno. I don't know him really. All I know is that Isabel trusts him.'

'So what about Alf?'

'Too small.'

'No!' It was my turn to be the smart one. 'I mean why isn't she worried about Alf's safety?'

'I dunno, but maybe that's because Alice hardly lets him out of her sight now, unless he's with her.'

'So that leaves Laura.'

'Yes, and she's always been the mother hen who looks after them all. She's a very unlikely killer.'

'Well, we've eliminated everybody.'

'There's one more person.'

'Who? Oh, I know, there was another car there. Someone from outside the family. I saw an MG there. I think I'd seen it earlier in the day, on the road back from here.'

'Yes, that's another possibility.'

'Do you know whose car it is?'

'Yes, Isabel says it belongs to a woman called Beth.'

'Beth! I met her in the pub. She's disabled.'

'Apparently, but fairly nimble and certainly capable of firing a rifle.'

'But what connection does she have with the Whites? And why on earth would she want to kill me? I'm a complete stranger to her. She's only just met me. She'd have no reason.'

'I know. I can't see why either. But if she was in the house, she must be a suspect, however unlikely. And if we're eliminating everyone else, then it becomes more likely it could be her.'

'Lily, I didn't come here to play detective. I never dreamt I'd be caught up in some kind of murder mystery.' As I said this, I remembered that Isabel has said I was being 'detected', not a detective.

'I know, and we can't be sure anyone has been murdered. All we know is that there have been at least two nasty accidents, in which people died, and someone seems to have tried to kill you yesterday.'

'At least two?'

'Yes, no one knows where Martin is. Anything could have happened to him. And we can't be certain Stuart is alive. Someone could be faking his ID.'

'Do you think so?'

'Could be. I don't think we should rule that possibility out. Anyway, let me tell you what I do know. I did some hacking, into Alice's laptop, which it seems everyone has been using.'

'That's right. What did you find out?'

'Well, someone wrote to Stuart's account from The Weavers just before you arrived, telling him that you'd be coming.'

'Yes? Who?'

'That's where it gets more difficult. It was sent from Alice's machine and an account set up in a name that sounds like it's hers: awhiteteapot@cabinet.com, but I don't think it was her.'

'Sounds more like the kind of name Uncle Wilf would dream up, but it couldn't be him, because he's not computer literate. So Alice is the most likely sender then?'

'I suppose so. But I'm not sure about that. It's all a bit bizarre. I think we are either dealing with a crazy person, or a very cunning one. Maybe both. And there's something else. I think that it could be the same person who wrote to you as Stuart.'

'I don't quite get you. Why would anyone do that? And in that case the person would be writing to themselves, wouldn't they?'

'Well, it could either be someone trying to lay a false trail to allay suspicion, or a person with a warped mind, or a complete lunatic. Maybe someone with a split identity. But I don't think it was Stuart. It all seems crazy.'

'Well, everyone in the White family seems crazy in one way or another, however much we love them.'

At that moment there was a clamour at the door, shuffling feet, the sound of running footsteps and Annie was with us, with Spike just behind.

'Uncle Sam, Uncle Sam. You came back!'

'Yes, Annie. I'm here. I've been dying to see you again.'

Lilith tried to check her enthusiasm. 'We have to be a bit careful with Uncle Sam, sweetheart. He nearly had a nasty accident.'

'Oh!' But she was only momentarily taken aback. 'He looks alright to me, Mum. He said he's dying, but he's not really dying, is he?'

I tapped the side of my head, where the hair had been singed. 'Just a scratch. Not dying, but dying to see *you*.'

'Let me see the scratch. Oh, that's not nice, but don't worry. I think we can fix that. Judy and me.'

'Who's Judy?' I was clearly ignorant again.

'Judy is my imaginary friend,' and she put her hand out to escort invisible Judy across the room. 'Judy, kiss Uncle Sam's head better.' I'm not sure whether Judy obliged, but Annie deposited a big kiss on the side of my head where the bullet had parted the hair and told me authoritatively, 'Now you will get better in two shakes of a horsey's tail.'

Lilith tried to correct her, 'The expression is in two shakes of a cow's tail, dear.'

But Annie was having none of this, 'I know *that*. Everybody knows *that*. But I mean two shakes of a horsey's tail. I think horses shake their tails faster than cows.' Even Lilith had to laugh at this logic.

'How is Horncastle, Annie?'

'He is very well, thank you, though he sometimes gets a bit lonely when I am at school.' She drawled the vowel sound in 'school' to convey a degree of disapproval: 'schoooooooool'.

'Are the summer holidays coming soon?'

She nodded, cautiously, not prepared to demonstrate too much dissatisfaction with school.

'She's a star student, you know,' said Spike. 'She's nearly top of the class in everything.'

'Except 'rithmetic,' added Annie ruefully. 'Judy and I hate 'rithmetic.'

'Well, we can't be good at everything.' But even as I said this, I was wanting Annie to excel in every area of life.

And her father wasn't going to let her put herself down in any way. 'She's good at arithmetic, you know. Just because she's not top of the class in it, she's not keen on it, but she does well with sums. What's 12 times 9?'

'108.' Quick as a flash.

'And who is the best speller in her class?'

Annie pointed at herself. And then nodding to her left, 'Judy is a good speller too.'

'As good as you?' I winked.

'Not quite. But nearly. She's pretty good. Uncle Sam? She can spell "carnivorous".'

'Wow. That's a hard word.'

'Yes, it is.'

'Can you spell it too?'

And she smiled. She'd caught me in her trap. 'Nope. I won't touch it. I'm a vegetarian. Uncle Sam?'

'Yes, dear.'

'Will you come to see the Imp with me?'

'Yes, of course.'

'But not today, sweetheart. Uncle Sam needs to rest today. Maybe tomorrow.'

'Don't be a spoilsport, Mummy. Uncle Sam would like to come *now*, I know. And I could show him Tom and Da Vinci.'

'Da Vinci? Is he like Tennyson?' I'd never heard of a Leonardo in this part of the world, but might there be some kind of commemorative plaque or statue?

Lilith explained. 'She loves Tom Hanks and they filmed bits of *The Da Vinci Code* here in the cathedral. We were up there, coming home from her school on one of the days when they were shooting, three or four years ago. You wouldn't believe how many vans they had there. She thinks she saw Tom Hanks, but I'm not sure. We certainly saw someone who looked a bit like him and she's never forgotten it. They couldn't get permission to film in Westminster Abbey and so Lincoln Cathedral stood in for it.'

Spike seized on this. 'Yeah, it just shows to go you. Just like I said. They are a really dodgy bunch up there at the cathedral. Down in Westminster they thought it was blasphemy, but this lot up here didn't have so many scruples. They keep screwing up you know. A while back, they sent their copy of the Magna Carta on a tour of Australia and there was an almighty ruckus when they lost money on it. A real can of worms.'

Lilith was more earnest. 'Well, there are two sides to every story. But Spike is right about it being a can of worms! Clerical politics! It was like something out of a Trollope novel.'

Annie was above controversy. 'We can see the Imp, Uncle Sam, and I will show you where I saw Tom.'

'I can't wait, sweetheart.'

'Then let's go now. Mummy, pleeeeeeease say we can go now. The cathedral is still open. I know it is, I know it is. It's open in the evenings in summer. Ask Judy. She'll tell you. And Uncle Sam says he can't wait.'

'I think Uncle Sam is being polite, dear.'

'No, he isn't, he isn't. He really wants to go now. You do, Uncle Sam, don't you?'

'I do, Annie, I do, I do, but we must do as your Mum and Dad say.'

'Oh, Dad will let us go. We just have to get Mum's permission.'

Spike came to her rescue. 'I have to go to see my mate, Dermot, and he lives up near the cathedral. So maybe I could take you up after we've had our tea.' And then to me and more seriously, 'If you should feel at all ill iffy, Sam, you can give me a bell and I'll be with you in two shakes ...'.

'Of a horsey's tail,' Annie chuckled.

To my surprise Lilith agreed. 'OK, then, but you must have your tea first and not stay out too long.' Looking at Spike, she was sterner, 'And that applies to you, too.'

'No worries, darling. I will bring them home safe and sound and we won't be too long.' And then to me, 'We can take the car, so you don't have to walk too much, matey. We don't use it much, unless we're going out of Lincoln. It's no real advantage in town and then there's the parking. It's the old banger parked over there.' He gestured out of the window to a gaudily coloured Volkswagen Beetle parked across the road. 'That's the one. The Volkswagen outside No. 39.'

'The yellow, white and red one.'

''Fraid so, matey. Eggs and ketchup. You can see why I don't say too much about it. A man doesn't always want to boast about his car, when he's got one like that. But it's unique and it goes.' He nodded feverishly, in a manner reminiscent of Kermit the Frog. 'It gets us from A to B – usually.'

'Well, sometimes anyway,' said Lilith sardonically. And then she dropped her voice and said to me, 'And while you're gone, I'll do some more of the homework you asked me to help with. Maybe I'll know a bit more by the time you get back.'

Annie was ecstatic. 'We're going, we're going in the car. Our car is really nice, Uncle Sam. We have the nicest car in the whole of Lincoln. Sometimes Daddy drives me to school in it and all my friends are very jealous. Their Mums and Dads only have black cars or red cars or silver cars. No one has a car with colours like ours.'

Imp

'Don't forget, Sam', said Spike as he dropped us off at the side of the cathedral. 'Just call me, if you feel at all funny. I'm not sure this is a good idea, you being out so soon. But what do I know? And make sure you get your money's worth. They charge an arm and a leg to go round this place. Still trying to make up for the Magna Carta fiasco if you ask me, and that was donkey's years ago. Remember, call me if you need me. The Spikemobile will get me here in a flash.'

Annie grabbed my hand and started tugging me towards the cathedral. 'What's the magnet carter, Uncle Sam?'

'Oh, I don't know exactly. Some old document about what kings should do and what they shouldn't do and what people could expect and what people shouldn't expect.'

'It sounds like hist'ry. Is it very very old?'

'I think so, sweetheart, but I don't know all that stuff like your Mum.'

Annie nodded. She understood. 'Yes, Mum knows everything. I bet the magnet carter isn't older than the Imp, though.'

'How old is the Imp? Do you know?'

'Oh, that's hist'ry too. Thousands and thousands of years old. Med-yeval, I think.'

'Well, I think the Magna Carta is about the same. That's med-yeval too.'

We'd come to Minster Yard and were near the main entrance. 'I'm cheap, you know, Uncle Sam. I don't have to pay much. They have children's prices.'

'Well, that's wonderful news, especially when you're going to be my tour guide.'

She put her finger in her mouth. 'Only for the Imp, though. I know where it is and I can tell you *all* about that. But I don't know as much as Mum about the rest of the things, you know.' Then she became very animated and added, 'After we come out, I can show you where I saw Tom.'

'That sounds like fun. Did you see him in the movie too? *The Da Vinci Code*?'

'Yes, Mum and Dad took me. Afterwards. Two times.'

'And did you like it?'

'Yes,' nodding vigorously. 'I didn't understand all of it, you know, but I liked Tom, and Audrey was nice too. There was just one thing I didn't like.'

'What was that?'

'No Imp,' and she laughed at me for not anticipating what she was going to say. 'But it wasn't really Lincoln, you know. It was some other place. Well, I mean it was Lincoln, because they filmed it here and Tom was here, but it was meant to be another place. Did you see it, the film?'

'Yes, I did.'

'Did you like it?' I realised that my answer was critical for how our relationship would develop over the next ten minutes or so.

'Well, so so, dear.' I didn't have the heart to tell her I'd thought it was godawful.

'I bet you liked Tom, though.' She smiled.

'Yes, I *loved* Tom.'

Her smile broadened. I was safe. 'I always like Tom, you know. He's my favourite. I liked him in *Forrest Grump* too. Did you see that?'

'Yes, *Forrest Grump* was great.'

My inquisition wasn't over yet, though. 'What about Audrey? Did you like her?'

'Yes, she was good too. Did you see her when she was here?'

'No, but I don't care. I like Tom best and I saw him. Do you think he'll come back, Uncle Sam?'

'Well, you never know. If he liked Lincoln, maybe he'll tell his people he wants to do another film here.'

'I think he should. It's ages since he was here, you know. I was small when he came and I think I would like to see him even more now.'

We'd come to the main entrance. We paid our admission fees and went inside. Annie grabbed my hand and started tugging me again. 'The Imp is this way. Right down the end.'

'Your Dad said we should try to see as much as possible.'

'Yes, but we have to see the Imp first.'

The Imp was at the far end behind the main altar, nestled high up on a pillar. Seen from below it was tiny and, although Annie pointed directly at it, I couldn't see it at first. Then she fished in a pocket, brought out a coin, put it in a slot and the Imp lit up. It had four large demonic ears and a mouth that stretched the full width of its face in a mischievous grin. Half comic, half menacing. One of its legs was crossed over the other one, so that it looked as though it was sitting on a stick. A truly strange apparition and I remembered what Lilith had said about the medieval attempt to make sure everything in the world was *inside* the cathedral. For Annie, though, there was no need to reconcile apparent opposites. To her it was entirely natural for it to be there.

'Shall I tell you the story of the Imp, Uncle Sam?'

'I would *love* to hear the story of the Imp.'

She pointed towards a pew from which the Imp was still visible. We sat down there.

'Well,' she said and drew a deep breath. 'It all began like this. Once upon a time there were two imps.'

'*Two*?' I was incredulous.

'Yes, two. Definitely. I think they were twins, because they were both the same size and they looked identical. Not everybody tells the story the same, you know, but there were definitely two. In med-yeval times. And somehow they got into the cathedral. I don't know exactly how, but somehow they got in. P'raps they crept in through a window at night when everyone was sleeping.'

I nodded energetically.

'Well, anyway once they were in the cathedral, no-one could get them out and they ran round and round, being very bad. I don't think even Tom could have controlled them, but well, we don't know, because Tom wasn't here then.'

'What did the imps do?'

'They were really bad.' She giggled. 'They smashed things up and they sang rude songs, and they were very, very naughty. They did dances too, and then an angel came and told them not to do what they were doing and well, the next thing was they had a fight with the angel and the angel was winning, you know.'

'That's good. I think angels usually beat imps, don't they?'

'Yes, they do. Anyway, the angel was winning the fight and the one imp was smarter than the other imp and he had a witch to help him and so he flew away with the witch on her broomstick. But the other imp wasn't so fast and that's the one that's here.' She nodded to the top of the pillar, where the Imp was no longer illuminated. 'He threw things at the angel, but he couldn't win the fight, you know, and she caught him and in the end she turned him into stone. And he's been here like that ever since.'

'For hundreds of years?'

'Thousands. Since med-yeval times. And you know something else?'

'What's that, Annie?'

'He was grinning at the angel and that made her mad and I think that was why she turned him into stone and he has been there grinning ever since. He's not nice, but his grin is ….' She paused trying to find the right word.

'Yes?'

'It's, it's … funny. I know he was very naughty, but I still like him, you know. I wish he could come alive again, but then if he did, he might run away and then I couldn't come to see him. Uncle Sam?'

'Yes?'

'Do you know much about angels?'

'No, not very much, I'm afraid.'

'Well, can I ask you an angel question?'

'Of course. I may not be able to answer it, but I'll try.'

'Well, I was wondering. The imps were boy imps and the angel was a girl angel. Do they have boy angels as well as girl angels?'

'Oh, I can answer that one. Yes, they do. There are some famous men angels. There's Gabriel and there's Michael and maybe lots of others.'

'That's good then. And what about imps?'

'You mean, are there boy imps and girl imps? That's a harder question.'

'Yes, I know, but do you know the answer?'

'Well, I'm not so sure about that, Annie. Most of the imps I've ever heard of are boy imps, but I think there could be girl imps too.'

'I think so. I mean, I know ladies are very nice and little girls are sugar and spice and all things nice, but …'

'But what, dear?'

'Some of the girls in my class aren't very nice, you know. They say rude words, like the imps. But don't tell anyone. It's a secret. I don't want anyone to know I told on them. Linda Smith and Cheryl Workington. They say rude words.'

'Don't worry, I won't tell. My lips are sealed. It's our secret.'

'For always?'

'For ever and ever.'

She smiled. 'You know, those two imps that were so bad in the cathedral. I'm almost sure they were twins.'

'Really?'

'Yes, I asked Mum and Dad about it.'

'What did they think?'

'Well,' and she gave a big sigh that let me know in advance that they had done what adults often do and complicated the issue unnecessarily. 'Mum said something to Dad about them being double-gangers and then she told me I was right. They might be twins.'

'Doppelgänger?'

'Yes double-gangers. I think that means they were a gang of two people. But anyway they were probably twins too. So the other one may still be running around in the world, doing bad things. He's probably started a new gang.'

'That's a worry, sweetheart.'

'But maybe he changed his ways after the fight with the angel. Or she changed *her* ways, if there's girl imps and it was one.'

'Let's hope so.'

'Sometimes I wish I had a twin, you know, or even a brother or sister. But I do have Judy. So I say she is my twin. And I have two penguins too, you know, and they are like twins. They're both pairs too, pairs of … pyjamas.' She was enjoying teasing me. 'There's a good pair and a bad pair.' She paused and then changed tack. 'You know what else I heard? I heard there can be bad angels, like Bellzebub. I think he was a he, you know. I don't think there can be any bad lady angels.'

'I think you're right. I think lady angels are always good angels.'

'But witches. They're different. They are always ladies, aren't they?'

'Yes, they are. Male witches are called warlocks.'

She giggled. 'War…locks. That's a funny name. Did you ever meet a war …lock?'

'No, I never did. And I hope I never do.'

'Me too. I think it would be very scary. I could sit here for hours looking at the Imp, you know?'

'You don't get bored?'

'Well, sometimes, but not usually.'

'Are there other bits of the cathedral you like?'

'Not really. Well a bit, but not like I like the Imp. Some of the windows are nice. They're roses windows, you know. And I can show you the closed-toor, if you like. That's nice too?'

'The closed door?'

'Yes, the closed-toor.'

'What's behind the door, dear? Does anyone ever open it?'

'No, silly. It's not a closed door. It's a closed-toor. Let me show you.'

She grabbed my hand and I pretended that the force of her grip was pulling me up from the pew. 'Come on,' she said. 'We can go down there now. And if we turn off to the right, I can show you some angels. They're in St Huge's Choir.'

'St Huge?'

'Yes. He's very famous. The most famous person there ever was in Lincoln, and he had a swan and he was very big. That's why they called him St Huge.'

'Was he more famous than the Imp?'

'Probably. He was certainly bigger. The Imp is so small and he must have been very big, I think. Look, here are the angels. They're playing music too.' The choir stalls had wooden carvings of angels with harps and a drum. 'One of them is probably the one who turned the Imp to stone. But ….'

'But what, Annie?'

'Well, if I'm right, after the angel turned the Imp to stone, she must have got turned to wood.'

'Who could have done such a thing, Annie?'

'I expect it was St Huge. This is his choir and she's here. So it was probably him. I think he liked her and wanted to keep her here. I don't know for sure, but I reckon that's what happened.'

At the end of the choir there was a splendid brass lectern, with a Bible mounted on the wings of an eagle and beneath the eagle a globe. There was no doubt about it. There was only one book that was ever going to lay claim to that position and putting the earth underneath it made it clear where power lay. I remembered the *Mappa Mundi* in Martin's cabinet and was going to say something to Annie about 'med-yeval' geography, but she was eager to get to the cloister and two minutes later we were there. An inner haven of peace within the general seclusion and otherworldliness of the cathedral.

'It's very nice here, Annie.'

'Yes.' She didn't sound too sure. Then she winked, 'But no imps.'

'No, no imps.' We laughed together. At that moment my mobile vibrated in my pocket. I'd put it on silent. I had no idea what the protocols were for using phones in a cathedral cloister, but I decided it wasn't the most absolute holy of holies and so I'd take the call. Lilith.

'Come back as soon as you can, David. I've something to tell you.'

'What is it?'

'I'll tell you in a few minutes. There's something to show you too. Spike is coming to pick you up. He'll meet you by the small post office on Eastgate. Ask Annie where it is. I think she'll know, but if she's not sure, just go out of the West Front of the cathedral, the main entrance, go forwards towards the castle and turn right into the Bailgate. I think you can see the post office from there. It's just one minute. On the corner. Past the White Hart Hotel. It's the nearest place Spike can bring a car. And David.'

'Yes?'

'Get there quickly, and don't worry if Spike isn't waiting. He'll be there before you, but he may not be able to park, and if that happens, he'll circle around. He's under strict instructions.'

'OK, Lily.' For a second I felt glad I wasn't under her 'strict instructions', but then on reflection it occurred to me that I was.

'It's your Mum, Annie. She wants us home. Your Dad is coming to pick us up.'

'Oh! Well, that's OK, I s'pose. You didn't get to see everything Uncle Sam, but you saw the Imp, didn't you?'

'Yes, and you told me the story and so I know all about it, don't I?'

'Can we can see it again on the way out?'

'Lead on, dear. We'll go round by it again, but we can't stop. Your Dad may be waiting for us. We have to meet him by the post office … on Eastgate. Do you know where that is?'

'I don't really know Eastgate, but I know where the post office is. Mummy buys stamps there sometimes.' And then more decisively, 'I can get us there, but we have to see where I saw Tom too.'

'Is that on the way to the post office?'

'Nope,' she said sulkily, 'It was round the other side of the cathedral. It wouldn't take long to go that way.'

'Next time, Annie. Your Mum wants us to be back quickly. If you can get us to the post office, that will be wonderful.' And she did, with a minor detour via the Imp. On the way she asked me again about my names. Why did I have two names? Why did her Mum call me 'David', when my name was Sam? I didn't have an easy answer.

'Don't worry, Uncle Sam. I know about these things. We can't always explain them, but they happen. There are all kinds of twoses in the world, aren't there? There were two imps and I have two pairs of penguins. They're twins and Judy and me are like twins too. Uncle Sam?'

'Yes, sweetheart?'

'I think you must be a double-ganger, if you've got two names. But you're not an imp are you.' And she burst out laughing.

Spike was waiting, parked by the post office.

Inside the car I asked him, 'Did Lily tell you what she's found out?'

'Haven't got a clue, matey. All she said was to get you home ASAP. I think it may be big-time trouble, but you never know. Anyway, don't worry too much. She's great in a crisis, just as long as it's not *her* crisis.'

Wilf

I'm OK now, Sherry. Please don't fret. No worries, sweetheart, though I never thought it would come to this. It's good that Sam hasn't come back here from the hospital. It was much too close for comfort. I still have to show him the rest of the cabinets, of course. And now I have to worry about little Alf. It's a bit hard at my age, looking after the young ones, but it keeps me busy and that's good. And I have you to help. I'm glad you aren't a puppy anymore, Sherry, because you are wise and you understand. Oh yes, of course. I know. You were the loveliest puppy in the world. Yes, you were, and you are such a beauty now.

Perhaps I should send Sam a message. Very handy this modern technology, Sherry. Maybe I will teach you how to compute tomorrow. Then you can send messages to the butcher and if you are a very good dog, you can use my debit card for an order. And you can buy fillet steak and chicken and maybe a bone or two. Only the best for the working classes. But make sure you don't buy too many bones! And no chicken bones at all. They splinter. Yes, you're very beautiful.

Penguins

Lilith was keen to put Annie to bed as soon as we got back. Annie had other ideas.

'Mum, could Uncle Sam come up with me and tuck us in? Horncastle and me? Then I know we will sleep better.'

I was flattered to have become her favourite of the moment, but surprised that Lilith agreed. 'OK, but just two minutes, darling. I have something important to talk to him about.'

'Could I stay then, Mum? Is it a secret? You know I love secrets!'

'No, it's boring stuff, but he can take you up. Just as long as you don't keep him more than a couple of minutes.' Spike came to Lilith's aid. 'I think Mum wants to talk about some grown-up things, and grown-up things can be really really boring. I get so bored I yawn and yawn and fall asleep.'

'Then if I heard the things, they might make me sleepy.'

'No, darling, and Uncle Sam can't stay with you more than two minutes. Your Dad will come up with him to see he isn't too long.'

Spike saluted ironically. Upstairs, he said he was going to clean his teeth and Annie tried several ploys to keep me with her. I had to tuck Judy into bed, as well as Horncastle and her, and I had to see her twin pairs of penguin pyjamas.

'Are your penguin pyjamas really twins?'

'Yes,' she nodded slowly and purposefully. She crossed the room and pulled two identical pairs of pyjamas out of a drawer. 'They look the same, but they're not, you know?' She winked.

'They're not? They're different?' I couldn't have been more surprised.

'Well, they may not *look* different, but one is a good penguin and the other one is a bad penguin. Just like the imps. Their names are Happy and Humpty.'

'One good and one bad, like the imps? Is Happy the good one.'

Another confirmatory nod. 'I like Happy best, but some nights, if I feel naughty, I like to put on the Humpty pyjamas. Humpty is like the bad penguin in Wallace and Grow-mick, but not quite so nasty. Judy says it's risky to play at being naughty. She says I might turn into a bad person, but I tell her that won't happen, because it's only a game. I think it's nice to be two people. And one time … one time I even put both pairs of pyjamas on at the same time, so I could be two people at once.'

'And what happened?'

She laughed and shook her head this time. 'Nothing happened. I got very hot and I had to take one pair off. But maybe if I'd kept them on, I could have been good and bad at the same time.'

'Tell me, dear. Did you ever go to the Weavers with your Mum?'

'What's Weavers?'

'It's a house. It's where Aunty Isabel lives.'

'And Alf lives there too?'

'Yes, that's right, with his Mummy, Alice.'

'Yes, I've been there. I played with Alf.'

'What was it like? Where did you play?'

'Oh, I think … I think we played in Aunty Alice's room.'

'Her cabinet room?'

'I don't know. It was a room full of guns. Bang, bang.' She pretend-shot me with her finger.

'Guns? Are you sure?'

'Mmm, yes. Definitely, definitely, definitely.'

'And the two of you just played there on your own?'

'Well Mum and Aunty Isabel were there some of the time, but then we were on our own too and we had fun. I like Alf. He's funny.'

'What games did you play, dear?'

'Oh guns, and things, you know. But only pretend.'

'You didn't really shoot the guns?'

'Course not. But Alf said they were fired one time, and somebody got killed.'

'Really?'

She nodded.

'Who was it got killed? Was it his brother? His big brother, Glen?'

'Oh no, but he's dead too, you know. He got drownded.'

'That's what I heard, but I wondered if it was true. Do you know who was shot, Annie dear?'

'Well I only know what Alf said and he said it was one of his uncles.'

'Did he say the uncle's name?'

'I think so.' Sucking her thumb now, acting babyish.

'Do you remember who it was, dear? Was it Steve or maybe Martin?'

'P'raps. I don't remember.'

'Did Alf know who did the shooting? Did he tell you?'

'No, he didn't say that. He didn't say who she was.'

'*She*? He said it was a she?'

'Mmm, I think so. But p'raps not. I don't know if Alf told me, but I know it was a she.'

'You do know that?'

'Well, I think so. *Somebody* said so. I remember that.'

And at that moment her father came back and, realising she was being interrogated, frowned, uncharacteristically. 'It's Annie's bedtime, Uncle Sam. She's got to go bye-byes now.'

'Can we kiss Horncastle goodnight, Dad?'

'Did you do a good job of tucking him in?'

'Yes, but he wants to be kissed too.'

'OK.'

'By everybody. Everybody has to kiss him. You and me *and* Uncle Sam.'

Horncastle found himself the object of outpourings of affection and Annie was satisfied. As we went down the stairs, Spike said, 'You were getting a little bit heavy with her there, matey. A lot of questions for a little 'un.'

'I'm sorry. I didn't think, but once I realised she knew something, I couldn't stop myself.'

'I don't think she knows much. She was only over at the House of Horrors two or three times.'

'She thinks one of Alf's uncles was shot.'

'I know. I heard what she told you.'

'Do you think that's right?'

Spike shrugged, 'Search me. I haven't got a clue.'

'She said that.'

'Yes, I heard what she said. Let's go and ask She Who Must Be Obeyed.'

'Lily?'

'Yes, Lily, you tosser. She found out something while we were gone. Remember? Hope she lets me in on the secret this time.'

Back with Lilith, Spike went into one of his routines, becoming mock-servile and she said he could stay. She came straight to the point. She'd found the three folders as files on Alice's laptop. They seem to have been there all along. What you've read was probably printed out from there.'

'Have you read the third folder?'

'Yes, and the other two. All three files were there. It was easy to find them.'

'Were they downloaded from e-mails?'

'It doesn't look like it. I think they were written on that machine.'

'So you think they may not be from Stuart?'

'Well, I'm not completely sure, but there's no trace of any e-mails from him in any of the accounts I could find, except for the message you read and I don't think that was from him. And the documents I found were dated just before Isabel sent you the first e-mail. So I'm guessing that they've been put there recently and I don't think they're copies.'

'Do you think Isabel could be doing all this? Controlling everything?'

'No, I don't think so, though I suppose it's possible. They could have been written by anyone in the house.'

'Has someone else has been hacking in, like you?'

'No, I mean it wouldn't even need that. They're sharing Alice's computer and if they know her password, they could be straight into everything on that computer. And maybe other people's accounts. They've all been using that laptop, it seems. There are no real safeguards.'

'S-so can we guess who is involved?'

'Well, putting two and two together, someone in the house wrote the documents, the three folders, on the laptop, just before Isabel started e-mailing you. Maybe it was her, maybe Alice, maybe someone else. It doesn't look as though they were sent by Stuart unless they were transcribed or their origin has been covered up. And I'm guessing that what happened is that someone read Isabel's e-mails to you and got worried you were coming, or read the folders and felt they would give the game away. Or maybe that person read both. I think that person sent you the e-mail that seemed to be from "Stuart". I don't think he's had a hand in any of this. I think everything that's happened was within the house and cyberspace has been used as a cover-up – a kind of alibi.'

'So we need to know who wrote the folders *and* who read them?'

'Yes.'

Spike chimed in, 'I think it's time for both of you to have a guess and if you don't agree with one another, then I'll have the casting vote. I'll be your super-sleuth.'

'Like Hercule Poirot?' I was remembering that *I* wasn't supposed to be playing detective.

'No, too corny. This may seem like a country house mystery, but I'm more of a Raymond Chandler man myself. Not this time, though. Let's just say I'm your Precious Ramotswe. We need a bit more basic common sense here and if Annie says a woman is behind this, then maybe we need some female intuition to work it out, even if it means me getting into cross-dressing.'

Lilith said nothing, but I sensed that her analytical intelligence – forget about 'female intuition' – was likely to solve the mystery, if she hadn't already. She handed me a stapled print-out. The third folder. 'Bedtime reading. See what you think, David. Oh, and I forgot to say. Isabel phoned and she's bringing Uncle Wilf here first thing tomorrow. So I think you can work it all out overnight and then we can talk about it once they get here. Then we have to decide what to do.'

'You've got a good idea of what's happened, haven't you?'

She nodded, reluctantly, but didn't elaborate. 'You should have too, once you've finished reading the folders. Isabel wants you to find out what's happened on your own. She's been really worried for you and she's very worried about Uncle Wilf, too. She wants to get him out of there.'

'I know. She's very, very worried. While I was there, she wanted us to take turns watching him. Me, her and Jules.'

'It wasn't an Alka-Seltzer then?'

'I don't think so. When he told us that, I half-believed it, but then Isabel still thought he was in danger and now it seems clear they've been playing around with me over the folders.'

I went up to my bedroom and started reading the third folder. It was also prefaced by a few words from 'Stuart':

Here's what I imagine happened when the nightmare began. It was a long time after the older man took the child and it was a long time after the husband had returned.

It had gone on for years and years and now it was uncontainable. There are moments when the baked beans in one's head begin to wander, moments when the toast of one's life has no butter, moments when one has two knives and no forks and so if one used the sharp one for other purposes, there would still be one to cut toast with. But she will not use the knife this evening.

He comes home. He always comes home. It wouldn't be so bad, if he would only stay away forever. If he would stay with one of his women. One of those, like the dark one who brought the usurper to her doorstep on that night. But then she must belong to his past. He would have another one now.

He always comes back. She can't be rid of him. He neither flaunts his behaviour, not apologises. He continues as though this is part of the natural order. If this is normal in this world, then it is time to travel into other worlds. And this is the night when everything snaps. This is the night when she speaks of his time among the leviathans of the southern oceans, the square-faced extra-terrestrials on the planet gorgonzola, the yellow haloed demons of the fifth moon of Jupiter and the fairground curiosities that he believes make a life.

And he is amazed, for the first time in all their years together and all their months apart, by the poetry and passion of her words. He could almost love her again. It is too late, but he comes close to her. As if she were one of his women. As if she could be. As if she ever would be again. And she strikes him with the first thing that comes to hand. A plastic kitchen server. A ridiculous weapon. He has no weapon, but to her surprise he hits her back, hard across the face and he draws blood from her lips, like a barefisted boxer in a fairground booth. Like something out of his ludicrous collection. That's what he is. A circus freak.

She smells the perfume on his clothes, and as he looms above her, his palm open, ready to slap her again, she screams, the loudest scream of her life, a life lived according to the rules, a proper life, a decent life. She screams the single word, 'GO!' She screams it long and loud and it stops him. He is even more amazed by her and for a second he hesitates, but then he obeys and he is gone into the night. Gone to one of his whores, she supposes, but she will never know. Hours later, the news of the crash comes. He has been pronounced dead at the scene. She wonders exactly how the police pronounced the word. He may have been driving recklessly. He seems to have gone off the road when there was no other car near him. Nothing is certain, except that she knows she is responsible. She laughs with joy at what she has achieved. A perfect murder, because it is no murder at all, unless the thought has engendered the deed. She never realised that she was seeking revenge, but now she knows that that desire has been there for years, festering relentlessly, and now she is free. Free not just of him, but free to do as she wishes. This is the beginning of her new life. Her respectability of decades is her guarantee of safety. He is dead and she has the perfect alibi. She is innocent. A murderess only in her thoughts. She smiles to herself at her power. At what she has achieved. Anything is possible now.

She hates his collection, but she'll leave it as a testament to his absurdity. They all collect. All of them. She will never have a room like them. Never did. Never will. Let the maggot cheeses of their minds rot, until she sends them away. The older man can be spared, because he saved her from the usurper and age will claim him in due course. The girls and women can be spared, so that they can suffer as she has suffered. As women suffer. But the men must go. Men and boys. One at a time. No hurry. Then she will be truly free. Accidents will be best, and as long as she is patient there will be opportunities. She can take her time. This can be a work of years, giving her life a purpose again. An invisible gallery of the disappeared. She can learn a thousand ways to make them vanish. If she is respectable, no one will ever suspect. And the old man, who can read her mind, can be relied on. He loves them all and will be sure to keep the secrets he finds in the charnel house of her mind.

And here 'Stuart' wrote: *She was wrong, of course.* His manuscript continued:

No one suspected her of killing her husband and she hadn't. It was only later, when the little boy died, that they understood, though there had been other deaths before this. Even the dog knew that she had drowned the little boy. That was the night she came into the house, muttering 'Usurper, usurper. Another usurper. He had to go.' And her wild eyes turned on her sons.

For several years, her thirdborn son, the usurper's twin, had known what had happened on that night many years before. That night when the woman had come to the house, with his usurper twin. One evening, the older man had told the thirdborn about that night. And later the thirdborn went looking for the dark woman who had brought the child to the house on that night. She was easy to find. The older man had given him a small piece of pink paper. A name. An address. It was harder to find the twin, but the thirdborn knew who he was and after a time he traced him. He went to meet him, accidentally, on purpose. The thirdborn was confused, because there had been days when he thought he was the usurper, though he was the one who had always lived in his father's house. He needed this encounter to understand himself. He found his twin and became his friend, without saying who he was. He imagined a story into being. If you imagined hard enough, you could make a story real. It came alive. It was a story in which he brought the three of them together. At a college, in a restaurant. He spun his own web of intrigue. He involved his favourite sister in his plot. But there was no happy ending. He spoke to the dark woman, but she was hardened. She had abandoned her child for all time and would never acknowledge him. There was a day when she spoke words of rejection to her child, now on the threshold of manhood, though he never knew who she was. The thirdborn was silent. His dream of reconciliation had failed.

The thirdborn's father had died. He went home. His mother was sedate, calm, composed. But he saw the danger. He stayed because of his sisters and he had the illusion he could save his mother. But he was impotent. And then his oldest brother was shot. There is more than one way to 'disappear'. No one knew what she did with the body. A shallow grave? A burial at sea? No burial at all? He told his favourite sister what he knew. And then another brother vanished. There is more than one way to 'disappear'. Gradually they came to realise that she was no longer their protector, that she saw them as enemies now. She was no longer protecting them, but they protected her. They closed ranks to protect her, knowing she needed help, imagining she was no real threat to them. They believed this, because the older man told them it was so. And then the little boy drowned and the thirdborn told his sisters they must bind together, for everyone's sake. That was his wish, but he failed again. He stopped sleeping at night. And after a while he went away.

He wrote to one of his sisters about his feelings for his twin, the orphan, the usurper. It was his twin's right to know and the older man should see the twin before he died. That man was the twin's real father, because he had chosen his future, when he carried him away. He wrote short messages. He disguised them, though he made certain the sister would know he had written them. That sister wrote these pages. She is 'Stuart' now. She told the other sister, his favourite sister, what she had written and they argued over whether they should tell the twin about his parentage. The favourite sister said the usurper had been usurped. It was time he should come home. She said it would be too dangerous. They agreed to keep the secret. Then the favourite sister wrote without telling her. She had spoken to the older man and he said it was time. The mother was in a calm phase. A queen bee happy at the obeisance of her drones. It should be safe. So the favourite sister sent the twin e-mails. Eventually he came.

There the manuscript ended. Lilith and Spike were still up and so I went downstairs to them. 'So Alice wrote these folders?'

Lilith was at her most serious, 'It seems so and the pieces fit together, but…'

'But what?' Spike said what I was thinking.

'Well, if this is right, Laura is obviously very disturbed and they've been collectively covering up for her. So it almost doesn't matter who wrote what exactly. And remember whoever has been writing this says themself that this is how they imagine it. But it would seem as though it draws on knowledge only Uncle Wilf and Stuart could have had, whoever they told it to.'

'Do you really think this is all possible? That Milly is my mother and Stuart was conspiring to re-unite me with her. I mean, did he really find us both and persuade me to go to a college, where my mother was just around the corner? It seems far-fetched. Even if he *could* have done it, *would* he have done it?'

'It's hard for me to say. You know Stuart better than me.'

'*Knew*. I don't really know him now. I haven't seen him in years. He's the absence in this story. I don't even know for sure that he's alive. And anyway, why wouldn't he just let sleeping dogs lie? If this story is right, my Dad is dead and his wife might want to murder me. It'd be crazy to invite me up to The Weavers.'

'But Stuart didn't invite you,' and she hesitated, 'He tried to get your birth mother to acknowledge you years ago and that didn't work. Then he tried to protect Laura and that didn't work either. And now either Isabel or Alice, or both of them, decided to get you up here. It looks as though Alice wrote the stuff in the folders and it's Isabel who decided to get you up to Bubbleby. Stuart probably hasn't been involved at all.'

Spike had been silent. He leaned forward, his chin resting on a hand, supported by an elbow on his knee. 'I love a good murder mystery, especially when there's a foundling involved too.'

'This is David's life we're talking about, Spike.'

'I know, and a bloody good life it is too, if you ask me. I think it's about to get even better, just as long as he doesn't get bumped off in the next twenty-four hours.'

Lilith and I smiled nervously. I asked her, 'Do you think that they will be willing to shop their mother now? It'd be for her own good. She needs looking after.'

'I don't know. But that assumes that what we've just read is true. We can't know and we don't really know who wrote it. And goodness knows how much evidence there is to prove any of these supposed crimes. The car crash seems to have been an accident, even if it happened after an argument. And I think the police investigated Glen's drowning thoroughly and didn't come up with anything. So all that really leaves is an allegation that Laura murdered Martin, and there's no body or anything else to confirm that happened. We don't even know whether he's alive or dead.'

'Well, someone certainly tried to kill me yesterday, right after they'd had a go at poisoning Wilf.'

'Maybe. I mean maybe someone tried to poison Wilf. The only thing that's certain is that someone shot you and police have been crawling over every inch of The Weavers and the garden yesterday and today. That's the only hard evidence they *may* have to go on.'

There was a creak on a loose floorboard behind us. Annie had come downstairs, clutching her bear. 'Horncastle can't sleep, Mummy. He needs a glass of milk.'

'And what about Annie? Does she need milk too?', her father asked. I admired Spike's capacity to switch registers, but then perhaps this was a gift that came naturally to good parents. I didn't know.

'Mmm, yes, a glass of milk and some television and I think I *might* feel sleepy.'

She managed to stay wide awake for an hour or more, until one of her favourite television programmes had finished. When she finally went back to bed, I tried to revive our conversation. Lilith looked as though she'd had enough for one day. 'Why don't we leave it until Isabel and Uncle Wilf get here? They should arrive pretty early.'

'I think we'd better do what the lady says, matey. But what does it feel like to know who your Mummy and Daddy were?'

'I don't know what to believe anymore. But it doesn't s-sound as though I'm much better off. If all of this is right, my father is dead, my mother doesn't want me and my father's wife is trying to kill me.'

Spike gave me a dummy punch. 'I suppose so, but look on the bright side. You've just found your long-lost siblings.'

At that moment the landline rang shrilly. No one except Annie was to get much sleep that night.

Wilf

We're going tomorrow then, sweetheart, and I'll tell him. It's only right the boy should know. I've protected her too long. She needed help. She's such a frail flower. She was like my own daughter and she had such hard times. She was a battler, but after a while she simply followed her instincts. Just like you, when you sniff out food, Sherry. She never meant any harm. It was very hard for her. I've tried to protect them all.

I know you sometimes get hot in the car, but we'll have lots of water and you will be with your Aunty Isabel and me tomorrow, my smart dog. And we will both look after you so well, just like home. You would be so unhappy if you got hungry and there was no one here all day long to give you your dinner, wouldn't you? So it's best you come, my better-than-any-winner of Cruft's. You are such a clever dog. Do you remember little Annie, who came to see you? Of course, you do. She will be so pleased to see you again. You are a great favourite with all the children, Sherry dear. What's that? Yes, of course. That's right. You are popular with everyone. You are top dog with everybody in the whole wide world.

Let's have some pieces of your chicken. Are you ready to catch? Oh yes, that's a good catch. Now sit and you can have more. That's a good dog. Just small pieces. Here comes another one. Well caught! You are such a clever dog. More? OK, there's more. Twenty small pieces and this one is number nine. I know, yes, you haven't missed one yet. You are a champion catcher. What are you hearing, dear? Maybe it's your Aunty Isabel coming back to see us and I really wanted her to have an early night. I told her there was no need to guard me all the time. She might hurt Jules or little Alf, but she would never harm me. I'm the one she's relied on all these years. But then Sam's coming back hasn't been good for her. It's been a shock to her, poor soul. Anyone can see that. Yes, you can see it too, Sherry. I know. Mirror mirror on the wall. Who is the smartest one of all. And the mirror says it's … Sherry. Now sit down again, dear. Every family needs one intelligent person and you are ours, sweetheart.

Maybe Sam shouldn't be here, but he is and it's only right that the boy should know. The girls are very pleased he's come, though Alice doesn't always show it and she was against it until he arrived. I'm glad I wrote some of it down in those folders. I had to pretend it wasn't me, of course, because she has always relied on me. Maybe I'll write some more. It's hard to speak to people about these things. I have to be someone else to do it. And yes, dear Sherry, you're right. I am a very good ventriloquist, just like you are a champion eater and a very good barker. We both know how to protect people, don't we? I had to be Stuart or Alice or anyone but myself. I had to write it down, because I'm the only one who knows it all, though I don't know exactly what happened when Stuart went looking for Sam's mother. He told me a bit, but I had to make the rest up. Don't tell them I can compute, Sherry. That's our secret, isn't it?

What is it you're hearing, dear? Your ears are better than mine.

Steve

I sometimes think I should have gone further away. Perhaps I'm still too close to her here. The day she found out her face went white, but I think I became safe then. She didn't seem to see Eric as a threat. I worry for Jules. He's smart with books and things, but not smart with people. Everyone else can see she's off her trolley.

It's been better since I came out. Eric used to think Grimsby was grim, but now we both have jobs here and we can afford the rent and live with a bit of style, he's OK about it. And there is a scene, if you know where to find it. Mostly, though, people just leave you alone and it's better being in a town than in a village. Of course, I miss the others and sometimes I'm tempted to go back, being so near, but I never do. Jules came to see me two or three times, but not recently. He disapproves of Eric. He's OK about me being the way I am, and I think he'd be fine if I was with someone else. He just doesn't like Eric.

I thought about going to the police after Alice's little boy was drowned. But then I wasn't there and so all I had was suspicions. Still I knew all the same. He didn't deserve that. He was such a nice little lad. I hope he didn't suffer. I wonder how she did it. I hope it was quick. She'd spent all those years learning about poisons, practising at rifle ranges, becoming an expert archer, too. I think that's how she killed Martin, but perhaps she shot him. No one knows. He's just gone. Eric says that serial killers usually have the same m.o., but I don't think she does. Perhaps she wants to make it seem like several different people have been responsible, but if they nail one on her that'll be enough. Anyway, there are only two of her: my mother and the monster.

Laura

Lilith picked up the phone. She didn't say much, but her face appeared to turn paler than ever under her pasty Goth make-up.

'Yes … yes … I see … Is it serious? … Oh no! … No! … No! That's terrible! That's awful!… I can't believe it. … Yes, yes, of course. … How are *you*? … No, no, don't blame yourself. … You did everything you could. … OK. … Yes. … Yes, I'll come right away and I'll bring him. … Take care.' She hung up.

'She stabbed him. Wilf. Laura stabbed him.' She paused, trying to absorb the news, just as we were. 'He's gone. And the police have taken Laura away. She wants me there. Isabel wants me there. And you, David.'

After the initial shock had sunk in, Spike asked her if she would be alright, driving their car along the country roads to Bubbleby at that time of night. She didn't hesitate. She'd be fine in that respect and it was better to take their car than for me to drive. Just in case. In fact, she wondered if I should go at all, but Isabel had specifically asked her to bring me. I was sure I'd be OK. As Spike had said, Lilith was great in a crisis. Driving out of Lincoln and along the main roads, she was thinking of everyone but herself. Poor Isabel: she'd tried to do everything right and now she'd lost her favourite uncle and she'd be losing her mother. Uncle Wilf: gone, so suddenly. If only, he'd admitted to having been nearly poisoned. Laura: all those years of inner torment, drowning a little boy, trying to shoot me and now the plunge of the knife into Uncle Wilf's heart. Little Alf: thank goodness he was safe. Alice and Jules: how were they taking it? Was I really alright and not just putting on a brave face? And hopefully Annie would go back to sleep, not knowing anything about any of this. She mentioned Stuart, Sherry, Beth, Steve. They'd all had their problems. Yes, even Sherry, who had been having monthly visits to the vet's for a heart condition.

A torrent of words that encompassed everyone, except … Spike. Spike, who was as faithful to her as the spaniel side of Sherry's nature had made her to Uncle Wilf. Spike who had asked me to put in a good word for him and who shouldn't have needed an intermediary. Ineffectual though I am, I knew I must try, but now wasn't the moment. And I was finding it hard to talk to her about the subject uppermost in our minds. So I asked her about the car. Was it difficult to drive? No. It was just like any other car. Easy as pie, once you got to know it and that hadn't taken long. Was Annie really good at arithmetic? Yes, she was. But talking about the events at The Weavers was unavoidable and we came back to them quickly. My mind was bubbling and most of all I kept thinking how much poorer a place the world was going to be without Wilf. Crazy, when I'd hardly known him, but my thinking of him as a kind of grandfather did now make a kind of sense. And crazier still, I was blurring identities and thinking that *my* mother was a killer.

'What else did you find out, Lily?'

'There were some more e-mails. They were from Uncle Wilf. We never dreamt he was computer literate, but he was. He didn't send a lot, but he wrote to a few friends. He'd written to Beth, asking her to come up to the house and there were replies from her too. She was Laura's friend, one of the people she used to visit. And she was also in Wilf's confidence and I think he'd asked her to come up to the house, because he was worried Laura might go over the edge again.'

'So she knew everything? Beth?'

'It's hard to say, but something in one of the messages suggests she knew who your mother was. Wilf must have told her.'

'And did he say it was Milly, the wife of the Italian café owner.'

'Well, he didn't name her, but yes. He said Stuart had gone looking for her and engineered that whole situation. Getting you to go to the college and trying to put the two of you in one another's way, hoping that might bring you together. But it didn't work. She loves her husband too much. I only remember him a bit, but not too well. Do you?'

'I remember him. We laughed at him, but he was a very nice man.'

'Just think then. If things had turned out differently, he might have been your stepdad.'

'And it was in their café that I told you my real name. My other name.'

'Yes, I know. That's one of the few things I remember about the place.'

'And where is Stuart now? Could you tell?'

'No, there were no clues. Really. Perhaps Isabel can tell us, but I don't think so. I don't think he's been in touch with anyone in ages.'

'And he wasn't summoning me, after all?'

'No, or at least it seems not. It seems as though he tried to reunite you with your mother all those years ago. It seems Uncle Wilf told him who she was and I think the folders were all written by Wilf too, though he tried to make out that Alice had written them. Then Alice and Isabel debated whether to get you up here or not.'

Seems, seems, seems. I listened to Lilith attentively as we neared Bubbleby. She was a superb driver. She took sharp bends at just the right speed, braked at the perfect moment and accelerated smoothly as she came out of the bends and changed up. She extracted the best possible performance from the 'Spikemobile', which I could tell *was* a difficult car to drive. As we approached The Weavers, she negotiated the turns and potholes in the narrow lane like someone who drove them every day. Sitting beside her I remembered my awkwardness as I'd driven the same route four days before in broad daylight. Bubbleby and its surroundings had made me feel a novice in every respect. On the final stretch a police car, its flashing lights and siren shattering the rural quiet, sped past us at a spot where I wouldn't have believed it was possible to overtake. It was one of two parked outside The Weavers when we arrived.

Isabel came out to meet us. A winter coat thrown over light summer nightclothes, adrenalin flowing, talking rapidly in the cool night air. 'It's so terrible. Poor Uncle Wilf! And it's my fault. All my fault. Dear Uncle Wilf. I shouldn't have got you up here. It was bound to bring things to a head. Alice said I shouldn't. And I shouldn't have left him, not even for a minute. I knew he shouldn't be alone and I left him. And the police. They're doing a good job, but it's all too much. Police everywhere. I didn't really think she'd try something else so soon. He'd always supported her, but I think she found out he was divulging what he knew. He wrote the folders, you know. He couldn't bring himself to tell you directly. He's so used to hiding behind a mask. I guess that was the only way he could do it. Pretending to be Alice, pretending to be Stuart. It's easy to be a ventriloquist on the Internet. Just like what he said about the radio.

'The police wanted to talk to you earlier. They were going to come to the hospital, but then you got discharged and they didn't catch up with where you were right away and then this happened. It was all too quick. They would have come tomorrow. They're from Lincoln anyway.'

'What exactly happened?'

'The first thing I knew was that Sherry was whimpering at my door.' She took a deep breath, bracing herself to give a clear account. 'Jules and I had left Uncle Wilf alone because he insisted, and I was going to be bringing him to Lilith and Spike's early tomorrow. Jules was supposed to go back and check on him every once in a while, but I think it happened before he even checked once. I'll never forgive myself. Sherry jumped on to my bed and began tugging at the sheet. She's not as agile as she used to be, but she was insistent. I should have known right away that something was wrong, but I was groggy. It took me fifteen seconds to surface and realise that she was trying to tell me something. Her tail was wagging, but not the way it usually does. Once she knew I was awake, she jumped off the bed and ran to the door, then back to me, then back to the door. She wanted me to follow her. I grabbed a bookend and followed her into the corridor, along to his room. There was a lot of blood and I think he was dead already. I rang for an ambulance right away. I think I got the same operator as the last time. I worried, a stupid thought really, that she might have thought I was a hoax caller – two calls in two days – but she didn't. She must have known the other call was genuine. Then I went downstairs and Mum was in the kitchen. The knife was on the table. Not one from Alice's cabinet, where the police say she took the rifle and the poison from. Just a kitchen knife. She was smiling and then she picked it up and started making a sandwich, spreading blood across cheese as though it was some kind of relish. She asked me if I was hungry and if I'd like her to make me one too. I wanted to scream, but I didn't. I suppose I was in shock. I just ran out and found Jules. He couldn't take it in at first. I'm not sure he has now. Then the police got here and arrested her. She smiled at them too. She was still smiling, when they took her away. She was telling them how much training she'd done for special occasions like this and that was a pity, because now some of it would be wasted. It didn't look as though she would ever be able to make use of her archery lessons. I couldn't speak to her and she didn't say another word to me.

'I feel so bad, Sam. I've been such a fool. I should never have asked you to come up here, but it seemed the right thing to do and I wanted to see you again so badly. And Alice is feeling terrible too. If she hadn't had all that stuff in her cabinet maybe none of this would have happened.'

'Of course it would,' said unfailingly practical Lilith. 'She did the stabbing with a kitchen knife. She must have drowned Glen with her bare hands. She'd always have found a way. Come here now, don't be silly.' And she threw her arms around Isabel and nodded to me to join in a communal hug. Jules, shy and shaken, made four with us. He was saying nothing and I think he was the most shocked of all.

'Where's Alice?', I asked.

'In Uncle Wilf's cabinet with Alf. Trying to keep him away from all this. Thank goodness he's safe.'

'Did she kill Martin and Steve too? And is Stuart OK?

'He's OK, I'm sure. I don't know where he is, but I know he's OK. In here.' She tapped her forehead. 'Steve is OK, too. He's fine. We think she killed Martin, though we're not sure. Not Steve, though. Steve was smart enough to get out, and he has a good partner he's happy with. I think she was less hostile to him, because he's gay. But it's hard to know what was going on in her mind. Anyway, Steve sure as hell didn't want to take any chances. He got out. He's smart.

'She's been reading all our messages, you know. Uncle Wilf wrote that story of what happened, and she read the folders. We don't know, if it all happened exactly like that, but he had a pretty good idea. He was there, and he invented what he didn't know for sure. In a style that was meant to suggest Stuart, and he'd told Stuart about your mother. So it was plausible that Stuart could have written it all. He threw up a smokescreen, calling himself 'the older man' and things like that. Then he added another layer to make it seem like Alice had written it all. His whole life was a disguise and in the folders he was coming clean and telling what had happened, more or less, even if some of it was guesswork. But he had to find another facade for that. He needed a voice that would throw her off the trail, if she saw the folders. And she did. She read everything. We didn't know she was getting into our mails. I had no idea she was seeing my messages to you. She's very computer savvy, but I never dreamt she'd do that. My own Mum! I should have realised. It's stupid of me, when I knew what she was like. And then, when I did realise, I didn't know what to do, and it still didn't register that she'd seen the folders and what Wilf wrote too. I forgot the files were still on the laptop. I was thinking of them as just hard copy. And, after you'd read the first one, Uncle Wilf and I thought that if we moved the other two, you wouldn't know and she wouldn't know and everything would be OK. I wanted you to come so much, but Alice didn't think it was safe and then I wondered if it was right.

'She's been so placid recently. I was confused, but I thought I could make it all come right. That was stupid of me, I know. And we've always protected her, because she's our Mum. And you can see how she is. She's Mrs Perfect most of the time. I never imagined she would go so far off the rails all of a sudden. It's my fault, for getting you up here. I think that pushed her over the brink.' She talked and talked, repeating herself. A kind of confessional? A kind of exorcism?

'Don't blame yourself, but why didn't you tell me more of this before? And why the need to pretend it was Stuart who had left the papers.' I said this as gently as possible.

'Well, Uncle Wilf had used Stuart's identity to start with and I thought I'd carry it on. I thought you'd be more likely to come, if Stuart was calling you. He was your friend.'

'It's terrible what's happened, but I'm glad you did get me here. I've never really had a family.'

'Apart from your wife?'

'Well, yes, but even that wasn't a very big part of my life. For some reason I went and made it seem like it was a bit more than it was, when I spoke to you about it.'

'You made it sound pretty insignificant.'

I blushed. 'It was even more meaningless than I let on. More like a brief affair, though we were married.'

At that moment. Sherry came running out of the house and rushed up to welcome Lilith and me. Excited! Visitors! It was hard to tell whether she was distressed over Uncle Wilf. Her manner was the same as ever, desperate for attention. So I picked her up and cradled her in my arms while we carried on talking. She licked my nose. After a while, Lilith took her from me.

'That woman Beth. What was she doing here on the day I was shot?'

'Nothing much. She's a friend of Mum's. She comes up here occasionally. She's a nice woman.'

'Right, I see. For a moment I thought she was the one who had shot me. By a process of elimination.'

'No, no way. She's not that kind of woman. Well, Mum isn't either, I suppose. You know, in one sense no one could have brought us up better.'

'Yes. You know in a funny way, I feel she might have been my mother.'

'She's your sister's mother. It would be nice if you could have known Dad. He was one of the world's good guys, even if he gave her a bad time.'

'Was he as promiscuous as the folders suggest?'

'Who knows? I don't think so, though. He was here most of the time. But he does seem to have had a fling or two.'

'Do you know how he met my mother? I mean Milly.'

'No, I haven't the faintest idea, but he had a lot of contacts from his travelling days. Will you go looking for her now?'

'No, that's all in her past, and she rejected me second time around when Stuart tried to bring us together. It's enough, almost too much, that I've found all of you.'

I spent two more nights at The Weavers. Lilith stayed too, tactfully saying that Isabel needed her, though I could tell that she was also wanting to make sure that I was OK, now I'd found out that I'd been at the heart of the puzzle I'd imagined I might be helping to solve. She phoned Spike every hour and I waited for a moment when I might be able to try to get her to acknowledge her feelings. Meanwhile we focused on Isabel. We could both see that her grief was tempered with relief, now that the nightmare of protecting Laura was over. She said very little about her, talking instead about Wilf and wanting to start on funeral arrangements, though the police made it clear it would be a long time before his body would be released. Alice and Jules went to see their mother. They came back, saying she had been mute and oblivious to their presence, appearing not even to recognise them. She had retreated inwards, like the cringing animal Wilf had described in the folders. She'd been charged with his murder, but nothing else as yet.

Choosing what seemed like an opportune moment on the second day back at The Weavers, I seized on one of Lilith's phone conversations to try to intervene on Spike's behalf.

'He's great, isn't he? And so devoted to Annie.'

'Of course he's devoted to Annie. Who wouldn't be?'

'He's devoted to you too, you know?'

'Yes, of course, I know that, David. Do you think I'm stupid? And before you say any more, I think he's wonderful too. I could never love anyone in the world more.'

'Then where's the problem?'

'The problem is *me*. I'm just not good enough for him. Can't you see that?'

'No, I can't. You're an extraordinary person yourself.' I thought I could distinguish the hint of a blush beneath her Pierrot whiteface. 'He loves you to pieces. Annie wants to see you two married again. What more do you need to persuade you?'

'I think if ....'

'If what?'

'If he could just stop acting like an idiot for a while, then I could take him seriously. He's another one who hides beneath camouflage, you know. If he'd just come out into the open, then I'd know that he's really forgiven me for the way I treated him.'

And I found myself taking an initiative. 'OK, I'm coming back to Lincoln with you, when we leave here and we're going to make sure you know he's mad enough about you to start being serious. How long does he have to stop goofing around, before you believe that?'

'Oh, I don't know. It's hard to put a time limit on it. I think maybe forty-eight hours, but who knows how I'd feel at the end of that. I just wish he didn't play-act all the time.'

'But we all act. You do.'

'Me? No, I don't think so.'

'Yes, you do. You're the white-faced clown, who's his straight man, straight woman. Only most of the time you don't really play the part.' And finally I seemed to be getting through to her.

'I suppose you could see it like that.'

'Yes, definitely.' I was surprised at my assertiveness. 'You hide under that make-up. We all play roles. Uncle Wilf did, Laura did. Isabel does.'

'I don't think Isabel does consciously.'

'I think she does.' I was remembering the e-mails she'd sent me. And shackled to Bubbleby for most of her life, her imaginative evocations of places she'd never been to seemed like a form of role play. She'd been living beneath many layers. What I didn't know was that she had a further surprise in store for me.

The police had found the rifle in Laura's room. It had obviously been fired from there, and they said they would be questioning me. The evidence against her appeared to be overwhelming, but first they wanted the pathologist's report on

Wilf. She arrived quickly: a no-nonsense, serious-looking woman, as befitted her profession. As she was walking away from the body, I half-heartedly asked her what she had found, not expecting to get a reply. Surprisingly she answered, 'Blood tells many stories'. Then she clammed up. I took it as a comment on what she'd seen on Wilf's body, but afterwards wondered whether I was right. Perhaps she knew the whole story and the remark was directed at me. Or perhaps it was a remark on our existential situation. However it was intended, for me it frustrated closure. The story that I'd seen unravelling so quickly that there had been no real time for reflection had seemed to have arrived at a tight resolution, but her words made me feel there were loose ends. 'If you put a razor in your mouth, you will spit blood.' The saying came back to me and I remembered its source. I'd heard it in Nigeria, when I'd been investigating corruption in the oil industry.

Jules, who was struggling to come to terms with what had happened, thought that Laura could plead insanity. Alice didn't think she'd be capable of pleading at all. Steve, whose old room I'd been sleeping in, came to The Weavers on the morning of the day that I left and so I met another half-brother. As they'd said, he was intelligent and he struck me as the most down-to-earth member of the White family. He joked about his cabinet and his 'purely academic' fascination with female nudes. He was shrewd, extravert, affable, a pleasure to be with, though I could tell that beneath his easy manners he was another deeply private person.

Now that I'd found my 'family', I knew I'd be making major adjustments to my life, but I couldn't imagine what they would be. As the sun went down that evening, we joked nervously about how we'd behaved to one another in recent days. I told Isabel, 'I thought you were trying to seduce me when you came to my room the other night.'

She replied, 'Yep, but I guess I just couldn't go through with it, though I *know* you were ready to play along!'

Alice chimed in, 'And just in case you're wondering whether I was flirting with you or not, of course I was, but I wouldn't have let it go very far. My own brother! I'm not that hard up … yet.' Then, she added, more enigmatically, 'If you're looking for *that* kind of relationship, you'd better try Isabel.'

Steve had a lighter touch: 'If you're available, look out for me, Sam.'

Only Jules kept apart from this banter, unable it seemed to dispel his belief that nothing out of the ordinary ever happened in his world. He alone had genuinely believed in his mother. He hadn't been covering up for her and it was now dawning on him just how much danger he'd been in.

Isabel said she'd show me her cabinet. I wasn't as enthusiastic as before, but I was curious to know what it contained. Alice said she would get rid of her arsenal. Jules said he wanted to get rid of the house, but that wasn't going to be easy as the title was in Laura's name and now she was refusing to see or speak to anyone. Steve teased them both, saying he didn't really have much to get rid of, but maybe they could dispose of Laura's bees, before someone got stung.

I felt my life wouldn't return to normal until I left Bubbleby, but in the meantime I searched my e-mails, hoping to find the ordinariness that had so stubbornly eluded me in Lincolnshire. My uncle (my 'mother's' brother) was still complaining about his colonoscopy, but it seemed that that was receding into history, now that he had 'this agonising pain from a late middle-aged wisdom tooth'. My former colleague was back from Greece and that seemed to be receding into history, now that he had joined the local gym and was 'definitely going to get in shape before the winter'. My ex-wife was stubbornly refusing to recede into history, but she became more reasonable when I told her £1,000 ('all I can spare at the moment') was on its way to her.

I remembered Beth's card and something prompted me to ring her. She came up to The Weavers to see me. She'd been Laura's friend and had known how troubled her mind was, but had seen her as a victim rather than a perpetrator, and had only now grasped the full extent of her psychosis. Like Lilith, she was a repository of common sense.

I brought up a subject that had lingered in my mind, since I'd last seen her. 'You know you said people like you and me have to stick together? Did you just mean we're outsiders here?'

'Bless you. Course, we're outsiders. Everyone's an outsider here in one way or another. It's like that everywhere. Here's no different, though some people think so. No one has been here forever. This part of England, the whole of the eastern side really, has seen waves and waves of people coming in. Even the oh-so pure Whites can trace their ancestry back to Huguenots. So you and me, we're nothing too special really, are we? But well ....' She smiled at my ingenuousness, pointed to her brown skin and put her bare arm beside mine. 'We've got that in common too, you and I, haven't we? They're all invisible minorities, but with you and me it sticks out a bit, doesn't it? We couldn't fool anybody if we tried. Maybe it doesn't get noticed any more in the world you come from, Sam. Here people still see it, though. But it's changing, thank goodness. There's more and more room for mongrels. You know, you could almost have been *my* son, couldn't you?'

I grinned and walked towards her MG with her. 'What about your chickens, Beth?'

'The purest of the pure, or so we have to pretend. I'll love you and leave you, Sam. You'll be alright now, dear. You'll all be alright, but take care of Isabel. She's the one who needs looking after the most now.'

On my last morning at The Weavers, Isabel took me to see her cabinet. I suppose I shouldn't have been surprised to see two walls covered with Michael Jackson photos and memorabilia, but I'd forgotten about the oddity of the way he had burst into her e-mails and I was momentarily taken aback. Michael at various phases in his life. Young Michael, with his brothers, in the Jackson Five. An older Michael, snapped just a year or two before his death, with an unhealthy ghoulish face. Black Michael, white Michael. Michael with an Afro, long-haired Michael, Michael with a cocked hat. Michael on crutches with a mask over his mouth. Michael dangling a baby over a balcony. Prince Michael III? Was this an adopted child or his biological son? Another dimension to be added the enigmas surrounding Michael that Isabel had written to me about.

She was staring at me, her hands on her hips, her head on one side, waiting to see how I'd respond. She no longer seemed a distraught daughter, but rather someone who was taking control of a situation.

'Are you trying to tell me something?'

'Uh-huh.' She smiled. 'There are other walls.' She nodded to the right.

I looked at the wall to my right and had my biggest shock of all. There were more photos, but not of Michael Jackson. The photos were of me. Mostly alone, but sometimes with Stuart. The majority were from my student days, but some had been taken when I was younger.

'I don't understand. Where did you get these from? Who took them?'

'Stuart took most of them. I took one or two. Those ones over there are from the day we went to Woodhall Spa. I took those. I like them all, but I like the ones of you as a boy most. Don't you look handsome in them?' Teasing me now.

'I don't know. I look young.'

'Uh-huh.' She smiled.

'I don't understand. You have pictures of me from when I was a boy.'

'Yes, Stuart got them from your mother.'

'Not Milly?'

'No. She brought you here and left you. Stuart got them from your other mother. The one who brought you up. He found her when he found you. All the pix of you when you were young are from her, except these two.' And in the darkest corner of this wall, there were two baby pictures. 'Uncle Wilf took those two. He thought Desmond might want them, but I don't know what happened. Maybe he never did. Anyway Uncle Wilf hung on to them. He gave them to me fairly recently. They're the newest additions to my collection. I'm glad I got them before you came, Sam. You must admit, I've a pretty good photo gallery of you. All I need is some more recent pictures to bring it up to date. I think I fell in love with you from looking at your pictures.'

Fell *in* love. I'd fantasized when she'd come to my room that first night, after we'd come back from The Hope Inn. But she'd turned away and later, when I found out she was my half-sister, it all made sense. Love. But now *in* love. The language was getting confusing.

She was looking at me strangely. 'There's one more wall to see.'

It was the wall to the left of the door, immediately next to us, but I hadn't looked that way as we'd entered the cabinet. It was devoted to a montage of photos of Isabel herself. A sequence documenting her growth from a small baby to the woman who stood beside me, a more complete portrait gallery than her collection of photos of me. She had about fifty photos of me, but there were at least two hundred of her, vying for space on this wall. So the story they told was more complete, but also more puzzling. She was with Laura, Uncle Wilf and her brothers and sisters in many of the photos, but there were also some of her as a very young child in which she was with other adults.

'We've so much in common, Sam.'

'I don't understand.'

'Work it out. It's not rocket science.' She was smiling, but more nervous now. Less assured.

'I gave you a hint. We've more in common than you realised.'

'You mean …?'

'Yes?'

'You were adopted too?'

She clapped ironically. 'You made it. I knew you'd get there sooner or later. Yes, exactly. It's taken you quite a while to work things out here. You're not good at Happy Families, are you?'

'*Happy*! But I still don't understand. How? Why?'

'Well, I don't know the hows and whys of it, but obviously my biological Mum and Dad didn't want me or couldn't keep me for some reason and so they put me up on the adoption market and along came Laura, the epitome of middle-class respectability, and snapped me up.'

'That easily?'

'Well, no, I don't imagine it was nearly that easy. But think about it. A nice house, a stable family (she laughed as she said this) and a mother straight out of *Good Housekeeping*. I imagine she had no trouble fooling them, when they were vetting her. She wouldn't even have had to do it consciously. She just had to be herself. The self she was 99.9% of the time. The textbook mother. She was wonderful, you know. She brought us all up perfectly.'

'Did she tell you that you were adopted?'

'Yes, she did, and of course she even handled that supremely well, too. I never felt a jot less loved or wanted than her own children. Everything was hunky dory until Stuart found out about you from Uncle Wilf and set out to track you down. And then, it's hard to put it into words, but that was when I felt I *was* you. I mean we'd both been uprooted and put in a new family, and I think that maybe

Mum adopted me to replace you. I don't know, but something like that anyway. You weren't hers, but I think that there may have been moments when she felt guilty and thought she should have taken you in, after all. So she got me instead. To atone. To make up for you. And I think that's why I've felt so close to you. Funny, I know, but that's how I've been ever since I knew about you. I'd always known I was adopted, but I had no idea you existed and were out there somewhere in the world, waiting to be found. Then when Stuart discovered you, I wanted so much to be close to you. It may seem bizarre, but I feel closer to you than anyone in the world.'

'So you're like my twin? Not Stuart?'

'Well, yes, that's one way of putting it. Stuart got you to follow him to college and when I knew you were there, I had to come down too. I was longing for the moment when everything would be out in the open. But then Dad died and I knew I had to be at home with Mum. I knew something was seriously wrong with her. She was such a wonderful mother. We had to protect her, but … well, after these last few days, there's nothing more to be done.'

'You told incredible stories about faraway places.'

'I know, I know. I still can, but they're all in my imagination. I think I do it to make myself more interesting than I really am. I'm an attention seeker, you know.'

'You don't need to make yourself more interesting. You're great as you are.'

'Well, thanks, but that's not true. I've never been anywhere, except London.'

'And Woodhall Spa, and Lincoln.'

'Well, yes, and a few other places around here. I've even been to Stamford.' She laughed. 'But no, I've not travelled anywhere much. I'm very dull.'

'Travel doesn't make a person interesting. It just …'

'Broadens the mind?'

'Well, yes, but that's not what I was going to say. I was going to say that I think it just makes a person mixed up about where home is.'

'I suppose I had this sure sense of where home was and now it's gone. We can't stay here now. The house will be haunted by her forever.'

'You know, I came here thinking this must be one of the most settled places in England. But it's not, is it?'

'I don't know. You tell me. I've never really been anywhere else.'

'The house isn't going to be easy to sell. No one local will want to touch it with a barge pole.'

'Maybe there's a niche market. Just imagine the estate agent's blurb. Jake could do a great job with this, you know. Large period residence, with spooky pond and well-documented recent murder history. There are probably people out there who go for that kind of thing. No need to go on a murder mystery weekend break. You could have it all at home. Day in, day out.'

We laughed and the tension that had been between us for days was fast evaporating.

'Maybe we could sell it off complete with curios?'

'But not our photos. They're ours. Ours only. They bring us together. Sam? I'm glad you're not my brother. We'll still be closer than close.'

'Yes, of course. And I'm glad you're not my sister.'

'I'm the real outsider now, aren't I? *You* have a lot of new brothers and sisters.'

'Yes, but you've grown up with them. I think that they belong to you more than me. What'll you do now? Will you get a job? Will you stay here?'

'I don't know. It's too soon, but yes, I guess I'll get a job again. I don't have anyone to "protect" anymore, though I think I'll be the one who'll be looking after Sherry.'

'Maybe you could get a job down south, somewhere near me?'

'Perhaps. She smiled. I might even have a career. It'd beat Butlin's or the Hope Inn, much as I love the people at the Hope.'

We went back to the others to have lunch and while we were eating Alice asked if I'd stay a while.

'I think I'll go back to Lincoln and spend a bit more time with Spike and Lily, if that's OK with you. But now I know that we're … family, I'll be back regularly, whether or not you and the others decide to stay in the house. One way or another, you'll be seeing a lot of me.'

'Soon?'

'I've got an assignment that's going to keep me busy for a month or two. That job I told you about. Then I'll be here so much, you'll be sick of the sight of me.'

'Never,' said Alice, mocking me by batting her eyelashes rapidly.

'There's just one thing that's still puzzling me.'

'What's that? I mean there's a lot of stuff we don't know, but what's the *one* thing?', asked Isabel.

'Van Morrison. I kept hearing his songs.'

Lilith had the same answer as before. 'Life is full of coincidences. This may just be one of them. One of the one in a million chances that just happen to come together, when the other million minus one possible coincidences never do. The radio was playing his records. He was a favourite of Stuart's. Nothing more than that.'

'But were the BBC having a Van Morrison day, or something?'

'I don't know. Why don't you google it, or maybe send them a message?', Isabel suggested.

And later when I was alone with Isabel again, she asked 'Will you come for Uncle Wilf's funeral? It'll be a sad occasion, but we'd feel so much better if you were here. I mean, *I'd* feel so much better with you beside me.'

'I'll try. It depends when it is.'

'Who knows? I guess there will be an inquest, but don't say "try". Just do it.' I recognised the Isabel of the e-mails and now it felt good to have her back.

'Say "Yes, Iz, I'll be with you," even if it means you have to leave that all-important assignment you've got coming up for twenty-four hours. Nothing could be more important than this.'

'OK, I'll be here with you.'

'Good. I knew you'd see sense.'

'You know, when the job is over, there's something I'd like to do.'

'Uh-huh. I know.'

'I'd like to go looking for Stuart.'

'Uh-huh. I know.' Isabel was smiling broadly. It seemed she'd read my mind.

'Do you think you could put what you're going to do in the future on hold for a while? Then maybe ....'

'Uh-huh?'

'Maybe we can we go and find him together?'

'Uh-huh.'

Annie

Dad, Dad, look, there's the car. Daaaaaad! Come quick! Mum is home. And she's got Uncle Sam with her. And someone else I think. No, it's not a person. It's a dog. It's Sherrrrry! Dad, Dad, Dad, I think we're going to look after Sherrrrry. Maybe we can keep her all through the summer holidays and I can take her for walks. Me and Judy. Dad, can I feed her? Can she sleep with me? Say yes, Dad, pleeeeeease. I promise to be good, if you let me. Linda and Cheryl will be really really jealous. They don't have a dog like Sherry.

Will Uncle Sam stay long, Dad? It's so exciting. I thought the summer was going to be borrrrrring, borrrrrring, borrrrrring. But now I will be so busy, I won't have any spare time. I won't be able to do any house jobs, Dad, unless I can do them with Sherry. And I have to take Uncle Sam back to the cathedral to show him where I saw Tom. And Sherry must come too. She will love to smell the spot where I saw Tom. I don't think they let dogs inside the cathedral, though. So, if not, p'raps it will be hard for her to see the Imp. Unless we pretend she's a guide dog. If they don't let just any dog in, I betcha they allow guide dogs. Dad, do you think I could pretend to be blind? I could buy a white stick.